Sabrina looked dully at the woman reflected in the mirror.

The image still looked radiant, cheeks flushed, eyes bright, hair golden. Diamond-cut crystal winked at one ear, scattering the light of the room. For this moment in time, she looked elegant. She looked like a woman who belonged here.

But she wasn't. Deep in her heart she wasn't. She was a woman who wore faded jeans and walked the gutters of the city at night to see what souls she could save. She wasn't a woman of glitter. She was a woman of the streets.

It was ending, she thought. Because this was Thomas's world. She thought of how well he moved in these circles, knowing what kind of wine to order, what things to say, what steps to dance. He belonged here. And he belonged with a woman of this world, too.

A woman who could give him his laughing children, his suburban dreams.

A woman who could give him a future.

Dear Reader,

The year is coming to a close, so here at Silhouette Intimate Moments we decided to go out with a bang. Once again, we've got a banner lineup of books for you.

Take this month's American Hero, Micah Parish, in *Cherokee Thunder.* You met him in the first book of author Rachel Lee's Conard County series, *Exile's End,* and now he's back with a story of his own. Without meaning to, he finds himself protecting woman-on-the-run Faith Williams and her unborn child, and suddenly this man who shunned emotion is head over heels in love. He's an American Hero you won't want to miss.

Reader favorite Ann Williams puts her own spin on an innovative plot in *Shades of Wyoming.* I don't want to give anything away, so all I'll say is beware of believing that things are what they seem. In *Castle of Dreams,* author Maura Seger takes a predicament right out of the headlines—the difficulties a returning hostage faces in readjusting to the world—and makes it the catalyst for a compelling romance. Award-winner Dee Holmes checks in with another of her deeply moving tales in *Without Price,* while March Madness find Rebecca Daniels writes a suspenseful tale of a couple thrown together and definitely in danger in *Fog City.* Finally, welcome new author Alicia Scott—a college student—whose *Walking After Midnight* takes gritty reality and turns it into irresistible romance.

And 1993 won't bring any letup in the excitement. Look for more of your favorite authors, as well as a Tenth Anniversary lineup in May that you definitely won't want to miss. As always, I hope you enjoy each and every one of our Silhouette Intimate Moments novels.

Yours,

Leslie Wainger
Senior Editor and Editorial Coordinator

WALKING AFTER MIDNIGHT

Alicia Scott

Published by Silhouette Books New York
America's Publisher of Contemporary Romance

SILHOUETTE BOOKS
300 East 42nd St., New York, N.Y. 10017

WALKING AFTER MIDNIGHT

ISBN: 0-373-07466-2

First Silhouette Books printing December 1992

Printed in the U.S.A.

ALICIA SCOTT

is thrilled that her dream of being published has finally come true. Born in Hawaii but a native of Oregon, she is now living in Philadelphia and studying at the University of Pennsylvania.

Majoring in International Relations, she has a deep appreciation for different peoples and cultures. And while reading and writing romances is one of her favorite hobbies, she also enjoys traveling and just talking to people—so much so that in her junior year of high school she entered a contest for impromptu speaking and won eighth in the nation!

She's been to exotic locales such as Venezuela, Ecuador and Mexico, and intends on using them all in future books. Alicia brings her natural enthusiam for life to her stories, and believes that the power of love can conquer *anything* as long as one's faith is strong enough.

To my family for all their support

Y para mi pelado, te amo

Prologue

The night was cool and cloudy, wind whipping lightly through the long alleyways, carelessly tossing the debris of a downtrodden neighborhood. But the woman who walked alone didn't pay much attention to the havoc. The wind and the silent night, like the deserted streets, were much too familiar to her for that.

She walked with ease, none of the hunched shoulders or scurrying steps one would have expected in such an area, looking straight ahead, chin held high. A more ignorant person would have branded her a fool.

This was not the best part of town for a casual stroll nor was it the ideal time for such luxuries since it was one in the morning. As a matter of fact, the woman was very aware of all of this, but chose to dismiss it. This might be the other side of the gleaming Willamette river, the side without the ballets and condos. This might be the side of graffiti and gangs, pimps and pushers. But this was her side of town.

Here, on the edge of darkness.

Once, in a lifetime that Sabrina Duncan preferred not to think about but knew she must remember for all it had taught her, this had been her world, as well. It had been all she'd known—a dark, teaming world that walked a fine line between civilization and savagery.

She knew the evil it harbored all too well, and even now, after eight years, it still made her shiver. She knew the potential of these streets. She knew how rich and poor men alike, depraved men, often came and bartered for the soul of a child, simply for the twisted amusement of it. She had watched the streets seize people, bleed them of hope, and spit back out empty shells. Lost souls, lost lives.

Even now, she felt the pain.

But she kept walking forward, steps still casual and smooth. She had no destination, and upon further reflection, decided that was probably the problem.

Eleven years now, three in hell, eight in rebirth, and still no place to go. She had lots of things to do, her shelter kept her mercifully busy. It was her life, her passion. And yet on these dark, long nights, when all the kids were gone, it was she who had no place to go.

It was she who restlessly roamed the yawning frame of her lonely house, going from room to room, finding nothing but the emptiness that scared her more than she wanted to admit. All these years, all these miles, and still the emptiness.

A dry leaf crossed her path, and she paused long enough to kick at it, but even the leaf managed to avoid her, the wind pushing it out of her range. The restlessness swelled up again, almost choking her in the despair brought along with it. Hard on its heels came the pain.

There was no choice. She started walking again.

She knew the pain well by now, just as she knew that it would never completely go away. It was the sort of pain that ran far too deep to ever be completely exorcised. But with time and patience, it could be borne. She knew because she'd done it, and still did. Until afternoons like this afternoon, and long nights like this night when the pain swelled and grew, becoming a raging ache in the pit of her stomach that could not be ignored.

She wanted to ignore it. God, she wanted to. She wanted to think of anything but the pain and Jessie.

Her feet moved faster now, and she tried to outwalk the ache. Step one: no use crying over spilled milk. Step two:

you did everything you could. Step three: you cannot be responsible for everyone's life. Step four: life goes on.

Then she started all over again, taking bigger steps, moving a little faster, the regretfully familiar litany still echoing in her head.

Step one. Step two. Step three. Step four.

And just when she thought she was going to win the war, just when she thought she had a ghost of a chance, a sharp pang skirted up from her soul and with its insidious message, struck home in the dark recesses of her mind.

Jessie hadn't been able to outrun the pain, either.

The one thought effectively crushed all barriers, shattering her nerves, until she was forced to stop and lean over, holding her arms across her middle, on the brink of breaking down in the middle of the street.

Her hands were cold and trembling, and for one long and bitter moment she cursed the last eight years that had taught her how to feel, taking away the only protection she had ever had.

"Oh, Jessie," she whispered. "I'm so sorry."

And then it was too late, for with her moment of weakness the thoughts came, the memories, and she couldn't keep them away.

Nathan, earlier today, with beaten shoulders and hanging head. "Jessie sent me," he'd said, and she'd seen the sadness in his eyes.

Nathan had loved Jessie, too. They all had.

All kinds of kids came to the shelter. Those that had run from abusive parents and those without parents. Those that sold their body simply to buy a meal and those that ran drugs to pay the rent. Those that were drawn to the city like moths to the flame, desperately in search of excitement. But Jessie, Jessie had defied all of the categories, creating one all for himself. Jessie had always been distinctly himself.

He had no shadows in his past, only bloodlines filled with a gypsy spirit that refused to rest. By the time he'd first come to the shelter, he'd already hit thirty-five major cities, and he was only fifteen. He paved his way with fingers as restless as his soul, easily lightening the pockets of the unwary.

The police had caught him once, but not even they had been able to hold him. Nothing could. Nothing, no one.

In the end that was what killed him.

This time he had only been at the shelter two days when he'd announced that it was time to move on.

"I have to go," he'd said, shrugging off Sabrina's concern. "I can't stay. I have to move on. It's just the way I am."

"Settling down isn't a bad thing," she'd tried to reason. "We love you here. Stay with us."

Jessie had merely shaken his head, but she'd seen the hint of a bleak despair in his eyes when he'd looked back up.

She'd understood then. Understood that while some of the kids were addicted to drugs, so Jessie was to being on the move. Nothing could hold him down, and even Jessie didn't seem to know what he was searching for.

So on to Seattle he'd gone. And in Seattle the rebellious young boy who'd hidden the softness in him had taken it upon himself to interfere with a pimp beating a prostitute. A flash of knife and it had all been over.

Her gypsy had become a statistic, along with all the other street children who'd been swallowed up before him, and all those who would no doubt follow.

The despair was back, choking her. At times like this, she wished she could cry, get it all over with, once and for all. But she had lost the ability a long time ago.

"Let him go," she told herself with clenched fists. "You've got to learn to let them go."

And that, she knew, was the heart of her problem. She wouldn't let go. She wanted to save every child, rebuild every life. And she just couldn't do it.

"Damn it," she swore out loud, but somehow it came out as more of a whimper than a curse.

She drew a shaky hand through her short, golden curls, straightened her spine, and started walking again.

There were those things in life that could never be undone, prices that would always be paid. Life wasn't easy, nor was it fair, but it could be survived.

She ignored the small voice inside her that cried out for more than just survival.

Rounding a corner, she headed toward the flashing lights of one of the main strips. A block ahead under a streetlamp, leaned a scarlet-clad prostitute.

She was much too old, Sabrina thought. Even at this distance she could see the sagging lines on the woman's heavily painted face. Her hair was a badly dyed fire-engine red, and her tight black spandex pants revealed the full effects of gravity on her hips.

The prostitute looked up at the sound of Sabrina's footsteps, and for one instant, their eyes met. For Sabrina it was like staring into an empty pool, a vacant sea of nothingness. She stopped suddenly, taken aback, struck by the stark hopelessness in that gaze.

She had to fight the impulse to rush immediately forward and give the woman a good hard shake, to scream at her not to give up, not to sell herself so short.

But understanding reined in her impulses, and she knew she'd have to go slowly, find the right words.

After all, eight years ago, this could have been her.

But just as she was about to step forward, the moment—and her opportunity—passed. The light clip-clop of dress shoes rang out in the cool night, and a well-dressed man appeared up ahead. Immediately the prostitute turned away from Sabrina, arranging her expression into a blatantly beckoning one, straightening the straps of her blouse.

She turned slightly, showing her best side, and walked out of the harsh glow of the street lamp with an exaggerated wiggle.

Sabrina wanted to call out, wanted to tell the woman to stop, but she was all alone in the side street, and there were two of them. Instead she watched helplessly as the woman laid a hand on the man's arm, preparing to lead him away.

For a moment he hesitated, and Sabrina could see him dimly in the shadows. Nicely dressed, he was tall and thin, with a hawkish nose. He looked up then, perhaps sensing her gaze in the night, and it seemed to her that he stared right at her, even though she was certain the night hid her well enough. His stare felt cold and oddly intense, making her shiver.

Then, even as she watched, he turned back to the woman and they walked away, swallowed up by the night.

Hours later, she let herself into an old house in a run-down neighborhood. Finally exhausted, she took a shower, and collapsed on her bed.

Sabrina slept soundly until the alarm went off three hours later, at six. She stumbled into the kitchen for her coffee.

It was then she came face-to-face with the garish woman in black lace again. Only this time the woman was on the front page of the morning paper. And the vacant eyes were dead.

Chapter 1

Lieutenant Thomas Lain wasn't having a good night. Quite frankly, he was nearing the point of total exhaustion.

After putting in a fifteen-hour day of tracking down dead-end leads on his various cases, he'd tumbled into bed at one in the morning. Such were the joys of working in Portland, Oregon, a city that just a few years ago had outranked Los Angeles for crime. And as his nights usually went, just two hours after hitting the bed his phone rang shrilly in his ear. After twenty years on the force, he should have been used to it by now, but he wasn't. Funny thing about murder and mayhem, they seemed to keep odd hours.

Groggy and half numb with fatigue, his mind and body automatically switched into mechanical overdrive. With smooth efficiency bred of experience, he slid into his clothes, wearily patted his dog, and headed out.

Despite his speed, by the time he arrived on the gray, drizzly scene, spectators and the press were already there, vying for the prime view. He eyed them with something akin to distaste. Gore fanatics were bad enough, but what bothered him the most was that, no matter how many spectators were present, no one had ever seen anything.

It didn't take Thomas long to spot his partner, Seth Stein, hunched over a shrouded shape lying on the street. His brow heavily furrowed, Seth was mumbling something to the young rookie next to him. Seth looked up abruptly as he saw his partner approaching.

"Hey, man," Seth called out. "What took you so long? Are you getting old or something?"

Thomas merely grunted in reply, the verbal ribbing a familiar routine by now. Seth was ten years his junior and worse yet, a morning person. All that aside, they made a good team.

"So what do we have here?" he asked grimly.

Seth gestured to the covered body as an answer. Thomas leaned over and pulled up the sheet. Underneath was a heavily painted woman with bright red hair. Her throat had been viciously slashed, but he barely paused at the sight, his eyes drifting lower to her chest. There, resting on the cheap and flashy material of her bodice, lay a perfect black rose.

He glanced up at Seth, but Seth was already shaking his head. "I've tried," Seth said, throwing his hands up. "But I can't think of a single gang, pimp, anyone or anything that's symbolized by a black rose."

Since Thomas couldn't, either, he let it slide for the moment, moving on. Automatically his mind began to fill in vital statistics. Probable age, race, height and a full description of her facial features, carefully noting any distinguishable marks that might help them identify her later. He didn't know how long he'd been dispassionately cataloging her when he heard a noise behind him.

The rookie was hunched over, being violently ill. For a moment Thomas was taken aback. He searched his memory, trying to remember if, as a rookie on his first crime scene, he'd ever been sick. Probably. As a rookie he'd still had the idealism that allowed him to feel offended by any violence. Now hundreds, possibly thousands of murders later, he didn't have the time or space left for feelings, just for the facts.

Looking at the prostitute again, he forced himself to *really* look at her, really see the jagged wound that had taken her life. His stomach remained perfectly calm, unaffected.

Finally he felt a sinking sensation that had nothing to do with the murder. The fact that he didn't feel anything was sobering. This job was getting to him.

He forced himself back to business. Four in the morning was no time for being profound. "What's the story?" he asked Seth.

"One of the 'girls' over there said her name was Sally," Seth supplied. "Supposedly she'd been a hooker for about ten years, though they've only seen her hereabouts for the last one. Her pimp's name is Willy. He showed up just before you got here—I've questioned him once. He claims to have been with two of his girls all night and they hardly refute it. And, of course..." Seth wrapped it up with a sigh. "Nobody saw anything."

Thomas simply nodded, his eyes roving the crowd before him. The group was mostly prostitutes, crowding around in skin-tight spandex and short, neon-colored tops. Glittery eyelids winked at him and huge plastic earrings dangled in the gray light. They looked like a group of neon peacocks set against the drab, gray buildings. White graffiti bravely flashed back from the broken structures. Like the makeup on the women, it stole away all chances for dignity.

The prostitutes were craning their necks, trying to get a last look at the body. Still leaning over the body, he wondered if it would make a difference, if seeing such an end would make them reconsider their chosen occupation. He doubted it. For them death and violence were simply a matter of life. Grimly he realized that he was no better. Once there had been a time when he'd had the energy to wish that things could be different. There'd been a time when he had believed that by getting up at three in the morning, he could change someone's life. But that had been fifteen years and more than a hundred murders ago. Now he knew, from long experience and little sleep, that nothing would change. These girls would look at this body now, and walk the streets later. They had no choice, it was their livelihood, and no amount of sermonizing or example-setting would alter the cold hard facts of survival. He only hoped that he caught the murderer before the murderer caught them.

He realized that the odds were against it, though. Street crimes seemed to have amazingly few witnesses, and amazingly few leads. According to Seth the crowd tonight was no different. These people didn't want to look closely at their customers and they didn't want to know their real names.

Rising, he felt a queer sensation beginning to build in the base of his spine, almost as if someone was watching him. Scrutinizing the crowd, he saw no one who stuck out. With a frown, he turned away. He *had* been at this too long.

The next few hours were spent interrogating the surrounding girls, checking the scene for clues and prints, and generally drinking bad coffee. Finally Thomas and Seth called it quits. There was little more that could be done, they might as well return to the station. At least the coffee there was better.

Five hours and five cups of coffee later, Thomas didn't feel any better off. His eyes were so blurred with exhaustion that he could barely read the autopsy report before him. In the past four days he'd been lucky to catch ten hours' worth of sleep, and he knew it was beginning to affect him. Worse, neither he nor Seth had anything to show for it. It looked as if the gang-related murder they'd been working on was about to join the tremendous ranks of unsolved cases. There had been a witness, a horribly scared teenage kid, but he'd turned out to be as scared of the police as he'd been of the gang. Time and again he'd refused police protection, and had managed to skillfully avoid the police tags Thomas had assigned to him anyway. A drive-by shooting had taken the boy out of the game early yesterday morning. They'd pumped him full of nearly a pound of lead. As usual, no one had seen anything, and the murder weapon had been found, wiped clean, a block from the scene of the crime. A quick check had revealed that the .22 calibre had belonged to the boy. He'd been killed with his own gun.

Thomas felt the frustration begin to bubble up, and forced his mind back on track. Frustration, he knew by now, got him nowhere.

With that in mind, he was peering intently at the report when his buzzer sounded.

"Sabrina Duncan here to see you."

Sabrina Duncan? He searched his mind in vain, coming up with a complete blank. Surprise, surprise, he thought wryly.

As if sensing his confusion, the voice on the intercom supplied, "She's here about the prostitute killing. She called earlier."

He didn't remember that, either, and felt the frustration rise.

"Hell," he said with a sigh, "I've got to start getting some sleep."

At a loss for anything better to say, he instructed the desk sergeant to let the woman in. That accomplished, he went back to deciphering the medical jargon in front of him.

When he looked up thirty seconds later at the petite figure standing uncertainly in the doorway, he barely restrained a groan.

Standing before him was a miniature figure in faded jeans and an emerald green, plaid shirt. She was probably a hundred pounds soaking wet, and with her short, blond hair, she could pass as anybody's kid sister. Worn tennis shoes completed the disparaging picture, and all his hopes sank.

Great, just great, he thought. Practically no sleep and now he had to interrogate Tinkerbell.

Sabrina wasn't feeling so hot herself. A hundred times this morning she'd told herself that there had to be another way. Anything but voluntarily coming to a police station. It had been a good while since she'd been to one, and despite the fact that she was now on the same side, years of distrust died hard. The first time she'd seen the inside of a station, it hadn't been to talk to a cop. She had been booked by one instead.

And the cop sitting on the other side of the desk did very little to reassure her. A giant lug of a man, he looked like he'd crawled right out from under his bed and was still nursing a hangover. Dark blond hair in complete disarray capped bloodshot eyes. Two days' worth of stubble littered his cheeks. Frankly, he looked like he had the temper of a grizzly.

She wondered if it was too late to leave, but knew as soon as she thought it that she couldn't. For the same reason that she'd repeated to herself more than once already. She should have helped the woman last night. Now all she could do was try to find some justice for the woman in death that she probably had never had in life.

Squaring her shoulders, Sabrina marched toward the desk.

"I'm here about the murder," she declared. "I talked to someone about it earlier on the phone. A Seth Stein, I believe."

"That explains it," mumbled the man in front of her, but before she could ask what he was talking about, he abruptly waved his hand in the air.

"Go ahead," he said briskly, impatience clear in his voice.

Sabrina hesitated, unsure of what to say. "Well, around one last night, I was walking around and I saw the woman."

She paused, waiting for him to ask her a question or lead her in some direction, but he simply returned her look. She began to feel annoyed. She searched for what to say next.

"A man approached her, a john, and she led him away."

"Did you see where they went?" he asked almost indifferently.

Sabrina hesitated. "No."

"Did you get a good look at the man?" he continued automatically, looking down at the papers in front of him.

Sabrina felt her face become warm with embarrassment. "Well, no. He was too far into the shadows to get a good look."

"Height?" Now he was looking at her, firing questions with forced patience.

"I don't know. A little over six feet, probably six-one, I guess."

"Weight?"

"Not heavy. He was thin, very thin."

"Distinguishing marks?"

"I don't know."

"Beard? Mustache?"

"I didn't see his face."

Thomas bit back an impatient sigh. Well, technically speaking, it was a start. God knows a witness was more than he'd ever dared hope for. Then again, a witness who hadn't seen the face of the killer wasn't much to go by. He could post the information, but gut instinct told him it wouldn't narrow the search down much.

"Look," he said curtly, his mind already moving on to the pile of reports in front of him. "Thanks very much, and I promise to include this information in my report, but frankly, without a good view of his face, there's little you can help us with. I can give you my card. Call if anything else comes to you."

Without glancing up again, his right hand found the stack of cards on his cluttered desk and passed one across. Once more engrossed in the autopsy report, he didn't notice that she hadn't left.

As for Sabrina, she could only stare at him, dumbfounded. Somehow, in all the times she'd run through this scene in her mind, this hadn't been the way things were supposed to go. He was supposed to be pleased with her information. He was supposed to be excited, to thank her for coming forth. He was *supposed* to use her information and magically catch the killer before the killer got someone else.

There definitely *wasn't* supposed to be some overgrown oaf of a man who simply dismissed her without even looking at her. Damn it, she deserved better than that and so did the victim. The more she thought about it, the madder she got. And for a tiny thing, she could be awesome when infuriated. As one Lieutenant Lain was about to learn.

"So that's it?" she demanded to know, straightening up to her full height of five feet in her anger. "So that's simply it? Just go home and *forget about it?*"

Thomas looked at the woman before him, who seemed to have suddenly gone from Tinkerbell to a spitting wildcat when his attention had wandered, and a tiny piece of his mind—the part that could still function on the little sleep he'd had—told him he was handling this badly. But the rest of him, the part that couldn't function on ten hours of sleep in four days, simply nodded.

And right before his eyes, just across the desk, the wildcat exploded.

"Obviously that's easy for you to do," the woman spat out. "Well, you listen to me for just one minute of your precious time." Her anger carried her forward until she stood at the edge of his desk, her violet eyes flashing, her tiny fists clenched. Yet even standing, she had to look up to make eye contact with him. A fact he found vaguely intriguing, but apparently enraged her all the more.

"That woman out there is dead," the wildcat continued savagely. "And maybe she's just another hooker to you, but she had a name and a life and probably a dream or two. She didn't deserve to have all that put to an end, to have her throat slashed like an animal, just because of her profession. And she definitely doesn't deserve to be dismissed by the likes of you. It's your *job* to help her, and if you don't, then you really aren't any better than the butcher who killed her."

In that last breath of anger Sabrina had the satisfaction of seeing the Lieutenant's green eyes widen and his jaw drop slightly. But then, as quickly as it had come, her anger drained, leaving her shaky and unsure. She spun around, cursing her temper even more than she cursed him as she strode for the door.

"Don't."

The command in the voice stopped her momentarily and now that his system had been rudely jolted awake for the first time this morning, Thomas searched for the right words. He couldn't just let her go like this.

"Please," he said quietly. "Please stay, and let's try this again."

She turned back around, warily looking into the serious gaze of the man behind the desk. He seemed sincerely apologetic, apparently prepared to really listen this time around. Sensing that this was one man who didn't apologize often, she released the last of her pent-up breath. If he was willing to start over, she was, too.

He rose and extended his hand. "I'm Lieutenant Thomas Lain. Now, how can I help you?"

She refused his hand, but it wasn't due to any lingering resentment. As a rule she avoided all unnecessary social "touches." She kept to herself, she preferred others do the same.

"All right," he said, letting his hand slowly sink to his side. She'd nodded politely instead of taking his hand, so he didn't take offense. In fact, he found her refusal rather interesting, just as he found the carefully controlled look that was beginning to shield her eyes intriguing. One minute passionately demanding his attention, the next, cool and calm. The wildcat not only had claws, but she was volatile, too.

"If you really want to help," he began cautiously, watching her reaction carefully, "you're going to have to search deeper in your mind. We need distinct details, ones that you couldn't have read in the paper." Sitting down in his chair again, he motioned for her to take the seat in front of his desk. "We'll start from the beginning. Where did you see the prostitute?"

Sabrina sat down, and in her mind's eye she recreated the scene, struggling to make out details. But there was no clear image, for the night had only been distinct in her memory due to her emotional state, not because of the surroundings. She could remember no street signs, only the despair. Poor Jessie... Abruptly she jerked her thoughts back under control. She couldn't help Jessie now, that was over and done with. She had to accept that and go on.

"Burnside Avenue, about four blocks before the alley where the body was found," she said at last, hoping the huskiness in her voice would be taken for nerves.

Thomas looked at her sharply, picking up on the undercurrents in her voice, in her eyes. She returned his probing glance evenly, determined to reveal only what was necessary to the case at hand.

Eyes narrowed, he studied the petite woman before him. Even if her voice and eyes hadn't given her away—what was so special about last night, or even Burnside Avenue?—her posture would have. She was stiff as a board. Well, the lady wasn't telling and he wasn't asking... for now.

"Describe the prostitute," he ordered.

"Red hair, dyed. She was wearing a short, cheap red top with black lace. Skin-tight black spandex pants. Black heels."

Thomas shook his head. "Not good enough, dig deeper. Can you think of any distinguishing marks?"

Sabrina's head began to hurt. God, she wished she had a cigarette.

Faintly, something stirred in her memory. She closed her eyes and pressed her palms against her temple, concentrating harder.

"She had some kind of mark on her arm, high up. The arm facing me, the left arm. Like, like some sort of tattoo, maybe."

This time Thomas nodded, and felt the first faint prickings of excitement. The hooker did indeed have a tattoo—a flowering vine on her left arm—something the department had purposely kept out of the info released to the media. I'll be damned, he thought to himself. We may have a real witness after all. *Witness.* Suddenly the picture of a teenage boy's body, riddled with bullets and blood, flashed through his mind. Then the image flickered, this time showing a woman in the boy's place, sprawled on the sidewalk. A fragile woman with blond hair... Cutting the mental image off quickly, he told himself *this* witness wasn't in any danger. The killer, after all, wouldn't know he'd been made until it was too late.

"Tell me what you can about the customer," he asked evenly, carefully measuring Sabrina's reply.

Closing her eyes tightly, Sabrina was nonetheless able to come up with only a description of a tall, shadowy man in a dark overcoat. They had both almost given up when she remembered the scarf.

"It was blue."

For a moment Thomas simply looked at her, and then slowly the words penetrated. A blue scarf. Of course. The autopsy report mentioned that traces of blue woolen thread had been found at the woman's wrists, as well as fabric burns. Clever. A scarf, no one would think twice about it in this chilly weather, and yet what better to tie someone's hands with?

And, by God, if they didn't have an honest-to-goodness witness. The excitement, so rare these days, steadily increased. But he carefully schooled his features, keeping them neutral. This had to be handled carefully, he wouldn't be doing anyone any favors by "leading the witness."

"I'd like you to work with the station's artist for a bit and see if you can't come up with something more."

There was very little change in his voice, but it was enough. Relief flowed through Sabrina. So they were taking her seriously. Finally they were getting somewhere. She allowed herself a weak smile of triumph. Not only had she gotten him to listen, but she had actually managed to help, as well. Perhaps it was her lucky day after all.

Buried in her own thoughts, Sabrina hardly noticed Lieutenant Lain rising and offering his hand, but this time, he didn't wait for her to offer her own. He simply took it.

The shock of his touch jerked her head up. It was so warm, rough and callused, engulfing her own. Confused, she angled her neck upward, to find his eyes looming above. They were dark with reluctant heat and something she was less sure of.

For one suspended instant, she felt a tiny flame leap deep in her stomach, reaching toward him, reaching toward...

With an oath she jumped back, almost stumbling, catching herself just in time. Her face felt overly hot, and her pulse much too fast. Mortification flooded through her, and she closed her eyes tightly. No, she told herself, I'm imagining things. I didn't feel a thing when he touched me. She took several deep breaths, mercifully, her control came back.

When she looked again, his eyes had gone blank, his face totally expressionless.

Throughout the rest of the interview, they were both careful not to touch.

After dropping off Sabrina with the artist, Thomas returned to his office and found himself once again rubbing the back of his neck. He wondered how he could have been so wrong.

For months now he'd been telling himself that he was not losing his edge, that he was just losing interest. Now he understood that they were one and the same.

He'd almost blown a lead today. For the first time in twenty years he'd almost thrown away a case without even trying to solve it. He knew that it wasn't because the victim was a prostitute. Miss Duncan had been wrong on that account. But after so many weeks, so many years, of fruitless hours and sleepless nights, it was much too easy to believe in failure and much too hard to believe in actual success.

Perhaps he *was* getting old. He'd been hunting down the bad guys for twenty years now, putting in later and later hours, having less and less of a real life. And what did he have to show for it? For two consecutive years he and Seth had won the awards for solving the most cases, yet the stack of unsolved cases continued to grow at an alarming rate. Every year more and more crimes, and less and less time to solve them.

Sometimes he even wondered if they were in control of the city at all. There were entire blocks of the city where crack houses and gangs had moved in with such strength that they carried weapons openly on the streets. The few elderly people who remained in the community, having supposedly retired to their safe homes, now spent their nights with rifles across their laps.

Time and again, narcotics and the rest of the station had cracked down hard on such areas. Only to have the gangs simply shift and pop up a few blocks away. It was a brutal war, ongoing, and the danger was increasing daily.

Last month one of the undercover narcs had been routinely searching a junky when he'd pricked his finger on a hypodermic needle in the junky's pocket. The whole station had waited all day to get the results back from the junkie's AIDS test, which he'd agreed to take shortly after being brought in. In the end the results had been negative, but it was enough to make you think, think real hard.

Thomas knew he didn't have to be a cop. Hell, with the kind of money his family had he really didn't have to be anything. But once upon a time it had seemed important to him to be something more. He hadn't wanted to introduce himself as "I'm Thomas Lain, and I'm rich." There had been pride, huge, glowing pride in being able to say "I'm a cop."

It sounded significant, as if he made a difference in the world. But maybe that had all been a sham. He was forty-two now and he had yet to see the change. Still way too many murderers, way too many people unable to stay alive to fulfill dreams and promises. On his good days it made him sad and determined. On his bad days, like today, it simply made him disgusted.

He sighed into the emptiness of the office and wished that Seth was back so he could talk to him. But he was out, checking other leads. Seth was worried about him, Thomas knew. He'd noticed the restlessness in Thomas long before Thomas himself had given name to it. He and Seth had been together for ten years now. They knew each other inside and out, better than most married couples, he imagined. After all, they spent more hours a day together than any couple he had ever heard of. They made a good team, they got things done. And for nothing in this world would Thomas ever let his partner down. But the nights were getting longer, the exhaustion stronger. He wasn't a young rookie anymore. Perhaps it was only a matter of time . . .

One night, one very rare night off, he'd bought a very good bottle of Scotch—Chivas Regal to be exact—and had proceeded to become very hammered. About halfway through the bottle and well on his way to oblivion, he'd decided that it was time to quit the force and marry one of the silk and satin ladies his mother was always setting him up with.

But he'd known, even in that drunken state, that he would never do it. After twenty years he couldn't just walk away. Just as his job threatened to destroy him, it was also his sanity. Without it, he was just Thomas Lain, rich and useless. Besides, when it got right down to it, he still believed in being a cop. He looked around himself every day at all the men and women wearing the badge, offering their lives to try and make a difference, and felt something akin to awe.

But believing it and *feeling* it were totally different things. If only he could get the magic back, get the old feelings to come alive again. He wanted to be able to wake up in the morning with the certainty that he was accomplishing something. That the endless hours and cold coffee really were worthwhile. Frustrated, he realized that he just didn't know how to do that. He just didn't know.

At least this case was progressing, he thought grudgingly, and found his mind drifting back to the petite Miss Duncan. She'd looked so delicate in the doorway, a mere shadow of a person. Come to think of it, with that short-cropped hair of hers and those huge violet eyes, she'd looked like a lost waif. But she'd been tough. That intrigued him. As for that one brief explosive touch...

He stopped abruptly. That line of thinking would get him nowhere. She was part of a case. That made her strictly off-limits. Besides, his reaction to her could be explained by any number of reasons. Not the least of which was that, if the truth were known, he hadn't been on so much as a date for the past nine months.

So that was it, in a nutshell. She was just part of a case and everything was well under control. He reached for a case file and buried his nose in it, intent on getting to work.

But ten minutes later he found himself staring off into space. Sabrina Duncan, he was thinking, what a beautiful name....

Smoke floated languorously up from the tip of the burning cigarette. Halfway across the room, Sabrina enviously watched the smoker lift the cigarette for another deep drag. As he inhaled, so did she, her mouth watering for the acrid taste of nicotine as her fingers drummed restlessly on the mug shots.

"How long ago did you quit?" came Thomas's deep grumble in her ear.

"Eighteen hours, thirty-four minutes and seven seconds ago," responded Sabrina, her eyes still glued to the distant cigarette.

"That long?" Thomas gently mocked. "Why?"

"It's a dirty habit," she responded automatically. *And I'm not a dirty woman.*

"Any luck with the mug shots?"

With a sigh, she tore her gaze away from the cigarette and instead focused her attention on him. He looked even worse close up, she decided. She pegged him at one hour's worth of sleep, maybe two if he'd been lucky. She suddenly felt bad for being so hard on him earlier. Obviously he was very tired, probably not his usual self.

"Mug shots," he prodded again.

"Oh, yeah." She sighed again and shook her head. "No luck."

They hadn't really expected any. The department's artist had suggested that she look at them on the off chance that one of them might trigger her memory. But she simply hadn't seen enough of the shadowed man. By her estimation, half of the book could very well be the killer.

"Well, then," Thomas was saying, "I need to ask you a few more questions to clear some things up."

Sabrina ran her fingers through her hair in agitation. She had been at the station for four hours now, helping with sketches and sifting through mug books. Her head hurt, her stomach was growling, and her whole body was crying out for nicotine.

"Oh sure," she grumbled. "Why not?"

Thomas chuckled at her sarcasm as he made himself comfortable in his desk chair.

"Full name?"

"Sabrina Marie Duncan. Yours?"

He paused, caught off guard. "Pardon?"

"Your full name?"

Mentally he shrugged. If asking him questions made her more comfortable, then it was fine with him.

"Thomas Anthony Lain, but my friends call me Thomas. Feel free to do the same. Now that we're officially acquainted, where were you born?"

Silence. He looked up to find her face once again completely blank and controlled. So, he thought, she's back to being mystery woman. Life was getting interesting. "Place of birth?" he repeated.

The raining gutters of the big city.

"Hopkins, Idaho," she said evenly, ignoring the cynical echoes of her mind. "And you?"

"Good ol' Gresham, Oregon. Social security number?"

She rattled off the nine digits and as he wrote them, he found himself asking casually, "So...is your whole family from Idaho?" Just making conversation, he told himself.

"I don't know," Sabrina said matter-of-factly. "I was abandoned at birth. And your family?"

For a moment he was at a loss for what to say. But then he clued in to how calm her voice had remained and how high her chin had tilted in her determination to appear normal. To call attention to her comment on being abandoned would only cause her to retreat even more than she'd done so already; he was certain of that. So instead of asking the questions that strangely burned within him, he went along with her game, and answered her question as if they were at some polite social function.

"My parents are Timothy and Janice Thomas. Only my mother is still alive, and she lives in a condo on the waterfront. I take it you grew up in a foster home."

The last slipped out despite his best intentions, and he was definitely veering away from the form he was filling out, but he couldn't seem to help himself. Something about this woman... What could it hurt? he asked himself. Besides, a little insight was always helpful in dealing with a witness.

Sabrina nodded. She found that her throat was tight and that it was suddenly harder for her to breathe. She wondered what he thought of her lack of family. Thomas Anthony Lain, unkempt as he appeared, was definitely a family man, she could see that clearly. In fact, she could see him growing up with the simple, normal routine of riding in a station wagon, older brother on one side, younger sister on the other. A big dog, a golden retriever, probably sitting in the back. Boy Scouts and Little League, she thought with a tremulous smile, and wondered why it hurt her so to picture him there. She ought to be glad for him. He'd obviously had a stable childhood, and would no doubt be a good father someday, raising happy children. She should be thankful for that, the world needed more good parents and happy children. But inside, she knew she had to face the truth. Thomas had been the boy every mother dreamed of having...and she had been the girl every mother hoped her boy didn't meet. Swallowing convulsively, she told herself fiercely that it didn't matter anymore. We're all big boys and girls now.

"Next question, Lieutenant."

Thomas looked blankly at the paper in his hand for a minute. He had been trying to read the expression in those huge eyes of hers, but she eluded him still. With an inner sigh he realized that it was hopeless and brought his focus back to the form.

"Address and telephone number?"

She gave him her address—the northeast section of town—causing him to frown in concern. It definitely was not the good end of town.

"My house is a shelter for homeless youths," she explained upon seeing the grim look on his face. "I can offer them food, shelter and, thanks to a few contacts of mine, sometimes jobs and permanent homes, as well. I also work in correlation with a main shelter which can provide counseling."

He still didn't like it. The teenager's body was suddenly back in his mind. And looking at her, at the petite golden frame, the concern became almost overwhelming.

"Look," he found himself saying. "As a witness to a murder, you're putting yourself on the line. Maybe you'd better stay someplace safer until we've gotten everything under control."

Once again her face closed. "You do your job, Lieutenant, and I'll do mine."

He didn't want to give it up. He wanted her agreement, and, irrational as it seemed, he wanted armed men around her at all times. But then logic reared cold and hard in his mind. This was a different case, a different person. There was nothing to indicate she was in any type of danger, and as long as that was the case, he wasn't authorized to do a single solitary thing.

"One last question," he said at last. "You said that you were out walking when you saw the victim. Any particular reason?"

"Just searching..." she began, and for a brief instant her guard went down and she looked at him with huge pool of violet vulnerability. But then she shrugged and gave him a small smile. "Just searching."

"Searching? For what?"

"I don't know, Lieutenant," she answered him softly. "I honestly don't know."

He looked at her hard for a moment, but her violet eyes were wide and sure under the pressure of his gaze. And suddenly he felt something he had never expected. He felt a kinship. So he wasn't the only one searching.

God. Brutally he pulled in the thoughts. She was a witness, he needed to think of her as such. This whole thing was becoming much too involved for him. Sternly he reminded himself that the forms and questions had been completed, and that was that.

"That will be all for now, Miss Duncan," he managed to say briskly. "We'll get in touch with you as soon as we know more."

Sabrina nodded politely at him as she rose to leave. She avoided shaking his hand carefully, the memory of their last handshake still too raw in her mind.

She swiftly weaved toward the station doors.

"Just one last thing, Miss Duncan," he found himself calling behind her. She turned and he ran his hand through his hair. He sighed as he took in her small, delicate build.

"Be careful."

She gave him another slight smile, and then she was gone.

"She's not your type."

Thomas turned to see that Seth had returned and was staring at him.

"You like them tall, willowy, and in silk," Seth was saying. "She's short, petite, and in cotton. Her hair is tomboyish, and I bet she bites her nails."

Thomas smiled slightly at his friend's observations and dismissed them with a casual shrug. "She's just part of the case, Seth. The star witness who didn't see enough unfortunately. Honestly, just part of the job."

But Seth merely gave his friend a knowing look. He'd seen Thomas's face when the "star witness" had left, and he might be a lot of things, but he wasn't stupid.

"I take it that is the illustrious Miss Duncan?"

Thomas nodded in confirmation.

"Well, then," said Seth, and felt a twinge of regret for what he had to do next. "As long as it's *purely* professional, why don't you take a look at the file I dug up on her?"

Thomas's eyes narrowed. "Got anything?"

Seth didn't reply. Wordlessly he dropped the file on Thomas's desk and walked away.

Thomas stared after his disappearing partner with a puzzled look. With a mental shrug, he opened the file on Sabrina Duncan and began to read.

This time, for the first time in a long while, his stomach did turn.

Sabrina opened the door of her darkened house to the fragrant smell of chicken noodle soup. Peering through the dim light of dusk, she focused her eyes past the living room directly in front of her to the kitchen that it opened onto, making out a young boy standing by the stove steadily stirring the contents in a pot. With his slight build and gray shirt, he easily blended into the shadows that were his namesake.

In a rush, a sense of relief overwhelmed her. So he had come back. Once again, Shadow had come back.

Standing in the near dark, his carefully controlled features showed none of the youth of his fourteen years. Instead he carried himself with an aloof brand of self-containment, totally in control. There was no haunted look in his eyes, nor were there sad lines around his mouth. Shadow always looked each person squarely in the eye, easily conveying the impression that he had not lost his childhood, but had found it beneath him.

Even now he leaned comfortably against the counter, barely giving Sabrina a glance. She didn't mind his insolence, she had rather missed it.

Wordlessly she shut and locked the door behind her, taking off her coat and hanging it up. She casually walked into the kitchen, still silent, never giving a sign as to how pleased she was that he was okay, that he'd returned to the shelter.

After materializing at her home for the first time three weeks ago, Shadow had pretty much come and gone as he pleased. The timing seemed to defy all rhyme or reason—he simply showed up—but it was usually when no one else was around. Normally he would fix a meal or just sit companionably with her in silence. In return for the meals or temporary shelter, he would cook, clean, or fix things around the house.

At the moment he seemed to be intent on fixing dinner, reaching silently with a long thin arm and turning off the burner. The motion momentarily tightened his pantleg against his calf, revealing the outline of the metal pipe she knew he kept taped there underneath. He saw her gaze at the telltale outline, but neither said anything. Both also knew about the knife in his back pocket, but tactically refused to mention it.

Without asking, he poured a second bowl full of the warm soup and gestured for her to take it. She smiled her thanks, crossing from the living room's entryway to the open expanse of the dining room. As she passed through the small dining area into the U-shaped kitchen and took the bowl, she scanned Shadow's face, but it was, as usual, a careful blank.

Moving back into the dining room, they both pulled out chairs and sat together in silence while they ate, a young woman and a small, lanky fourteen-year-old boy.

She wondered how long he would stay this time.

Later, they sat in the huge front room that dominated the left side of the house, and watched the old Westerns that he seemed to favor. They shared the couch, but Sabrina was careful to observe the three feet perimeter he required to feel comfortable. The first time he had come to the shelter, she'd made the mistake of trespassing over the invisible boundary. He hadn't looked scared or frightened, he'd simply pulled out his knife. She was careful not to make that mistake again.

She wondered sometimes if she would ever reach him, or if he would just continue to fade in and out of her shelter, until one day he didn't come back. She knew by now, however, that she couldn't push her luck. The biggest thing these kids needed was time and it was certainly the hardest to give them. She wondered how many evenings like this they would have left, simply sitting and being together. She hoped that at some point in the next few hours she would give him what it was he needed or, if not, at least a respite from the wear and tear of survival. Maybe a good memory or two for when times got harder.

She really wished she had a cigarette.

On the TV screen John Wayne was galloping across the open prairie, closing in fast on the bad guys. Looking across at Shadow, she could see the faint hint of a smile around his mouth.

It warmed her for the first time all day.

Suddenly she found her thoughts drifting to another mouth, one she had no business thinking about at all. Lieutenant Lain's.

Never in her entire life had she responded to a man as she had to this virtual stranger. She found herself staring down at her fingertips, wondering if she'd imagined the soul-stirring heat elicited by the mere touch of his hand.

She'd never responded to a man like that. Or rather, she had never responded to *any* man. Intellectually she recognized the reasons, that it was due to circumstances, events in her life that had been beyond her control. After all, her first exposure to sex had been a brutal rape, and it certainly hadn't gotten any better from there. She'd eventually learned to separate her body from her mind, to—for the sake of survival—let the men use her body. But she'd never let them touch her soul. Counselors had assured her that with time and a 'normal' relationship, her frigidity, so to speak, could be overcome. But in the eight years since beginning the painful road to a "normal" life, she hadn't noticed any change. Even though she'd met a few good men, nice and considerate men, she hadn't felt so much as a twinge for any of them.

Until now. Until Lieutenant Thomas Lain.

But, she reminded herself sternly, it wouldn't do her any good to dwell on it. He was out of her league. He came from the perfect background with the perfect family and he certainly had no business being with the likes of her.

Still, insisted a small corner of her mind, she could dream, couldn't she?

When she had first gotten off the streets, when she was still struggling to fight off her past and find some measure of self-respect, she'd dreamed of the magic man who would appear one day to make it all worthwhile. But then she'd discovered a thing or two about society.

She'd learned—the hard way—that one could change their future, but never really escape their past. Not long after she had graduated from rehab, she'd been approached about giving speeches for the cause of homeless youths. At the time the thought had excited her. It seemed the perfect way to start her new life. She'd been a runaway herself. What better way to repay the society that had given her a second chance? What better way to help those who hadn't been as lucky as she had, who were *afraid* to believe there was a way out?

She'd left the poorer part of the city and crossed to the condos, ballets and theaters on the other side of the river. And she'd liked giving the speeches. She believed in the cause, passionately, and her own fervor had helped convince the audience. But then she'd started including her own experiences in those speeches mistakenly thinking it would lend credibility to her words.

Instead it had led to half the male contingency of her audiences hunting her down after every speech. Her past seemed to intrigue them and they had all seemed to want one thing. And they'd never taken her refusals very kindly.

But she'd learned. She'd learned to cut it out of her speeches and when that hadn't been enough, she'd simply gotten out of the speech business once and for all. She was through with feeling cheap.

But the experience had had its rewards. She'd met some wonderful, caring people, like Mrs. Jacquobi and Major Price, who had helped her with the down payment on this house. They also actively helped her find jobs and permanent homes for many of the kids who came to her shelter.

She'd done everything else on her own. She had put herself through night school, graduating after five years with a business degree. Then she had asked around, put together business cards and résumés, and managed to find enough clients for a small bookkeeping business. Now she simply worked out of the shelter, using the personal computer she'd bought. She would never be rich, but between her income and the donations she received she could keep the shelter operating. And that was her true career.

So things had worked out in the end. After rehab she'd gotten on the wrong track for a while, but she'd made it work in the end. And looking back to the pain that had been her existence before rehab, she knew she'd fought a long, hard battle, and was finally learning how to win.

The pride that flowed through her was still a new and fragile sensation. She'd stumbled upon it quite by accident when she'd signed the papers for this house and had realized that, finally, her dream was coming true.

Now, looking around herself at the faded brown sofa and cracked coffee table, she felt the pride grow. Looking at Shadow next to her, deeply enraptured by the magic of the old west, she felt it burst in her chest.

The credits were flashing across the screen as the movie wound to a close. With lithe but silent movements, Shadow stood and stretched slightly. Thirty seconds later he was gone.

Sabrina found herself praying for the next time. Praying that Shadow would come back, just once more. Maybe next time he would stay.

She was alone in the dark room.

"Take care of him," she whispered into the gloomy night. "Take care of him."

She wondered if that would be enough.

Chapter 2

He made it exactly one week.

One week of trying to forget her, one week of thinking of her constantly. Even now, she was haunting him still.

He knew because, at the moment, he should have been enjoying himself. And he wasn't. It was twilight, his favorite time, and he was lounging against the pillows, one arm thrown over his big mongrel, Woof, the other arm thrown over his head. The world was peaceful, quiet. From his vantage point in the loft, he could gaze through huge bay windows that seemed to overlook all of Portland. The sky was gray, clouds swirling darkly above, but it lent a certain mystery to the view. Beneath he could see the twinkling lights of the city at dusk.

It was beautiful, intriguing. Soft music played from the stereo across the room and an amber shot of fine Scotch rested on the nightstand next to him. He could smell the sharpness of the Chivas Regal. It tempted him into taking a sip and he felt it burn its way richly down his throat.

So here he was, the perfect time, the perfect view, the perfect music and the perfect drink. Even the perfect companion; he obligingly patted Woof on the head. He should be relaxed, savoring the rare moment of solitude. Instead he was restless beyond belief.

He'd tried very hard to get her out of his mind. He'd called up Raquel—a long-time dating acquaintance—and asked her out. The evening he'd spent with her should have been perfect as well. Raquel was tall and stunning in silk and suede. Her long blond hair, which tumbled luxuriously down her back, practically begged for a man's lingering touch. And in three-inch black heels, her legs could bring a man to his knees.

If her beauty wasn't enough, her conversation always ran witty and clever, covering everything from world events to current fashions. She was stunning and brilliant. In short, everything he had ever wanted in a woman, or at least, everything everyone said he should want.

But she didn't have violet eyes.

Oh, damn, he thought. Here we go again.

He really had thought that he'd gotten Violet Eyes out of his system by the time he'd picked Raquel up. He'd dressed carefully for the occasion, wearing a distinguished black suit. He'd even stopped and had his vintage red Mustang washed and polished.

The car ride had been pleasant enough. He'd complimented her on how she looked in an incredibly tight, black suede skirt and an electric blue, satin blouse. She in turn had complimented him. They had chatted briefly about how her modeling was going and then he'd turned into the Alexis, a very elegant Greek restaurant.

They'd shared moussaka and *spanikopita,* along with a fine bottle of white Robola. The conversation had been smooth, seemingly effortless.

But it *had* been an effort. His thoughts seemed to wander on their own, until he'd found himself wondering if Violet Eyes liked Greek food. Or drank white wine. He'd wondered how she would look, dressed up in heels and silk. He imagined that she would be more than stunning.

The ploy, quite simply, had not worked. Raquel had kept the conversation alive, sipping her wine and looking at him with thoughtful blue eyes. Then the meal had been over, the last bite of moussaka finished, the last drop of wine sipped. There had been nothing else to do but take her home.

They had done it before, of course—gone out, finished a pleasant evening with a nice night-cap. This hadn't been anything out of the ordinary. Except that he had broken out into a sweat long before he'd reached her apartment. The violet eyes simply wouldn't leave his mind.

In the end he'd been saved from a groping apology that would have hurt both of them. Raquel had leaned over and simply planted a gentle kiss on his cheek.

"You should go after her," she'd said softly, a wistful smile on her face. "Whoever she is, she must be special."

He hadn't known what to say, so he hadn't said anything. He'd just watched her enter her apartment, then had driven off alone into the night. How could he have explained that his thoughts were tied up on a woman he'd only met once and not even on a date? How could he even have begun to tell a gorgeous, intelligent woman that she'd been supplanted by a phantom he barely knew?

That had been three days ago and, even now, he was still trying to see the light. He kept trying to reason with himself, pointing out all the reasons Raquel was the woman for him. He could kiss her without breaking his neck, that wasn't an easy find for a man as tall as he was. She was extremely smart, keeping even him on his toes. She fit in well with his life, never demanding, very sophisticated.

But she didn't make his pulse race with an innocent touch. She didn't intrigue and infuriate him all in one breath. She didn't make him think hard about himself and his own actions.

However, he reminded himself cynically, she also didn't have a police rap sheet. Let's not forget that.

Unfortunately he couldn't forget it at all, and it was slowly driving him crazy. He didn't want to think of Sabrina, couldn't bear to think of Sabrina, as a former prostitute. He didn't want to picture all the men who had used her. It turned him cold.

He had seen enough in his years on the force to understand that she had been a victim. He knew that prostitutes were never born, but made. But he didn't know if that was enough for him to accept it. Then again, it obviously wasn't enough to make him forget her.

He felt as if he was smack dab in the middle of a war. On the one hand there was a single woman who attracted him very much. On the other hand, she was part of a case and had a past that twisted his gut every time he thought about it. Even now, he was plagued with doubts. What had she been doing, walking the streets all alone at that time of night in that part of town?

Searching . . . just searching.

The words she'd spoken lingered in his mind and they reached out to him, touching him deep inside in places he'd never known existed, in ways he didn't understand. And he could still see her eyes, those incredible eyes, so wide and so vulnerable.

He needed to see her again, he decided abruptly. As a cop, he would pursue the truth of her actions that night. As a man, he could decide if her eyes truly were as captivating as he remembered. Did her hips really sway gently as she walked? Was she really as beautiful as his imagination painted?

God, he had it bad, he thought. Really bad.

But it didn't make a difference. He would see her again. Tonight even. It was the perfect answer to all his problems. He could verify the credibility of his witness and get the attraction out of his system once and for all.

The thought so impressed him that he immediately abandoned the view, the dog and the Scotch. Five minutes later he was in front of the mirror, shaving off the last of his five o'clock shadow and contemplating how to comb his hair.

And for the first time all week, he was smiling.

Dusk came early to the streets of the city and with it came the cold. Eager shoppers clutched their bags closer and with hurried steps made their way home. Vagrants methodically unfolded newspapers to use as shields against the plummeting temperature. Prostitutes donned fake fur coats, trying valiantly to be both sexy and warm.

Sabrina watched it all as she walked the streets. Her blood quickened to combat the chill and welcome the night. For three long years this had been her world. Three years. Even now, the streets were still in her blood.

But her mission tonight, compared to those nights of long ago, was nowhere near the same. She came bearing handouts for the kids. Each pamphlet listed the area shelters, places to get food and places to go to for medical attention. Unfortunately the list was pathetically short. There were an estimated twelve hundred kids out there somewhere. They had beds for roughly forty. Most kids learned quickly to find places to sleep on their own. Doorways on abandoned streets and fire escapes became fair game. Those who felt rich could ride a bus out to the countryside and sleep peacefully in a field without fear of getting mugged. Sabrina had known one young man who would go to the waiting room of the maternity ward of the city hospital downtown, say he was waiting for his girlfriend and sleep there. Eventually, however, the hospital staff caught on, and he was forced to look elsewhere.

This severe shortage of housing had led Sabrina, with the aid of Mrs. Jacquobi and Major Price, to purchase the rundown house she lived in and offer the four spare bedrooms for any kids who needed them. Her house served as an intermediate shelter, one where kids could be assured of a clean bed, a warm shower and free food. She tried to direct them to counseling services, rehabilitation clinics, or employment services. Often she was able to help them find a job herself through the many contacts she'd made over the years. All in all, the shelter had worked out very well.

For the past week the rooms had remained empty, as a warm spell had hit the city and the kids hadn't needed shelter from the cold. But once again the temperatures were dropping to their usual February chill. She imagined she would have guests shortly.

As the temperature plummeted, she knew, the youths would get more and more desperate to fight off the cold. Some would try prostitution, searching for that one sugar daddy whose wealth and love would take them off the streets forever. Some would use drugs to find a whole new reality. Most would try both.

If she could reach them now, show them hope now, then perhaps she could save them from the three years of hell she'd gone through.

Rounding the corner she saw a group of kids in an alley. Ranging from ages ten to sixteen, they gave her sullen, defiant stares. Sabrina, however, was far from intimidated. Instead she handed each of them the list. None of them said a word. Most just glared as she promised them warm soup and coffee if they got too cold and wanted to stop by.

When she turned to leave she could almost hear their sullen grumbling. "Yeah, right, free shelter and food without strings attached. The lady's probably just some hooker for some pimp, rounding up kids for his stable."

One of the older boys, trying to be tough and macho, threw down the pamphlet and smashed it into the gutter with the heel of his worn tennis shoe.

Sabrina wasn't surprised by the reactions her offer brought. Eight years ago she would have done the same. But her heart went out to the group, trying so hard to pretend they didn't care. It would work for a while, they would be macho, be tough, just as she had. And then the day would come when they were no longer pretending. After years of merely surviving but never progressing, the acting would be over, and they truly would no longer care. She hoped to God that for them, that day would never come.

In her own mind, she knew there was no guarantee that they could be saved. These kids were lost, like many adults were lost—and if *they* hadn't done any better... What was worse, on the streets they had no past and no future. For these runaways time would blend into one never-ending present.

Some would make it—the ones with blind courage and good luck—some would destroy themselves. She had certainly tried. Some the streets would claim, like Jessie, dear sweet Jessie.

If only she could save them all. If only she could prove to them that they *did* have a future, that they could find all the love and self-respect they were so blindly searching for.

She could only hope that sooner or later, they would come to her.

Street people were not optimists. They firmly believed that nothing was free, no matter what people said. But sooner or later the drugs would be gone, the hoped-for sugar daddy still absent, and then the desperation would take hold. Then, and only then, the too-good-to-be-true offer from that strange lady would come back to them. And driven by desperation, maybe they would come to her.

That was all she could hope for. Once they were at the shelter she could prove her sincerity and offer help for those who were brave enough to grab it. For now all that she could do was wait.

It was fully dark by the time Sabrina made it back to the shelter. She was fighting the stubborn lock, which refused to let her key work, when she heard the voice behind her.

"Is this the shelter?" The voice was faint, mumbling.

Sabrina turned to see a young blonde in shredded clothes with a battered face staggering her way up the walk.

Sabrina finished opening the door, then rushed down to help the girl inside. Assessing the situation with one glance into frightened, pain-filled eyes, she quickly looked up and down the street, searching for signs of the girl's pursuer, who might not be too far behind, but the shadows remained still.

Closing the door behind them, Sabrina locked three different bolt locks, then hooked a chain into place. In this section of town, she never took chances. And with her latest guest, she couldn't afford to.

The young girl had moved away, sinking down onto the living room couch, her head falling back as she finally allowed herself, having reached safety, to slip into unconsciousness.

Sabrina grabbed a first-aid kit and went to work. The actual injuries were superficial. But just looking at the girl, Sabrina could guess enough to fill in her story. Wearing a minuscule, tight black skirt, three-inch spike heels, and a now-shredded, hot pink blouse, the girl was most obviously a hooker. The heavy makeup, clunky earrings and hopelessly overteased hair just underscored her "profession." Most likely she and her pimp had been fighting and he had decided to put her in her place. Judging by the girl's pupils, and the way she was shaking and mumbling, what was causing her the most pain right now was drugs. She was coming down very fast from a recent high.

Struggling, Sabrina half dragged, half carried the girl into a bedroom near the living room.

She applied a damp, cool cloth to the girl's face, then forced orange juice and aspirin down her throat. The girl's shivers and her mumbling seemed to subside a bit and she passed into an easier sleep.

Sabrina sat back with a sigh. The blonde on the bed looked incredibly young. Sixteen at the oldest. The streets hadn't worn her out yet. She still maintained a certain freshness in spite of the bruises. But for how long? Sabrina wondered. How long before the streets milked her dry and consigned her to the same fate as the prostitute in cheap black lace with the vacant eyes?

Wearily Sabrina rose to her feet and moved away from the bed. Sighing, she headed for the living room, leaving the bedroom door slightly ajar so she would hear the girl should she cry out in her sleep. Walking to the old battered desk in the corner, she reached for the phone to call Gord, the huge volunteer she worked with on occasion when she helped out at other shelters. At times physical strength and size became necessary in this business, and she certainly couldn't provide it. But before the phone call could even connect, violent banging sounded at her door.

Damn, she was out of time.

Having deduced that the girl was a hooker, Sabrina had figured that her pimp would show up sooner or later. After all, with at least fifty dollars a trick and sometimes as many as twelve customers a night, a girl brought in four to five thousand dollars a month, tax free. Nobody walked away from that kind of investment.

The pounding resumed and she quickly realized that facing him was inevitable. The decision made, she turned to the one locked drawer of her desk. Using the key she kept in her pocket, she opened the drawer and pulled out a small, gleaming gun.

Please, she prayed silently, please don't let this be necessary.

She was hoping that she could bluff, really. Pimps, like most wild animals, were encouraged by fear. And often, in the face of true determination, would be put off enough to back down. Or so she hoped.

"I know she's in there!" a high-pitched voice interrupted. "You can't keep her. She's mine, you hear? And I want her back, damn it."

When Sabrina remained silent on the other side, the pimp tried a new tact.

"I just want to talk to her," he said persuasively. "Come on, man, just a few minutes. I won't do anything, I promise."

But Sabrina already knew that he didn't have to. Pimps maintained incredible holds on their girls. After a five-minute conversation, the girl would probably follow him anywhere and think that was what she really wanted.

All right, Sabrina decided. It was time to find out what they were both made of. Bracing herself, she slowly began to unlock the first bolt lock. She could hear the sharp intake of breath on the other side of the door. He was just four inches away, separated from her by only three inches of plastic and wood.

Her throat became very dry, her breathing shallow. She drew back the second lock. She could practically hear his heartbeat, or perhaps it was just the echo of her own.

Just one left. Her fingers felt the smooth, cold metal. Here goes nothing, she thought, and let it slide open, as well.

She took one last breath, checked the security of the chain lock, gripped the door, then abruptly yanked it open a full three inches.

But the pimp had been waiting, as well. As the first crack appeared he leaped for the door, thrusting his foot into the opening. The chain brought him up short.

She could feel his breath across the brief gap, feel his rage at being immediately thwarted.

For a few vital seconds they simply stared at one another, his gaze murderous with anger, hers calm and controlled, not giving an inch.

Then he grinned—a wide, sickly grin that revealed gold-capped teeth. Looking down at the arm he held by his side, Sabrina saw the reason for his sudden confidence. Next to the pantleg of his gray silk suit, glittered the menacing blade of a knife.

She couldn't swallow, couldn't breathe, but her eyes remained level and even. Slowly, behind the door, her fingers tightened around the cold handle of her gun.

All at once the pimp brought up his arm, but even as he did, a shadow fell across the porch and a thick arm brought the smaller man up short.

"I wouldn't do that if I were you," a deep voice rumbled out of the darkness. "You see, if you hurt the lady, then I'll be forced to break every bone in your scrawny little body."

Startled, the pimp turned to find a huge, hulking man grinning down at him coldly. The knife fell harmlessly to the side as an iron grip clamped hard on his wrist. Eyes wide, the man suddenly realized he was in a battle he could no longer win. A true coward without his knife, he didn't waste any time. With a strangled yelp, the little man in silk turned and fled down the street.

Thomas watched him go with satisfaction. When he thought of what that undergrown piece of vermin had tried to do, it made his blood boil.

Then he looked down to meet the one wide violet eye staring at him through the crack in the door. His eyes narrowed dangerously as he remembered her tempting the armed man behind the flimsy safety of a cheap chain.

"What the hell did you think you were doing?" he ground out. "Do you have a death wish or what, lady?"

Sabrina stared at the menacing man before her, and for the first time realized just how pathetic the chain alone could be. If a man like Lieutenant Lain tried to attack, against such size and strength, the chain would be about as sturdy as sewing thread.

But she swallowed down her sudden fear even as her legs started to shake. On the edge of the fear, though, came anger. Behind the door she discreetly slipped the gun into her pocket. This was her house, damn it. He had no right to doubt her ability to protect herself.

"Why hello, Lieutenant," she responded coolly. "Fancy meeting you here. Well, as long as you're in the neighborhood, would you like to come in?"

She carefully drew back the infamous chain and opened the door fully. With the door open, she could now see all of him, and what she saw took her breath away all over again. Somehow, she'd managed to convince herself that he was smaller, much less forceful. But nothing could hide the truth now, not with the man in front of her, up close and *very* personal. Her mouth went dry and she found she had trouble *not* staring, so she didn't even try. He was now smoothly shaven, his dark blond, slightly bronzed hair combed back into waves. His eyes were no longer bloodshot, but burned into her, a clear, alert and disconcertingly fierce green. This time he had on gray slacks and a white dress shirt with gray pin stripes. A dark striped tie in subtle shades of deep wine and gray completed the commanding picture.

While she completed her inspection of him, he examined her through eyes still sharp with anger. But even as he wanted to strangle her in frustration, he had to admit that his imagination had failed to do her justice. Her eyes truly were as large and as intensely violet as he'd remembered them to be, although he'd forgotten how they were framed by thick, lush lashes. Her complexion was a natural, creamy white, devoid of all artifice or makeup. There were dark smudges under her eyes, but they only added to the intriguingly fragile quality about her. Her hair had apparently been combed haphazardly, spirited curls springing about. His eyes took their fill. Her form was as delicate as he remembered, looking even smaller in an extra-large T-shirt that hinted at the curves beneath. Once again she was wearing jeans and tennis shoes.

She looked absolutely wonderful and it made him even madder.

"You're nuts, lady, you know that?" he demanded. "You are absolutely, positively, one hundred percent nuts."

"Does that mean you'd like to come in?" she asked sarcastically, and gestured with her hand. "By all means."

He scowled at her tone, and brusquely pushed his way in.

"You're certifiable," he continued as he slammed the door shut behind him with one strong kick of his leg. "Do you have any idea what kind of danger you put yourself into just now? I know the man looked small, but you're a regular walking Lilliputian. And do you know the odds of thin chain versus man with knife?"

Sabrina gave him a chilling look. "Thank you for your concern, Lieutenant," she said flatly. "But as I believe I told you earlier, you do your job and I'll do mine."

Taking in her rigid posture, he found his anger slowly draining away and sighed in defeat. There was no use getting her on the defensive, no matter how small, she *had* managed to protect herself thus far without his help.

"Just be careful," he added a last warning, feeling suddenly worn. He was really too old for this.

Sabrina took pity on him then. The man really was just trying to do his job.

"Can I get you anything to drink?" she asked as a peace offering.

"Sure," he said, accepting her gesture with a look of relief. "What do you have?"

Sabrina headed toward the ancient kitchen. "Well, let's see...looks like orange juice, instant coffee, or water." She smiled apologetically at the limited options. She imagined that he was used to being offered selections from a full bar or, at least, a full refrigerator.

But he smiled easily and ordered orange juice.

The sight of his brilliant smile and the way it lit up his face nearly took her breath away again and, despite the tension-ridden moments just past, she found she couldn't help herself, and she smiled back. Somewhat tremulously, somewhat timidly, but an honest-to-goodness smile nonetheless. She turned around, feeling out of sorts, and headed for the kitchen, reminding herself to concentrate on the orange juice.

When a few minutes passed without her returning Thomas walked over to the kitchen to check things out. He found her fighting the lid on the jug with shaking fingers that refused to function.

"Hey," he said softly, and put his large hand over hers. "It's okay now."

His eyes were dark and warm with a tenderness that overwhelmed her until she felt she'd drowned in the emerald depths. Her lips parted on their own, searching for air, searching for things she didn't dare want.

Thomas felt his own breathing quicken as he felt her delicate hand shaking in his grasp. Sweet Jesus, she was even more beautiful than he'd remembered. She looked soft, inviting. He knew he shouldn't do what he was about to. Even as he leaned slowly over, he was reminding himself that she was part of a case. Business, just business. But it seemed he had been dreaming of her too long, wanting her too long.

He couldn't stop.

Lightly, tentatively, he brushed his lips over hers, exploring the texture, tasting her softness, lingering. Slowly he drew her into the circle of his arms, gently bringing her closer, parting her lips deeper, the moist recesses of her sweetness.

At the first contact she started a bit, unsure, slightly fearful. But his hold remained light, the kiss coaxing rather than demanding. With a soft sigh she relaxed into his arms, leaning into the warmth of his solid chest. She could feel the heated strength of him, protecting her, drawing her in to the pools of his passion.

Then suddenly the warm lips were gone, and he spun away, swearing vehemently. She stood there, dazed and uncertain. For one terrible moment, she felt the tears of rejection sting her eyes as she fought for control.

Thomas was cursing himself even as he marveled at the wonder of the kiss they'd just shared. He never should have done that. He knew that clearly as he knew that he would most likely do it again. Then the facts hit him, full force. She was part of a case, straight and simple, and she came with a questionable past. Kissing her again was *not* an option. He would have to use more control, although something told him finding that control would be less than easy.

Sabrina swallowed uneasily and stared blankly at the orange juice jug sitting on the counter. Though her fingers still shook, she managed to open it and pour them both a glass. The whole time, he remained with his back to her.

He knows, she thought suddenly. Of course. He had checked to see if she had a record.

She felt a horrible sinking feeling inside her. Of course he had pulled away. He didn't want to be involved with someone like her. He was Mr. All-American, while she...she was the girl he was never supposed to meet.

She swallowed again and felt resignation, seared into her by time and bitter experience, sink in. It was okay. She was strong, she could deal with this. She straightened her spine and held out the glass of orange juice to his back.

"Your orange juice, Lieutenant," she reminded him.

"Don't call me that," he snapped as he whirled back around, then could have bit off his tongue at his sharpness. She was giving him one of her cool, level looks. The sweetness was gone, her control now firmly in place, and he had lost all chance of exploring the woman underneath.

"I'm sorry, I didn't mean to snap," he said at last. "It wasn't your fault. I didn't—"

"I understand," she interrupted smoothly, not wanting to hear his groping apology. "We're both adults, it's quite all right. Now," she said briskly, closing the subject altogether, "what can I do for you?"

"Pardon?"

"Well, I highly doubt that you were just in the neighborhood," she supplied with an arched eyebrow. "So you must have come for a specific reason. Do you need more information, or has something new developed?"

His stomach sank to the bottom of his shoes. God, he didn't want to ask the question now. Not now, when he was still the man trying to understand the woman. He didn't have a choice, though. She had called him Lieutenant and she was right. He was a cop, and it was time he started acting like one.

She was looking at him with that perfectly calm look again, waiting. He swallowed hard, closed his eyes briefly, then got on with it.

"I have a few more questions," he replied, trying to make his voice sound as level as hers. "Why don't we sit down?"

She nodded and walked over to the living room and the faded couch, sensing his apprehension but unable to pinpoint its source. She watched him as he took a seat in the chair next to the sofa, her lips twisting wryly.

"The night of the murder..."

She nodded as he paused, urging him on as he hesitated.

"You said you were out walking. Could you clarify that please?"

For a moment she just looked out at him, not understanding. Then, in a blinding rush the insinuation sank in, burrowing deep.

You just can't stand it, can you? she thought vehemently. *You're attracted to a former prostitute and you can't stand it.* But another part of her wanted to cry like a child. She could never get beyond her past. Even after all these years, she was still proving herself to everyone, even to herself.

"Lieutenant Lain," she said at last, "has your life really been so perfect that you've never wanted for more? Haven't you ever been woken up suddenly, in the middle of the night, by a restlessness you couldn't pinpoint or a desire you couldn't name? If you haven't, then I congratulate you. You must certainly live a charmed life. But as for the rest of us..."

She let the words trail off, but he didn't seem to notice, his mind still focused on her words.

Haven't you ever been woken up suddenly... by a restlessness you couldn't pinpoint...

How had she known?

Searching... Just searching.

And in that instant he finally understood what he'd instinctively sensed that day in his office. Understood the restlessness, the yearning for something nameless, and most of all, the loneliness.

Searching... Just searching.

Yes. And perhaps he was, as well.

"What else would you like to know, Officer?" she said, scattering his thoughts. He noticed that she'd amended the last word from lieutenant, but had still managed to maintain the faintly derogatory tone. It made him feel like a green rookie with more shine on his shoes than tact. He had to hand it to her, she really knew how to get to a guy.

"Officer?" she prompted, impatience now clear in her voice.

Can I kiss you again?

He sat up abruptly, for a moment terrified that he'd actually spoken the wayward thought out loud. But she was still looking at him expectantly.

"Um," he mumbled, starting to lose his composure again. A thought drifted into his mind, and he pounced on it. "Did you ever meet the prostitute who was killed? Through the shelter, of course."

"No," she replied firmly. "I'd never met nor worked with this prostitute before. Mostly I see the younger ones. They tend to be less resigned to their lives, some still remember that they once lived better. Once someone has been on the streets long enough, it becomes a way of life for them and they stop hoping for anything more."

Thomas nodded, understanding her point, but then another thought struck him. According to the reports Sabrina had been nineteen when she'd entered rehabilitation. For a runaway turned prostitute, who, on the average, was between fourteen and sixteen years of age, nineteen was relatively old. What had given her hope at such a late date? He wanted to ask, but hesitated. Would she close up on him again? Well, there was only one way to find out. He asked her.

For a moment her face froze and then wariness clouded her eyes. "There's an exception to every rule, Lieutenant," she said rigidly, her chin once more up and ready for battle.

Frustrated because he knew he'd somehow hurt her, he decided to shelve the question. It would only make her retreat even further behind that cool well of oh-so-polite reserve. And in spite of his doubts regarding her activities that night, in spite of this insane attraction, she was his only witness. He couldn't afford to have her shut him out. Swiftly he changed the subject, intent on smoothing the waters between them. It was *not* because he was curious about the woman he'd held so closely just minutes before.

"What do you do to try and help the kids once they're here?" he asked.

She shrugged, somewhat confused by the question. "I give them shelter, food, a sample of what life could be for them. I try to find out if they do have homes that are safe for them to return to. If they do, I try to talk them into returning. But most don't. I try to help them find the self-respect and courage to change themselves, their lives. If I can get their commitment, I help them find counseling, job training, rehabilitation." Pausing, she saw genuine interest in his eyes and continued, this time with more fervor.

"This is just the first step, here. But in many ways it's the hardest. To change their lives, after everything they've been subjected to, takes more courage than most adults have. But then, these kids have to be strong, or they wouldn't have survived on the streets as long as they have."

Thomas nodded, finding himself caught up in what she was saying. As a cop he came into contact with street kids from time to time, though under completely different circumstances. He interrogated them, hauled them in for loitering, petty thievery and various other misdemeanors and more than a few times, investigated their deaths. In the end, though, they always made him sad, somewhat sickened at what life had done to such young kids. Kids who should have been in school, planning first dates and fighting with parents over homework, not stealing to survive or looking for a place to sleep on the streets. Once or twice, he'd delivered a particularly sick or needy child to one of the few shelters in the city. Other than that, he had never really become involved. He was beginning to realize that he should change that. This lady certainly had.

"Where are the kids you've taken in now?" he found himself asking. "I haven't seen any around."

She smiled wryly. "It's too early and too warm yet. Most of them have temporary spots they know of that aren't too uncomfortable if the weather isn't too bad. It's getting colder fast, though, so I'm sure I'll get visitors soon. Right now there's a young girl sleeping off the aftereffects of something—probably crack—in the other room. That was her pimp you so handily disposed of. She's beaten up pretty bad. I imagine she'll be around for a bit, at least until she heals. She's young yet. Hopefully I can use that time to give her a little hope."

Hope, that was the key word. When was the last time he'd felt hope?

"Do many of them wind up as prostitutes?" he asked.

His enthusiasm pulled at her even as she felt herself stiffen with resistance. She didn't want to talk about prostitution, didn't want to discuss the ugly details that reflected all the reasons he would never want a woman like her.

But it was also her job, her life. And remember, Sabrina, she reminded herself, the relationship was purely professional.

"At one point or another, almost all of them will sell their body for money," she said finally. "Most are runaways. Without an address, and most of them not even the legal working age, they can hardly go out and get a regular-paying job. And a young teenager can make fifty to one hundred dollars an hour on the streets—that's a far cry from minimum wage. Besides, the majority of these kids start out alone and afraid. They aren't sure how to find a place to sleep, or how to cook, or just generally take care of themselves.

"That's where the pimp comes in. He scopes out the areas most likely to have these kids coming in, like bus or train stations, although he finds them in other places, too. One thing is always the same. They're hungry, they're desperate and, coming from bad home situations, they're starved for love. He starts off simple, offering them friendship, a place to crash, some food, and lots of attention. In effect, he seduces them, even taking over and setting rules, administering punishment if they break those rules, being the parent they instinctively still want. Next he finds them a cheap apartment of their own, usually sharing with a few more of his 'friends.' Sometimes . . ." She paused and her eyes darkened momentarily, almost as if in remembered pain, but before he could ask what was wrong, she continued.

"Sometimes it's a lot harder than that, more violent. Some kids actually fight what they can see happening. But the end result is usually the same. Eventually the pimp lowers the boom, letting them know that they have to 'help out,' earn their keep. They do it—some think it's their only choice. How else are they going to survive? Others actually become convinced it's normal, that their new 'parent' really loves them."

She smiled sadly. "But then most of these kids never had loving parents to begin with, so they wouldn't know what normal is, or, for that matter, what real love is."

"Why did you do it?" His voice was soft, intense.

For a moment she almost refused to answer, but then she sighed. It didn't really matter, she supposed. He'd find out sooner or later anyway. Then again, she realized, how did you explain to Mr. All-American how it was to be sixteen and gullible? Sixteen and all alone in the world. Sixteen and believing that the two nice girls who'd offered to pick you up and take you to find a place to stay had done so because they honestly wanted to help? How did you tell a man like Thomas about having protested the moment it was clear what a helping hand would cost and being raped, again and again, by the man the girls delivered you to?

He wouldn't understand. When he'd been sixteen his biggest concerns had probably been whether he'd make the football team and what pretty girl he'd take to the prom. How could he possibly relate to the depths of desperation and despair that could send a kid running from their home and then lock them in a situation that was even worse but inescapable?

"Does it really make a difference?" she asked suddenly. He could see her eyes withdrawing from him once more. "What, does it make it more acceptable if I did it for drugs, because then I wasn't of 'sound mind' so to speak? Or if I was forced against my will? The end result is the same. In the end, it's all really the same."

The intensity of her words and the weary defiance in her eyes convinced Thomas that there was nothing he could say to that. He knew she was right. The exact why of that time in her life *didn't* matter. Not to the world at large and not to him in particular. Because either way he was looking at a woman with a very complicated past. His jaw tightened. All the more reason to remain uninvolved, no matter how tempting the thought of taking her into his arms again.

No, it wouldn't make a difference how she'd become a prostitute, Sabrina thought in resignation as she watched him. Because either way she was still the wrong woman for him. Dully, she wondered why that thought brought her such pain. It shouldn't, she shouldn't care.

He'd lost her, Thomas thought, a by now familiar surge of emotion—frustration mixed with equal parts anger and disgust at himself for hurting her—sweeping over him. He'd pushed the boundaries and now she had retreated to some dark corner of her mind where he couldn't follow. Cursing inwardly, he decided to regroup, move back to a safer topic.

"You know, it's nice for someone in my line of work to hear about programs like this. I've been in homicide for ten years now and it always seems I meet people when it's too late to help them. I spend my time piecing back together lives, finding out where it all went wrong, but the people are already dead. And there's nothing I can do about that."

Instinctively, she detected the bitterness lacing his words and it touched her in ways she couldn't explain. Disregarding the hurt he'd unknowingly caused when he'd shown her that her past still mattered—he had, after all, only reminded her of what she'd always known—she looked at him in amazement. How was it that this big man with the compellingly warm eyes couldn't see what she saw?

"But you do make a difference," Sabrina found herself arguing back. "Every time you catch a killer, you're saving someone else's life, or even deterring another person from killing because they're that much more afraid of being caught."

He smiled at her wryly. He'd given himself those same arguments a thousand times. Somehow, they sounded better coming from her. "Yeah," he said with a shrug of his shoulders. "I suppose so."

But his casual attitude didn't fool her. She could read the minute relaxing of his shoulders, the slight smoothing of his forehead. It brightened her own dark thoughts and she smiled, unduly pleased that she'd been able to help him.

For the first time in weeks, watching the wondrously beautiful smile on Sabrina's face, Thomas felt a small portion of the weight on his shoulders decrease. Looking into her earnest violet eyes, it was somehow easier to believe in his job again. It had been a long while since he'd seen it that way. Most of the time, he merely thought he was losing the war against the files on his desk. And sometimes, after a really grueling week, the savageness of it all threatened to overwhelm him. But Sabrina still had the hope that he'd given up on somewhere along the way. She was right, hope did make the difference. And perhaps, just perhaps, so did his job.

"Well, then," he declared with mock grandeur, "I propose a toast."

He raised his glass of orange juice into the air and a somewhat bewildered Sabrina followed suit.

"I propose a toast to all those people out there who are trying to make a difference."

Sabrina smiled as she clinked her glass against his and took a sip of her orange juice. The toast had included her, too, and she liked the idea of him finding something in her worth toasting.

Thomas set his glass firmly down on the unsteady coffee table.

"Well, I believe it's time to call it a night."

Sabrina nodded, and slowly uncurled from the sofa to lead him to the door. She was standing close to him, so close he imagined he could feel the warmth radiating from her delicate frame.

"I hope you got everything you needed," she said.

For a moment the double meaning behind the comment attacked his imagination. No, he thought, inhaling deeply of her light, clean fragrance, he hadn't gotten what he needed at all.

He looked down at her small hand poised on the doorknob, and wondered if it was realistic to think that he could hold out. He had already crossed over that invisible line, the line of reason and logic. His heartbeat accelerated at the possibilities—

With a jolt he felt reality kick in. The foolhardiness of a serious involvement—and with her his gut told him it would be no less—with a woman whose past was so complicated was potently clear. He thought of himself as a fairly liberal man, and it was obvious that Sabrina was a wonderful lady, but he didn't know if he could keep on kissing her, touching her, without wondering about all of the men that had come before him. It wasn't something he'd ever had to deal with.

But even as he acknowledged such thoughts, he was staring into eyes so violet, and so beautiful, that they stole his breath away. Even as he was thinking he should just walk away, he was wondering how soon he could return. She had touched him tonight, touched him in a totally unexpected way. For a brief period of time, she'd given him back hope.

Sabrina inhaled sharply at the fiercely intent look in Thomas's eyes as he gazed at her. Her mind was transported back to the kitchen, when his lips had been so warm and his arms so strong. Her pulse rate skyrocketed and her mouth went dry. She could no longer swallow.

Thomas cleared his throat noisily. "Well, thanks for everything." But the heat in his eyes spoke another message entirely.

"You're welcome," she replied faintly.

He edged closer to the door as the air began to crackle with the tension of unfinished business. He closed his eyes, and very stiffly walked out to his car. She stood watching him, unable to take her eyes from the strong figure vanishing in the night.

Chapter 3

He made it one block before the CB on the dashboard crackled to life. He felt the sinking sensation even before he answered the call. After all these years, he wasn't wrong. Thirty seconds later he made a quick U-turn and raced off to the murder scene.

Pulling in, he felt a curious sense of déjà vu. This time flashing lights tried valiantly to combat the darkness. A gray February mist hooded the lights, obscuring the boarded-up houses, and dimming the reflections off the streaked graffiti. The lights exposed the crowd, a wet collection of running mascara and skintight neon. Red sirens flashed off the blanketed body, still holding the place of honor in the middle of the street. Yellow crime tape glowed in the darkness, framing the gruesome picture.

Taking it all in, Thomas felt a strange foreboding creep up on him. Silently he prayed. For once he wanted to be wrong. But it wasn't enough.

Even before he pulled back the sheet covering the body he knew what he would see. This time the hair color was different, a cheap peroxide blond that badly needed touching up. The makeup glared back from a worn face, now passive in death.

Her throat was slit.

And laying perfectly centered on her chest was the black rose.

There was only one more thing left to check. He glanced at the wrists. It took a few seconds, but he found them. Blue threads.

Oh, Jesus, he thought. Oh, Jesus.

"It's the same, isn't it?"

Thomas didn't have to look up to know it was his partner. Nor did he have to answer the question. They both knew the answer.

A muscle flexing in his jaw, Thomas wordlessly pulled the sheet back over the dead woman's face and stood up. He and Seth exchanged grim looks. They had been too slow. Someone else was dead, and in the back of his mind, Thomas felt the weariness creep in. The department—*he*—was doing all they could, but without any more real clues... How many more sleepless nights were in store for them on this one?

When Thomas finally spoke, his voice was hard and flat, void of much hope. "Maybe there's another witness this time."

Seth just nodded, echoing tonelessly. "Maybe."

Thomas turned back to the crowd, whipping out a small notebook to start the bystander accounts.

"Come on," he said, motioning to Seth. "There might not be a witness this time, but we've got to find something. Or this won't be the last late-night call for us. Not by a long shot." With grim determination, both men faced the crowd of overpainted peacocks before them. One of the girls winked up at them with her silver-sparkled eye, and blew a bubble. Thomas could tell that it was going to be a long night.

Not more than five miles away Sabrina awoke in the middle of the night to a feverish and fighting boarder. As Thomas interrogated streetwalker after streetwalker, Sabrina raged her own war with a damp cloth, orange juice and aspirin. It took three hours and all her energy to finally break the fever, but when Sabrina finally fell asleep at four in the morning, it was with a satisfied smile on her face.

At least her night had been productive.

It was well after noon when Sabrina heard the first stirrings from the bedroom downstairs. She was just finishing up the books for another shelter downtown when she heard the clanging bang of the water pipes kicking to life. Sabrina didn't waste much time. The girl was probably hopelessly disorientated and confused. Better to welcome her right away.

Moments later, after taking a brief breather to compose herself, she walked into the bedroom downstairs.

"Well, you certainly look a lot better this morning," Sabrina said brightly as she spotted the girl sitting cross-legged and uncertain in the middle of the bed. "But those bruises will take a while to heal."

The girl self-consciously raised a hand to the hot and swollen flesh on her face as she stared at the tiny woman before her. The fear was apparent on her face, but Sabrina wasn't surprised. The girl had probably learned her distrust the hard way.

Maintaining her calm and friendly composure, Sabrina gave the girl a soft smile and held out her hand. Hadn't it been just last night that she'd been telling Thomas about how she'd tried to reach her runaways? It had sounded good then, she wasn't about to fail now.

"Hello," she told the girl gently. "My name is Sabrina Duncan. I don't believe we've officially met yet."

The girl hesitated, unsure. Then, awkwardly, she held out her hand to shake Sabrina's. "My name is Suzie," she said nervously.

Sabrina ignored the girl's discomfort and instead sat companionably down on the edge of the bed. She saw the girl tense, but remained where she was, knowing it would take time to get Suzie to relax.

"You haven't been on the streets long have you, Suzie?"

Suzie shook her head, her eyes still wide with caution and fear as she stared at the woman on her bed, sitting only five feet away.

"Six months," she said slowly.

Sabrina nodded. The girl had the fear and distrust of a street person, but none of the brassy bravado prostitutes developed in order to cover it. A part of the girl still worried about herself, she wasn't resigned enough to be indifferent. That was a good sign, Sabrina knew. As long as just a part of the girl wanted a safer future, Sabrina could use that, develop it, and hopefully get the girl off the streets.

For now she had to get more answers. "Did your pimp do that to you, Suzie?" she asked gently, wanting to get the girl to open up.

But Suzie only nodded again.

"Pimps do that a lot," Sabrina continued conversationally. "Looks like yours must have a pretty good right hook."

Suzie nodded, then, unable to hold back, burst out, "But Willy loves me."

"Does he love his other girls, too?"

Suzie shook her head furiously. "No, he just needs them for the money. I'm his favorite. He gives all the best things to me. And he takes care of me. He found a place for me to stay and he makes sure none of the customers beat me."

"So he can beat you himself?" Sabrina asked gently.

"Oh, but I deserved that," the girl said earnestly. She ducked her head down in shame. "I took all the money I earned and bought some drugs from this guy I know. I mean, I shouldn't have done that, taking Willy's money like that."

"But if he loved you, he wouldn't hit you."

The blonde just laughed, and Sabrina felt some of the hope in her die. This was going to be harder than she'd thought.

"Stay here for a bit," she said softly. "I'd really like for you to stay."

The teenager shook her head. "I can't. Willy loves me, I can't leave him. I need him. Besides," she said brightly, "he's probably calmed down by now, and he'll be so glad to have me back that he'll forgive me. You don't understand, I can't just leave him."

"Actually, I do," replied Sabrina after a pause. "And I'm sure you do, as well. There's no such thing as love on the streets, Suzie." Sabrina gave her a direct, hard look. "Even you know that."

Suzie shook her head in denial again, but her hand lingered on her battered face. "Look," she said softly. "I know you probably think I've made a real mess out of things, but I just know it will work out. I'm still young and pretty, and someday I'll meet some man and he'll want me enough that he'll keep me. And then I can escape Willy and the streets forever. Honest, it's going to work out."

Sabrina smiled softly down at the earnest girl. "Honey, I've been there, and trust me, it's not going to work out."

Suzie looked down, staring at the patterns on the pretty comforter. No, it probably wouldn't. But she didn't know what else to do.

"Suzie, do you have any parents?"

Suzie's head jerked back up, and she looked at Sabrina suspiciously. "Just my dad and he's worse than Willy."

Sabrina nodded, fully understanding.

"You know, Willy came by yesterday. He said he wanted to talk to you. He was very forceful about the issue, but we kept him away. You are safe here," she told the girl, and silently thanked the absent lieutenant for his part in making that true. "As long as you want to stay, I'll do everything I can to help you."

"In return for what?" The suspicion was back in the girl's eyes.

"This house is a shelter," Sabrina said steadily. "Its sole purpose is to help people like you. The only thing we want is to help you, to give you a second chance at life. Everyone deserves that. Give me a week, Suzie," she urged softly. "Just one week."

Suzie remained suspicious, Sabrina expected that. It would take time to ease her doubts. But finally, after a long pause, the girl shrugged. She really didn't have anyplace else to go.

Sabrina gave the girl and her grudging affirmative a brilliant smile. "You won't be sorry," she told her. "Now, how about some breakfast at two in the afternoon?"

"All right," Suzie replied with more enthusiasm this time. "But you have to cook, I can't even get cold cereal right."

"That's okay," whispered Sabrina confidentially. "I've been known to get it wrong myself."

Suzie smiled, her first real smile.

Seeing it, Sabrina felt herself breathe a little easier. It was just one smile, but for now, it was enough.

The phones kept ringing shrilly and the stacks of files kept threatening to topple over. Seth kept swearing and Thomas kept wishing he was anywhere but at the station.

He and Seth hadn't bothered to return home after filling out their reports last night. Instead they had grabbed a few hours' sleep on lumpy sofas, promising themselves an early evening for today. But so far, things were not going well. They had come up with exactly nothing since rolling off the sofas at seven this morning. No witnesses, no suspects, no leads.

They had been called into a meeting with the captain. It had mostly consisted of him yelling and Seth and Thomas nodding. The captain had also informed them that a psychiatrist would be brought in to help diagram a mental sketch of the killer.

Whatever, Thomas thought. At this point he would try anything. The frustration was overwhelming him and he'd already spotted four new gray hairs since morning.

He could remember Sabrina, with her wonderful violet eyes, telling him that he did make a difference. There had been sincerity, faith in her voice. He wondered what she would think now. The guy that was supposedly making a difference was thoroughly stymied and time was running out. Every day they didn't catch this guy, the chances were that somebody else would die. And they had nothing, absolutely nothing.

He put his head in his hands and groaned, feeling each and every muscle in his body knot up. He reached for the phone, as he already had at least twenty times today. And, as he had done all twenty times, he pulled his hand away at the last minute. He knew he should call Sabrina, tell her about the new murder. But he didn't want to call without having anything concrete to tell her. He wanted to call and say that he, the man she'd said made a difference, was on the verge of solving the case, of saving lives. He didn't want to face her knowing nothing, feeling helpless.

Seth had already asked him if he had learned anything at Sabrina's last night. To his chagrin, and Seth's never-ending amusement, Thomas had found himself blushing.

"Purely professional, huh?" Seth had taunted knowingly. But he had sobered quickly. "Be careful, okay? Be very careful."

Thomas hadn't needed Seth's warning. He already knew that he was flirting with trouble. But he couldn't seem to help himself.

The world was turning into madness, youths knifing each other in the streets, drugs pouring like water into the city. And against the backdrop of all the lunacy, his mind kept turning, time and again, to the sweet warmth of a certain lady. To the honeyed softness of her kiss. To the shining earnestness in her eyes as she talked of mending all those lives.

He wanted out of this place. He wanted to hit the road at a run, to burn up the blocks racing to one battered house filled with so much richness. He glanced down at his watch. No such luck. There were still hours to go.

Running a hand through already rumpled hair, he stared blankly at the list of florists he was supposed to call. He still wasn't sure what he was even supposed to ask. Somehow "Hello, do you sell dead flowers?" didn't seem appropriate.

Oh, hell, he thought.

But then he had an idea. The only problem was that it had very little to do with the murder at all. But it was a good idea, one that brought a smile to his lips.

A few minutes later, as he was making the calls, he found that he was actually humming.

The knock on the door startled Sabrina. She had just hung up the phone from talking to Maria, who ran a huge shelter that Sabrina often worked with and kept the books for. She'd hoped that Maria might have some information in the computer about Suzie. Maria didn't have any, but had promised to run a deeper check on Suzie.

Listening to Maria's tinkling voice, Sabrina had felt the tension of the past few days ease. Maria was hope incarnate. No matter how many kids, how understaffed, overworked and underbudgeted, she always got the job done. With a few dozen more just like her, they might actually win the war.

Thank God for the diligent, Sabrina was thinking as her hand lingered on the phone. Thank God for Maria.

The knocking persisted, and Sabrina roused herself from her thoughts to head cautiously for the door. It was already dark outside and memories of Suzie's pimp, Willy, floated near.

She eyed the door warily.

"Who is it?" she called.

"Santa Claus," responded a gruff voice she would have known anywhere.

Smiling in relief, and, in spite of herself, anticipation, Sabrina rapidly undid the three locks and the chain to throw open the door for Thomas.

"Well?" he asked.

"Well what?"

"Well, aren't you going to ask for ID?"

She laughed, a small almost shy sound that changed to a sighing "Ohhh" of delight when he brought his hand out from behind his back.

"Daffodils? In February?" she said in amazement, accepting them from him. "Wherever did you find them?"

At an amazingly expensive Holland greenhouse in the city, he thought. But he was pleased that he had spent the money just to see that look of childlike delight on her face. The lady needed to have more fun. All these shadows weren't good for her.

"A good cop never reveals his sources," he replied glibly.

She smiled slightly in response, her attention still focused on the soft, golden flowers before her. They were so amazingly beautiful and fragile. Her eyes grew moist and she turned away from him to hide the telltale sheen.

She had to swallow hard to relieve the lump that had gathered in her throat as she carefully arranged the flowers in a clean Tupperware pitcher. She wished she had a fine crystal vase to display them in. But she certainly didn't own any crystal, and actually, she didn't own any vases at all. There had never been any need, as no one had ever brought her flowers before. Her eyes threatened to overflow, but through the teary moisture, she kept smiling.

She turned back, but didn't dare meet his eyes. Instead, in a rare gesture that surprised them both, she leaned forward and gave him a quick little hug. Then just as quickly she withdrew, suddenly feeling even more nervous, her heart racing in her chest. She invited him inside, all the while warning herself to be careful. He brought you flowers tonight, but last night, just as quickly as he kissed you, he pulled away.

It was something she was having a hard time forgetting. She was a strong woman, but not so strong that she purposely went looking for ways to get hurt.

"Is tonight personal or professional, Lieutenant Thomas?" she asked softly.

"It's Thomas," he corrected her. "And I guess it's both," he responded quietly to her question. "Sabrina . . . there's been another murder, so I need to ask you a few more questions, maybe see if I can't jar your memory more. The daffodils are my way of apologizing for blowing up at you last night. I shouldn't have done that. But please promise me that you'll be more careful next time. This really isn't the safest part of town."

She gave him a wry smile. "I am aware of that, Lieutenant. Trust me."

He nodded. "Well, then. For starters, did you ever meet a prostitute named Marlys?"

Sabrina shook her head. "Is that the woman who was killed?" He nodded. "How old was she?"

"Almost thirty. The last woman was twenty-seven, but looked well over thirty."

"The life-style does take its toll."

"What about her pimp? His name is—" Thomas flipped through his small spiral notebook, which accompanied him everywhere "—Moonshine."

Sabrina nodded her head at that. "I've worked with a few of his girls before. I'm surprised he kept a woman that old. The last one I stole from him was fourteen."

"Think he's capable of murder?"

Sabrina gave him a narrow look, then nodded her head. "I'd say he's probably already committed one or two. But not with a knife. The man is big, and he likes using his fists."

"Well, I'll check into it. One last thing, I don't suppose there was any chance you were out 'searching' last night?"

Her reply was level and calm. "I spent the night trying to calm Suzie's raging fever. Trust me, I wasn't going anywhere."

"Suzie?"

"The girl who arrived last night. The one whose pimp you so handily disposed of. Thanks again," Sabrina said sincerely. "I know I probably didn't sound like it last night, but thank you."

"How's she doing now?" Thomas asked quietly.

"Better. She's pretty beat up, but she agreed to stay here for a bit, at least until she heals. Hopefully I can use that time to change her mind for good. We'll see."

"Still," Thomas said, and smiled wryly, "I'd say your night went a hell of a lot better than mine."

"The case?" she asked. "You haven't gotten that much further?"

Thomas shook his head in self-disgust. "We're getting absolutely nowhere. And I just know it won't end here. We now have a serial murderer on our hands, I have no idea when he'll stop and for the life of me, I can't get a grip on him. Now the only question is how many more women will die before I get my act together."

Sabrina gave him a quizzical glance. "You're awfully hard on yourself, you know. I thought only in the movies were cases solved in two hours or less."

"It's been a week."

"Still, average time must be much longer than that."

She was right, but the knowledge that he was batting average wasn't incredibly reassuring.

"You do your best," Sabrina said softly. "I'm sure you do. And I'd bet most of the time, you do find the culprit. So don't get too bogged down in just the failures. If you burn yourself out, who will help those people then?"

He didn't answer. Sometimes there was no way of helping. But then he looked at her, and he thought of the girl sleeping in the house right this minute, and he realized that he was wrong. Somehow, some way, it was still possible to make a difference. This woman could. God knows she already had him feeling slightly better. The words came out completely of their own volition. Before he could stop himself he asked, "I have some errands to run, would you care to accompany me?"

She looked shocked for a minute, slightly taken aback. She certainly hadn't expected this. But then, much to her own surprise, Sabrina found that she didn't want to say no. Still, there was the matter of Suzie.

"I don't know," she said honestly, a frown creasing her brow. "Suzie is still here. She's asleep now, and after everything she's been through, the poor girl probably won't wake up until well into tomorrow. But what if Willy comes back?"

"Is that likely?"

"I'm not sure," she responded with a shake of her head. "I know he'll try to get her back somehow, after all, she's worth a lot of money to him. He might try to catch her someday when she steps out, or he could call here, or pay a personal visit."

He nodded gravely, fully understanding. "There's a patrol car that's assigned to drive by here every thirty minutes and an unmarked car that's across the street right now—it'll be there until tomorrow morning. That might be enough to scare him away."

Sabrina gave him a sharp look. "Why the surveillance?"

"What do you mean, why?" he asked dryly. "You are the only witness to a murder, you live in a neighborhood only cockroaches could love, and you have an angry pimp after you. Why do you think?"

"You know," Sabrina replied evenly, "the kids around here are not stupid. They can spot an unmarked patrol car miles away. And I can't afford to have you scaring *them* away."

"Nor," Thomas pointed out, "can you afford to leave the one girl that has come here unprotected. And face it, you may have your resources, but you're still no match for a knife."

Her pride demanded she argue, but now wasn't the moment for it. In the end she nodded her head. Really, she could use some time away, and for the next few hours at least, Suzie would be safe. "All right," she said at last.

As further precaution, Sabrina left the lights and the TV on. Then she scribbled a quick note to Suzie, promising to be home soon, in the off chance that she did wake up.

Locking the multitude of locks behind her, she turned around and took a deep breath. She gave Thomas a nervous look out of the corner of her eye. He looked very nice tonight, in a dark green sweater that emphasized his emerald eyes and the bronze highlights in his hair. He was whistling softly as he stepped off the porch and led the way to his car.

She wondered if this qualified for a date and felt the fear pick up once more. She had never been on a date before, which was a ridiculous predicament for a twenty-seven-year-old woman to be in. But she hadn't. After rehabilitation and putting her life on track, she'd just never felt ready for that step. Actually, for a period of two years she hadn't wanted anything to do with the male sex at all. It had taken her a long while to separate the unsavory men she'd known from the entire male population.

Her experience in high society had done little to change her opinion, but gradually, mostly through her work at the shelter, she had encountered the other half of the male species, and decided that maybe there was hope for them after all. But there had hardly been any opportunities for dating.

She wondered what she was supposed to do or say. What were the dating rules for adults nowadays? They had already kissed and that hadn't been a date at all. Just how much was expected from her? Then again, how much did she want?

She wondered if it wasn't too late to call it off, but then Thomas was beside her, casually reaching for her hand and taking it into his comforting grip. She smiled at him somewhat weakly, but felt her nerves unwind a notch.

By now they were at the end of the block and she was about to give up altogether, when he pointed forward.

"That's my car."

It was a far cry from the blue sedan he had driven before. Instead it was a cherry red 1965 vintage Mustang. The paint glowed deep and warm in the night, the chrome flashing brightly.

"It's beautiful," she said, running her hand gently along the sleek curves.

"Thank you," he said, and smiled. "I built it myself when I was twenty-five. I'm sorry to make you walk so far, but I'm rather attached to the hub caps. I'd hate to find them missing."

She had to smile at that. In her neighborhood it would hardly have been a surprise. To avoid such problems, she stuck to the bus system.

Thomas moved forward and unlocked the door on one side. Then he held the door open and gestured for her to get in.

I can handle this, she told herself, sliding smoothly onto the black leather seat. She gave him another smile, hoping that it didn't reveal just how nervous she felt. Thomas neatly shut the door, then bounded around to the other side. He seemed to fill the car entirely as he got in. He had to bend his head slightly, then he slouched down low enough to fit in completely.

Sitting in the small car with such a huge man gave Sabrina another bout of anxiety. Maybe she shouldn't be doing this. She barely even knew this man, after all. She had talked to him twice, the first time in a police station. That hardly qualified. She was in over her head.

But even as the doubts assailed her, instinct took over. This man would never intentionally hurt her, she knew. He had touched her three times and each time it had been with gentle control. Perhaps she had physically seen him twice, but he had been on her mind for more than a week, like a nagging thought that refused to be dismissed.

Looking over at him, shifting the gears easily in the dark, she felt her muscles ease. This wasn't just any man. This was the type of man she had waited eight long years to find. Surely, for just a few hours, no one would begrudge her the opportunity to pretend that she wasn't the woman he was never supposed to meet.

Gliding along curvy roads thick with traffic, Thomas wasn't completely sure where he was going. Eventually they needed to go to the mall. But not just yet. He wanted more time with this elusive woman.

Sabrina was aware of the moment the car crossed the river separating the two sides of Portland, and she was immediately tense. She had once tried to live on this side, on the side with the condos and yachts. The side with the white picket fences, PTA meetings and Boy Scout clubs. Oh, there was darkness here, as well—homeless youths in the heart of the city, sleeping on fire escapes—but it still maintained its facade of bright lights and glitter. It was a contradiction she could never understand.

This was Thomas's side of the city. He had probably been born here, raised here. This was his life, not hers. It was a difference she had learned all too well early in life.

But then the car broke through the tunnel, climbing up the hill. In a matter of minutes it was turning onto a narrow, shrubbed road. As they broke into the first clearing, Thomas felt her gasp even before he heard the whispery sound.

Before them, laid out like a jeweled blanket, glittered all the lights of the city. And behind the lights, towering majestically in the background, rose the snowy shadow of Mt. Hood.

He pulled into a narrow parking spot, then reached over to take her hand.

"Welcome to the Rose Gardens."

She was speechless with awe as he helped her out of the car. She had heard of the Rose Gardens, they were a spot that had made Portland famous. But she had always pictured it in full bloom on a sunny day. She'd never imagined the view it would have at dusk. From this distance, the city seemed magical, a piece right out of a fairy tale. It beckoned to the onlooker with dreamy promises in each glittering light. *This* had been the city she had dreamed about when she'd been sixteen and so desperate to get away. She would have been better off if she'd stayed at this distance, where only the beauty, not the shabbiness, of the city showed.

But even having seen the ugliness, she could still appreciate its splendor as she walked arm in arm down grass slopes with Thomas. A large, geometrical artwork loomed to their right. In the darkness they could only hear the water that tinkled beneath it. Further to their right were the square sections of the different rose gardens. Cement and gravel paths wove through them. But for tonight, Thomas led her over to the amphitheater that had been carved into the side of the hill.

He helped her sit down, then seated himself next to her, automatically putting his arm around the delicate curves of her shoulders. The air was crisp and frosty with winter, causing her to huddle even closer to his warm frame.

"I used to come here a lot," he said, his eyes roaming beyond her to peer into the distance. "I always liked it by night, when it was quiet and hardly a soul was about. It's a good place for thinking."

"What kind of things did you think about?" she asked softly.

He gave her a small smile and their eyes met, clinging for breathless moments. Then he surprised himself by answering her question.

"I used to come hear to talk to my father after he died."

Sabrina remained quiet, simply leaning her head back onto his arm. He pulled her even closer against him, wrapping his arms securely around her. Purely for warmth, he told himself.

"See, when I was little," he found himself saying, "my dad liked to pack us all up on summer afternoons and drive out here to the gardens for a picnic lunch. He was crazy about this place. He'd bring the football and Frisbee and run us into the ground just like a little kid. God, he was wonderful."

"How old were you when he died?" she asked softly.

"Thirty. He went off to his construction firm one morning and just didn't come back. Had a heart attack sitting at his desk. But if he was going to die, that was the way for him to go. He loved life too much to ever slow down."

She nodded against the thick wool of his coat. "What things do you talk to him about?"

"Everything." He smiled slightly in the darkness. "I tell him how things are going at work. I tell him how Mom's doing and how Rich's last football game went. Tonight . . . tonight, I would tell him about this woman whom I've met, this woman who's given up so much of her life in order to reach out to others. I think my father would like that."

She was caught off guard, uncertain emotion clogging her throat. "Why would you say that?"

"Because my father believed firmly in making something of yourself. He believed in people trying their best and giving their all. And that's what you do."

"Oh." She couldn't think of anything else to say. She had never looked at her life quite that way. It gave her a warm feeling to know that Thomas would tell his father about her.

"You know," Thomas said, picking up the conversation softly in the dark. "My father bringing us here was part of a family tradition started by his own father. And someday, I want to bring my own son here and sit him down and tell him all about his grandfather. Play some catch, absorb some sunshine and carry on the tradition."

She nodded against the thick lining of his coat, suddenly unable to swallow and grateful for the protection of the night. She could almost see him, running around sunny gardens with a blond-haired little boy shrieking in pursuit. Maybe the child would slip and fall, and Thomas would be the first one there, brushing off the dirt, teasing away the pain. She could see him patiently teaching his son how to throw and catch. He was the kind of man that was meant to be a father. He had the patience and the love that were essential for fatherhood.

His son would be a very lucky boy, she thought. And his wife, some tall and slim, gorgeous and sophisticated model or socialite, would be a very lucky woman.

She swallowed the pain the images brought to her. Such were the dreams she'd given up a long time ago. Such was the price she'd paid. And for some mistakes, the tally never ended.

Eventually the chill got to them and so, reluctantly, they pulled apart and journeyed back to the car. On to the shopping.

It was almost eight o'clock by the time they arrived and the mall was nearly empty. There was only one jewelry store left open and Thomas headed straight for it.

"Do you mind telling me what we're looking for?" Sabrina panted as she struggled to keep up with his long strides.

"A locket. It'll be my mom's birthday in a month and I want the perfect locket for her."

She should have taken the "perfect" part as a forewarning. Evidently, nothing was perfect enough for Thomas. Finally, after dismissing the entire collection and causing the salesman to break out into a sweat, Thomas settled upon a plan. He would design the locket and the store would make it. The salesman tried to protest, explaining that the store used only its own artists. But the nervous man didn't stand a chance against six feet four of steely determination. He gave in gracefully, breaking open a new roll of antacids.

Thomas didn't notice. With swift, deft strokes, he outlined a simple oval locket, engraved with a single vine that bloomed into an elegant flower. In the center of the flower would rest a single diamond. Sabrina was enchanted in spite of herself. She never would have guessed that such huge hands could draw such a delicate and graceful piece of jewelry.

And when the salesman rang up the price, she thought she was going to choke. Obviously Thomas had invested his policeman's salary well. Or had he? She thought back to the excellent condition of the Mustang and the not-in-season and therefore obviously expensive flowers. She considered the almost arrogant way he moved, with the sure confidence of breeding. Then she remembered that he had said his dad had owned his own construction business. Damn, she thought as it all finally registered. The man must be rich.

The thought made her uncomfortable. She had a lot in common with an overworked detective, but a wealthy man? She had no idea what fork went with what dish or what kind of wine to serve. Her nervousness grew and she slowly began to edge away from him.

But Thomas was too quick for her. He snaked out one arm and pulled her close.

"Don't," he said quietly, having read the emotion filtering through her eyes. "Judging other people by their incomes is beneath you."

Reluctantly she nodded, recognizing the truth in his words. But the discomfort refused to fade completely. It was one more difference to chalk up. One more thing that put this man so far from her reach. One more reason she had not to fall under his charm. High society had only hurt her, she would not allow that to happen again. Besides, what was she thinking of? The kiss they'd shared, today, none of those things meant Thomas wanted a relationship with her. She would do well to remember that.

Perhaps he'd noticed her silence. Perhaps he'd noticed the years that had suddenly weighed heavily in her eyes. Perhaps he'd seen the encroaching darkness to the usually cheerful expression on her face.

She never knew what it was that had triggered it, but the next thing she knew, there was ice cream.

"We want a six-scoop sundae with caramel, butterscotch and hot fudge over rocky road, chocolate chip and pralines and cream ice cream. With lots of whipped cream. And nuts. I like nuts," Thomas told the wide-eyed server.

When the humongous—and decidedly gooey—concoction arrived, Sabrina thought she was going to be sick. But gamely, determined to make the best of it, she picked up a long spoon and dug in. The hot fudge was good, she decided after a bite. And it had been ages since she'd had whipped cream. The pralines and cream was far superior and, after a brief scuffle, she won the last bite of it. But there were still four scoops of ice cream left. Well, maybe three judging by the size of bite Thomas had just taken.

Unfortunately the spoonful was too big for even his mouth and he wound up with hot fudge on his nose and whipped cream on his cheek.

"Not bad," Sabrina informed him. "Highlights the cheekbones well."

With a careless shrug he nonchalantly reached over and planted a glob of butterscotch on the end of her nose. Surprised, she blinked, the earlier depressing thoughts receding a little, if only for the moment. She grinned mischievously. Sabrina definitely didn't know much about wealth, or wine, or table manners, but she did know a thing or two about food fights. When she was done with him, she decided, he would beg for mercy.

In the end it was the serving girl who did. With only thirty minutes before closing, she pleaded, she didn't want the parlor destroyed.

Taking pity, they relented and called a cease-fire, Sabrina watching in amazement as Thomas proceeded to inhale what remained of the sundae.

Then they both went to clean up. It was when they regrouped in the mall that she saw the sweater. Immediately she dragged Thomas into the store.

"It's perfect," she breathed. "Absolutely perfect."

Thomas stared at the soft blue sweater. It was a simple sweater, cut straight along the shoulders. He looked at it, then back to Sabrina.

"No," he said, frowning. "It's not you. Looks more like something a schoolgirl should wear."

"I know. I thought it would be perfect for Suzie."

"Do you normally buy them clothes?"

"No. And I'm actually not sure how she would take it. I don't want her to think I'm trying to bribe her or anything. That would only increase her suspicions on why I've taken her in. But still, it's perfect for her. You know," she said hurriedly. "She really doesn't have much to wear. Her blouse *is* pretty much shredded."

Thomas just nodded, at a loss for what to say, somehow deeply affected by the ever-increasing proof of this fragile woman's generosity, in spite of the coldness she'd been subjected to in her life. Sabrina saw the sale sign on the price tag and that decided the matter. Within minutes she was the proud owner of a new sweater.

After that their time was up. The shops brought down their metal gates in a pointed clang. Thomas reached for her hand in a natural way that he refused to analyze, and they walked out toward the car. At the sidewalk, however, Thomas abruptly dropped her hand and sprang off the curb.

"Race you," he called out as he dashed off.

It really was no contest, but she gamely took off running anyway. Halfway there, Thomas did a fairly good job of faking a stumble, allowing her to catch up with him. They both arrived at the car together, breathless, cheeks flushed.

And gazing down at her, Thomas couldn't remember ever having seen a woman so heart-stoppingly beautiful. The eyes that he had first thought of as being too closed, were now warm and vibrant. Suddenly he wanted to crush her to him in a passionate kiss, but tonight he wasn't sure if he would be able to pull away. She was too giving, too soft. And he didn't want to hurt her. The realization hit him like a sledgehammer and he stiffened. When had that happened?

When had the professional reasons for not becoming involved become so complicated? Suddenly he realized that his doubts about her past were still there, but that now they included a barrier that was just as immutable. Giving in to the temptation of his desire for her would hurt her in a way he couldn't—*wouldn't*—allow. Because even if she survived it, he suspected that he would not.

Sabrina could tell the turn his thoughts had taken. His eyes had darkened to a deep emerald and she could feel his hunger reaching out to her. She wondered if he would kiss her. The thought left her even more breathless, and her lips parted slightly.

Then his eyes clouded and he stepped back abruptly, breaking the sizzling eye contact that had threatened to start a blazing fire right there in the parking lot.

Thomas was the first to speak.

"Let's go home."

Chapter 4

The words hung in the air as they drove to Sabrina's house, ominously gaining import with each mile. She could feel her muscles tightening inch by inch as they smoothly covered the long blocks. Just ten blocks to go, now nine, now eight.

She risked a nervous glance to find his hands firm upon the wheel, his intent gaze peering out into the darkness of the night. Focusing on his hands, she studied them in fascination. He was a large man, but she imagined that he could be tender. His fingers were long, the pads rough with calluses. She could almost imagine how they would feel, skimming over her bare, soft skin. She swallowed convulsively. Four blocks to go.

He glanced over then and for one instant she could swear she saw the burning hunger in his eyes, reaching out to her like a physical touch. But then it disappeared, leaving her with the uncertainty that maybe she'd been imagining it....

I must be crazy, she thought. I don't even *know* this man.

But she did. She had known him forever, waited for him forever. Even now, she could feel the smooth warmth of his lips caressing hers. Teasing hers. Plundering. Heat suffused her cheeks and she turned her head away, looking out the window. Two blocks to go.

Her pulse seemed to have picked up speed of its own accord, racing like wildfire through her veins. Why now? she asked herself bitterly. After all the years of never feeling anything, why should she find passion now? And with a man she had no business being with?

No answer came to her as Thomas turned down the street to her house, the final block speeding by. She could see the dark outline of her house looming in the distance, just feet away. So this is it, she thought. After eight long years, this is it.

He pulled into the driveway.

The tension crackled in the tight confines of the car as each waited, uncertain of the next move.

Despite everything to the contrary, despite the knowledge that there was no future for them, she wanted him. For the first time in her life, Sabrina was feeling the irresistible and seductive pull of full-blown desire. It was against all rhyme or reason, against the certainty that she would only get hurt, but she could not deny it.

Back there, at the mall, despite his hesitation, she'd sensed that Thomas had wanted her as much as she wanted him. Yet now, actually sitting in the driveway, actually at the moment she had anticipated for miles now, she felt fear. Too many times, by too many men, she'd been perceived and treated as if she were some exotic toy. Just once, just this one time, she wanted it to be different. She wanted to take *this* man's face between her hands and force him to look at her. To *really* look at her. She wanted to beg, to plead for Thomas to see the woman underneath. The lonely woman who had struggled to crawl her way out of the gutters. The woman who was still unsure of her worth at times, scared no one would look beyond her past. The woman who had spent a seeming lifetime with endless, cold nights.

Thomas watched the emotions flicker like flames in her eyes, casting the violet depths with intriguing shadows. Her lips were parted, moist with a longing that threatened to drown him in its intensity. Barely banked passion flushed her cheeks, accelerated her breathing, until it was his cheeks that burned, his breath that labored.

His gut twisted over and over again. God, how he wanted her! It would be so simple, too. He could just reach over, one touch...that would be all it would take. But even as his body ached, the unbidden thought rose in his mind. *How many other men had ached just as he did now? How many others?*

There were no answers for questions like that, and perhaps a better man than he would be less obsessed with them. But the truth was that Thomas was only human. The truth was that even as the ache in his loins tightened into veritable knots, there was no escaping the fact that no matter what he felt, for her he would not be just another man. He would not be someone whose name and face she forgot somewhere along the line.

Backtracking, he tried to convince himself that this was a physical thing. And physical things came and went, like hunger that disappeared after eating a snack. In time, this would pass, as well.

But until then . . . God, he was going to lose his mind until then. Gritting his teeth against the desire, he turned to her.

"Thank you for the evening," he told her. "I honestly had a nice time."

Sabrina stared at him blankly for a moment as the words sank in. Somehow . . . somehow she hadn't quite expected everything to end this quickly. Hadn't he just been looking at her with desire? Hadn't she felt the intense, crackling tension in the car? And then, in that instant, it hit her. Of course he was attracted to her. He'd proven that beyond a shadow of a doubt when he'd kissed her in the kitchen. But he had also pulled back.

Because of her past, because she'd once been a prostitute. Unconsciously her spine stiffened and she sat a little straighter in the seat. Somewhere along the way she had lost sight of that little detail. Somewhere along the evening she had forgotten just who she was and just who he was. She had allowed herself to enjoy the evening, to perhaps even look at it as a date. She had forgotten that Mr. All-American would never date a woman like her.

But it didn't matter, she told herself fiercely. She had fought too long and too hard to feel ashamed about it now. So he would never consider having a relationship with her. *It didn't matter.* She was strong, she was proud, she could handle anything.

"I had a nice time, myself," she managed to say finally, determinedly ignoring the fact that the words came out slightly stilted. "Should you have any more questions about the case, feel free to call."

Then, not wanting to drag it out a minute longer, she reached for the car handle. Thomas looked at her curiously, noting the rigid lines of her face, the stiff set of her back. He watched her fingers curl around the metal handle, then pull it back. The door popped open with a little click.

Out of nowhere the desire hit him. He didn't want her to go, he didn't want the evening to end. The rational part of his mind warned him to keep to his side of the car, to let her go. But a deeper, more instinctive need tugged at his gut. Logic warred with primitive instinct. She was a former prostitute. She was a wonderful woman. She was part of a case. She taught him of hope. She wasn't his type of woman at all. She made him feel, for the first time in his whole life, at peace.

Over and over it went, tearing at him, pulling at him until he just couldn't take it anymore. He gave in to the battle, gave in to the frustration, and with a low groan he grabbed her arm and pulled her to his chest. She opened her mouth to protest, but he didn't give her a chance, his mouth swooping down onto hers with unerring accuracy.

His lips were hard, demanding, letting loose—without any of the requisite niceties of a slow seduction—all the passion he'd been trying to control. It was a bruising fire, threatening to consume her. But she wouldn't let it. Instead she abandoned the threads of her own control to anger, leaving behind her insecurities and fear to retaliate with equal fierceness, pushing him back against the seat, giving as good as she got.

His chest was rock-hard against her hands, hard and rippling with muscles that flexed and contracted under her sensitive fingertips. And his cheeks were slightly rough, rasping against the smoothness of her own until they were red and flushed.

He smelled of spices and tasted of heat. And to her own heightened senses, he was overwhelmingly male, wonderfully male. She realized dimly that she didn't want the kiss to end. And it didn't. It kept escalating, soaring higher and hotter. It had begun in anger, and where it would end, she didn't know. The fleeting thought—and her near submission to it, to the uncertainty behind all of this—made her blood run cold.

With a muttered imprecation, she tore herself away and flung herself as far away from him as she could. She sat perfectly still on the other seat, her breathing harsh, her eyes glowing hotly.

"Stop it," she said forcefully, trying frantically to subdue the quiver in her voice. "Just . . . stop all of this."

He looked at her in confusion, his pulse still hammering in his ears, his blood still soaring in his veins.

"Do you want to know what your problem is?" she demanded shakily. "You're attracted to a prostitute, and you can't stand it. You pull me close one minute only to pull away the next. Well I won't stand for that. I am not just some woman with a past, Thomas. I am a woman who's fought her way out of the gutter. I am a woman who is still fighting every day to make a difference out there. I'm a good person, Thomas. And I'm proud of who I am."

Her words were spoken with a passion that stunned him. She was right. She was a good person, and he should be able to see that, to look at the present instead of the past. But still the images of her with all those other men . . . The knowledge that they'd . . .

"I'm sorry," he said, his voice deep with emotion. "But you've got to look at this from my perspective, too. To be perfectly honest, I can't say I've ever come into contact, in my personal life, with someone who used to be a prostitute. I've never had to think about what it would be like to be attracted to someone with . . . your past. This is new for me, too, Sabrina, and if I'm not handling it perfectly, well, I'm not perfect."

"At last," she said sarcastically, hiding the pain his words brought, "we have something in common. You know what the real irony is, Lieutenant?" she bit out, laughing bitterly. "You can't stop wondering about all the men I'm supposed to have been with. And you know just how many there have been in the last eight years? *Zero,* Thomas. I haven't gone out on so much as a date in eight damn years."

Sabrina whirled away from him, and keeping her head high, she pushed herself out of the car, slamming the door behind her. Her spine ramrod-stiff, she walked proudly up the cracked driveway to the door. Then, as slowly and calmly as her shaking hands would allow, she unlocked the door, twisted the knob, and carefully walked through.

Behind her, still sitting in the tight confines of the sports car, Thomas pounded his fist vehemently on the steering wheel. *Damn, damn, damn.* It was just too disconcerting, too new for him, the feelings he was experiencing with Sabrina. He'd only known her a week. And all logic told him, as a man, as a cop, that he shouldn't be getting as close to her as he was getting.

So why was it so hard to listen to common sense. With another muttered curse, he roared the engine to life. Jamming into gear, the frustration riding high, he peeled out of the driveway and into the night.

Sabrina collapsed against the door as soon as she shut it, her eyes half wild, half fierce with anger and passion. Her lips were swollen and her hair tousled. The fire still threatened to burn her blood. With a harsh cry of frustration, she raced from room to room, opening each drawer, pawing through contents as she desperately searched for that last pack of cigarettes that she must have stashed somewhere.

In the upstairs dresser she found it. With shaking hands she lit one and inhaled deeply. The deep breathing soothed her, and she welcomed the nicotine. She inhaled again and again. But while her pulse eased to a reassuringly normal beat, her mind refused to be fettered. Time and again it replayed the events of the night. The softness, the sharing, the laughter, then the desire, and finally the anger. All at once the house was too big, too empty.

With a long sigh she sank down onto the edge of her bed. When all was said and done, she was still alone. Finally after all these years, she had met a man she wanted. And she could never have him. Their worlds were too far apart to ever meet. He had been raised with traditional values, traditional expectations. One of which was never to associate with a woman like herself, not on a public or meaningful level that is. And while she had retaliated with anger, perhaps what made her the angriest was that she did understand. Of course he had doubts. With her past, how could he not?

Even now, after all these years, she just couldn't escape it. Her heart would break, she knew that now. Knowing herself, she would fall hopelessly for him—was already dangerously close to doing so—and he would leave her in the end. Even if he got past her background it would never work. Because she simply couldn't give him the one thing he wanted, the one thing that he deserved most out of life.

In the silent bedroom, her hand came to rest on her stomach and the emptiness there. There was a price to be paid. Always, there was a price to be paid.

The cigarette burned out. She looked at it with regret for there was no other to take its place. She knew she would be grateful in the morning, but right now, alone in the darkness, the night stretched out endlessly before her. If only she could change it all, go back and find that one act that had made it all go wrong and fix it. If only...

She searched the dim memories, trying to pin it all together, but too much had been lost. Had she ever wanted to be a doctor or an astronaut or a veterinarian? If there had been any childhood dreams, they were lost to her now. She'd had no childhood. She'd been born one rainy day eight years ago, when a bum had offered her his coat as she lay huddled in a doorway, exhausted, hungry, and desperately afraid that Pretty Boy would find her there.

When she had first seen the bum, she'd scrunched back further in the scant shelter. But he'd already spotted her and had headed straight for her. A large scarecrow of a man, he'd had a ragged beard and bushy eyebrows that had hidden his eyes. She'd tensed, preparing for the worst.

But he'd only draped his coat over her frail shoulders. Then, wearing nothing but a scrap of a shirt, he had disappeared into the rain.

That single touch of humanity and compassion in the gutter had changed her life. But by then so much had already been lost. So many things she could never change. Now she would lose what she wanted the most; a loving man that would be there when the morning light came.

Suddenly she wanted desperately to disappear into the night. Out there her past meant nothing. Nobody cared who she was or where she'd been.

It would be so simple. Step into the shadows, where there was no past, no present, no reality. She could forget it all. All the trying, all the work. Trying to make it good with a past that was all bad. Wanting to be loved, but always being lonely. She could forget it all. Everything.

Just step into the shadows.

Forget deep emerald eyes, threatening to steal her soul. Forget strong arms and a warm embrace. Forget passionate kisses and fiery exchanges. Forget daffodils and ice cream.

Forget even hope. Lost it all in the uncaring shadows.

But in her heart, she knew that she couldn't do it. Last week, perhaps, she could have disappeared. But now, no matter where she went, the image of a tall, green-eyed man would always follow her. The streets had never left her blood, but now they were being replaced.

And her heart would break.

Exhausted by her thoughts, she quietly left her room and went down the stairs to the kitchen. There, still fresh, still golden, bloomed the daffodils.

Gently she touched the silky softness of their petals. And for the first time since that rainy night eight years ago, she put her head in her hands and wept.

Hours later, she was roused by steady pounding on the door. She glanced once at the clock, registering that it was midnight. She had crawled into bed around eleven after checking on Suzie. The girl had still been sleeping deeply. Sabrina just hoped the pounding didn't disturb her now. She fumbled with the belt on her worn terry-cloth robe. She had an easier time negotiating the darkened stairs, years of experience coming to her aid.

Thinking of Suzie's angry pimp, Sabrina took the precaution of looking through the peephole first. But there was no silk-clad man standing in the drizzly night. Instead she opened the door to two young boys.

As they stepped into the light, she instantly recognized Shadow and felt the familiar relief. The boy next to him, however, was unknown.

He was larger than Shadow, with a tall slouched frame. Black spandex shone through the numerous holes in his jeans, while a black leather jacket hung proudly over a faded T-shirt. Topping it off was an old blue baseball cap, worn backward over a mop of dishwater-blond hair.

From the looks of the scraggly beard on his face, she pegged his age at about seventeen.

Both boys returned her look from the entrance; Shadow looking as composed as ever, the new visitor looking sullen.

"All right," she said, more to the other boy than Shadow. "Here's the deal. My name is Sabrina and I can give you shelter for as long as you need and some warm food, as well. In return," she continued steadily, "you need to observe a few simple rules. All drugs are forbidden. You don't smoke it, you don't sell it while living in my house. The only other rule is to make sure you respect those around you. Start picking a lot of fights and I will ask you to leave. Is everything clear?"

The boy snickered, but nodded, his brown eyes sulky.

"Anything in particular you like to be called?"

He remained silent for a minute, slowly sizing her up. Then, with a careless shrug, he answered her.

"Mike."

She nodded, not pressing him for further details. There would be time enough for that in the morning.

"Hungry?"

Both boys nodded, Shadow automatically turning toward the kitchen.

Spying the dining room table to the left of the entryway, Mike headed straight for it, pulled out a rickety wooden chair and collapsed into it. He propped one foot up on the neighboring chair, revealing a relatively new high-top tennis shoe. He then bent his other knee, drumming his fingers restlessly on his thigh as he stared out the rainy window. Already lost in his own thoughts, his hand moved automatically into his inside jacket pocket. After a brief bit of fumbling, he withdrew a new pack of cigarettes, peeled it open, and lit up without so much as a glance in Sabrina's direction.

But she hardly noticed the cigarette, her gaze still focused on the tennis shoe. She recognized the brand, estimating the cost of the shoes as close to one hundred dollars. She didn't ask where he got the money. She already knew.

She swung her gaze sharply to Shadow, who was in the kitchen, silently slicing cheese for sandwiches. What was the connection between the two? she wondered. The other kid was most certainly a drug runner, she would have to watch him carefully. And Shadow? Had the two met through mutual friends or "business" associates?

She had long wondered how Shadow survived on the streets. He gave off an impression of total self-sufficiency, but she knew that everyone needed cash. She doubted that he'd ever resorted to selling his body, though, he was much too private, controlled for that. So what about drugs or theft? Thinking of the many weapons he carefully concealed, she felt a sinking sensation grow in her stomach.

Damn it, she didn't want him involved in that kind of business! She wanted him off the streets. She wanted to see his face relax just for one instant. She wanted him to look like the fourteen-year-old kid that he was.

The intensity of her gaze must have reached him, for he glanced over, his eyes measuring and appraising. And still giving away nothing. She couldn't stand it anymore. As Mike's attention was focused on the pouring rain, she quietly moved into the kitchen.

Shadow watched her approach with his expressionless eyes, eyes much too old for his fourteen years.

"Tell me, Shadow," she demanded softly. "I think I have a right to know. Are you into drugs, too?"

For a moment he just looked at her, his eyes narrowing slightly, judging, thinking. Then slowly, almost imperceptibly, he shook his head.

Her breath hissed out in a low sigh. "Thank you," she said quietly. "And, Shadow, please promise me that before you ever do, you'll come to me first. Please."

He simply shrugged, and after another small stare-down to impress him with the seriousness of her plea, he acknowledged it with a nod. At least he knew he had an option. That was a start.

He offered her a grilled-cheese sandwich, inclining his head slightly at her refusal, then he carried all six sandwiches over to the table.

Within a matter of minutes, the two boys had scarfed down the sandwiches. They ate with a ferocity and intensity that was almost frightening. As they were finishing, she poured them cups of coffee, watching Mike carefully as he took his cup.

Glancing around, he pinpointed the cracked ceramic bowl in the middle of the table. He raised the top questioningly, looking inside. Discovering that it was indeed sugar, he sat back, drawing it close.

Grabbing a nearby spoon, he began to heap spoonfuls into the coffee. After four, he stopped.

But Sabrina already knew that it was too many. A speed freak.

They loved sugar.

She wondered why he had come, if he really wanted help, or if he was hiding from someone. Tonight it didn't matter. As long as he obeyed her few simple requirements, for tonight he would have the shelter that he needed.

Tomorrow, they would worry about the future.

After they finished the sandwiches, Mike grudgingly did the dishes under Shadow's pointed gaze. While Mike was occupied, Shadow played with the old TV. Luck was with him, old Bonanza episodes were on.

They remained glued to the TV for the next few hours until finally, at four, their eyes began to droop.

Sabrina showed Mike to a small room downstairs, but Shadow refused a similar offer. He took the couch.

Later, after she finished wiping down the kitchen counter, checking the locks and turning off the lights, she walked through the small living room on her way to the stairs.

Lying in the glow of the moonlight was Shadow. He slept slightly curled, the blanket pulled close. The silver light from the window softened the angles on his face, easing the lines, smoothing the hollows. By the gentle glow of the night, he finally looked his fourteen years.

Sleep gave him back his innocence, for a fragile hour or two. But even sleep could not shake his control. Even curled in the moonlight, the soft face remained smooth and expressionless.

She wanted to reach out and softly stroke his cheek, tenderly ruffle his hair. Just like the mother he had lost somewhere along the way.

Her hand went quietly to her stomach. Alone in the moonlight with the sleeping child, she felt the bittersweet emptiness grow.

Quietly, oh, so quietly, she crept through the night and went upstairs to her lonely bed.

The sharp ringing was killing him. Blindly, a hand appeared to combat the noise. It groped clumsily for the source. Then, latching triumphantly on it, the hand threw the culprit across the room. The ringing came to an abrupt halt.

Safe now, a rumpled head appeared groggily next to the hand. Blinking its eyes owlishly, it tried to adjust to the light. No use. It gave up and disappeared again.

This time, wet slurping assaulted the hand. Valiantly the hand tried to fend the slime off, but the assault continued. Once again, the head appeared in dazed resentment. The blinking eyes met those of the very large dog that was still licking the hand.

"Woof," moaned the head, "I hate you."

But Woof took no offense, merely continuing to lick. The head gave up and with another groan, a whole body rolled out of bed.

God, he hated mornings.

Woof trotted on over to give his master a good morning kiss and Thomas spent several more minutes trying to avoid being slimed by his dog.

"Of all the people to wake up to in the morning," he grumbled, "I have to wake up to my dog."

Woof merely gave his funny master a quizzical look and one last slurp. Then he trotted across the floor of the small loft Thomas rented to stand pointedly in the kitchen. Thomas got the hint, but stepped into the shower first anyway.

Woof laid patiently back down in the kitchen to wait. He knew by now that his roommate didn't move too fast in the morning.

Twenty minutes later Thomas had managed to dress in semi-unwrinkled clothes and even made it into the kitchen for his badly needed cup of coffee.

Hunched over the steaming cup, he contemplated his dog, the floor tiles and life.

He hadn't slept well last night, tossing and turning restlessly until some odd hour of the morning. Now, even in the daylight, the restlessness remained.

The loft looked bigger somehow, bigger or maybe just emptier. A million times after the fight last night he had told himself to just let her go. He had only known her a week, and while he'd have to work with her from time to time because of the case, nothing personal needed to come from it. But then he remembered. More than anything, he remembered the fun they'd had racing along the hills of Portland. He remembered her quick hug when he'd given her the daffodils. He remembered her understanding eyes when he'd talked of his father. And he remembered her laughing when she'd landed a spoonful of ice cream on his chin.

Even now, he was sitting here wondering what it would be like to wake up next to a sleepy-eyed Sabrina. He could almost picture her padding around in nothing but an oversize T-shirt, pouring herself a cup of coffee, patting Woof indulgently on the head.

He felt a pang in his chest and gave Woof a sad look.

"Man, oh man, I've got it bad," he informed his dog. Woof barked once in agreement, then trotted over to rest his head sympathetically on Thomas's knee. He looked up with such doleful brown eyes that Thomas had to laugh and scratch his ears.

"Not only am I involved with the sole eye witness to a homicide, and a former prostitute at that," Thomas continued on to the now blissful Woof, "but I want to become more involved. Lots more. Who could have known," he said with a wry chuckle, "I'd be such a sucker for violet eyes? What do you think, have I lost my mind completely?"

Woof cocked one eye, which Thomas took for an affirmative. He patted the mongrel one last time, then heaved himself up.

"Sorry, buddy, but it's time to go to work."

He waited for the familiar feeling of exhaustion to come over him. But it didn't. Instead, for the first time in a long time, he felt a little more prepared, a little more determined. Perhaps Sabrina was right. He wasn't perfect, but he gave it his best shot. And maybe, if she could go on year after year trying to make a difference, so could he.

A little more than an hour later Sabrina's own alarm clock sounded. Without a dog for backup, she resisted throwing it across the room and instead attacked it with a book. Once the obnoxious ringing halted, she stumbled into the shower.

A bad taste lingered in her mouth and groggily she remembered smoking a cigarette the night before.

Then she remembered all the events leading up to that cigarette—the laughter... and then the fight, and she grimaced. Some things were best left behind, she told herself. Last night—what had happened with Thomas—would not happen again; she would make certain of that. She rinsed out her mouth. That at least took care of the cigarette.

Downstairs she could hear banging in the kitchen. It was still much too early for Shadow or Mike, so she surmised that Suzie must have finally roused herself from her sixteen-hour slumber. Good, Sabrina thought. It was Suzie's turn to fight with the cereal anyway.

Sabrina appeared downstairs ten minutes later, the box with the sweater firmly in hand. She glanced at the couch, coming up short. It was empty.

Two blankets lay neatly folded on the armrest, but no sign of Shadow could be found. He'd already gone. The disappointment was sharp. Somehow, she'd hoped he'd come to stay this time. She wondered if he would come again.

If only prayers were enough.

With a sigh she pulled herself together and checked on Mike. He was snoring soundly in the bed, leather jacket thrown over the back of a chair, but otherwise fully clothed. Quietly she shut the door.

Suzie's back was turned as Sabrina entered the kitchen and sat down. She set the box down next to a soggy bowl of cereal and waited.

Sensing Sabrina's presence, the girl turned around. Sabrina took in her shaking hands and nervous smile.

"Hi," the girl said, and flashed another awkward smile. "Would . . . would you like anything to eat? I mean, like cereal or something? I'm...I'm not too good at cooking." She shrugged helplessly down at her hands. Unsure of what to do with them, she stuck them into the pockets of the old robe Sabrina had lent her.

"Cereal would be great," Sabrina said, and flashed the girl a reassuring smile. "Did you sleep okay?"

"Yeah, sure. Everything's great," Suzie said, looking down shyly.

Sabrina nodded. "Just so you know, a kid named Mike arrived last night. He's sleeping in the bedroom a few doors down from yours. So if he comes wandering in here, don't be surprised. I don't know how long he's staying, or if he is at all. We'll see."

Sabrina waited for Suzie to look up again, then presented her with the box. It took a bit of gentle persuasion, but eventually the shy girl unfolded the blue sweater and disappeared down the hall to try it on. She emerged almost ten minutes later, just as Sabrina was beginning to get worried.

Suzie had swept her long blond hair forward in an attempt to hide her bruises, and the golden strands gleamed against the soft folds of the sweater. The simple style suited her, giving her a youthful elegance. Behind the curtain of her hair, her eyes appeared wider, a deep cornflower blue that reminded Sabrina of warm summer days.

Even with the bruises, even with her shoulders hunched and her face halfway hidden, she was pretty. Sabrina could picture her with shoulders back, face cleared to a pink perfection. She would look like anyone's daughter or the girl next door.

It was such a waste.

But not anymore. Not anymore.

Suzie was already beginning to shift uneasily under Sabrina's gaze when Sabrina's face finally relaxed into a deep smile.

"It looks very nice on you," she told the nervous girl. "Do you like it?"

Suzie only shrugged. "I don't know," she said softly. "I'm not sure it's me."

"I think it is," Sabrina countered gently. "And maybe you can't see that now, but eventually you will. Just give yourself some time."

The girl shrugged again, then looked at Sabrina with her large blue eyes. "Would it be all right for me to take a shower?" she asked tentatively.

Sabrina smiled. "Of course. There's no need to ask."

Suzie lingered a second longer, still looking nervous. Then, with a quick nod of her head, she turned and skittered back down the hall. She had no sooner left the room when a door swung open and a groggy-eyed Mike appeared.

He gave Sabrina what she figured was his traditional sullen look. She was beginning to wonder if he had any other. He didn't say a word, just marched over to the coffeepot and poured himself a cup. After adding his usual generous allotment of sugar, he tried to light a cigarette, but his hands were shaking too badly. With a curse, he threw his lighter on the table and contented himself with his coffee instead.

He'd be leaving soon, Sabrina thought silently, she would bet on it. His whole attitude reeked of rebellion. Well, she would give it a go anyway.

"Good morning, Mike," she said brightly, attempting polite conversation first. He just grunted in reply. So much for that. Perhaps the direct approach would be better.

She sat down directly across from him, waiting until she could catch his restless eyes.

"Mike, I know you have a drug problem. What I want to know is, do you want to do something about it?"

"Who the hell are you?" he snorted. "Some damn narc? Well forget it. I don't know anything or do anything."

She nearly smiled at his "tough man" attitude. "How much longer do you think you can go on like this?" she challenged him. "From what I've seen, I'd bet that you're running drugs, as well. That's a good way to get in trouble. Drug dealers have a tendency to see dependent runners as a liability after a while. But I'm sure you already know that. Is that why you came last night? Are you already in that much trouble?"

"None of your damn business."

"I know a place that can help you. They'll help you get off drugs, and they can help protect you, as well."

"Oh, I see. So that's your scoop. What? Do they pay you to deliver kids like me for them to work on? Hey, man, how much am I worth? If it's enough, I'll turn myself in and we can split the dough."

"Sorry, Mike, you're not getting off that easy today. I'm afraid I'm doing this out of the kindness of my heart."

"Well forget it lady. I don't need you and I don't need *kindness*. I happen to be doing just fine. I only came because it was raining and even I can appreciate a dry place to sleep. But, hey, it's looking pretty dry now. So maybe I'll just be on my way."

"On your way where, Mike? You can do a lot of running and still not get anywhere, you know. What's out there for you now that you didn't already do last night, or the night before, or the night before that? You don't have anything to lose anymore."

"Oh yeah, I do. At least I've got more to lose than some rundown dump of a house."

"You weren't complaining about the house last night."

"Well, I changed my mind."

"Yes, so change it again. Stay."

"No, man, no way. So I don't got a house, but at least I got freedom. You want to send me to some joint where they'll watch me twenty-four hours a day. Do you think I don't know about those programs? Think I'm that dumb? No thank you, I've been doin' just fine, I can take care of myself."

He was pulling himself out of his chair even as he spoke. Standing to his full height, he towered above Sabrina. He needed that, she knew. Needed to feel like he could look down on her.

He stared at her for a long minute, his eyes wild in his anger and frustration. Swearing, he turned to storm away, but she reached out and touched his arm.

He froze at the contact, his features growing hard and chiseled.

"What are you gonna do now," he sneered, "force me to stay?"

"No," she said quietly, keeping her eyes calm and serene. "I just wanted you to know that the offer stands indefinitely. If you ever need anything, you're welcome to come back, even if it's only for a night or two. Or if you get in any other trouble, if you need someone, just ask for Sabrina Duncan. Who knows? Maybe someday you will change your mind."

He nodded, but looked hard at her hand on his wrist. She let it go, watching him stride to the bedroom with quick steps. He stopped only to grab his leather jacket, then he was heading for the front door.

She wondered if she could have done anything differently. Maybe she should have stayed quiet, waited him out. But she had seen his hands, and he wouldn't have made it another night without a fix. He wasn't ready for her help yet. The first step, always, had to come from within.

Mike didn't pause at the door, she didn't expect him to. He flung it open with all his youthful strength. Then he was gone.

She had already moved on to other thoughts when she heard him call over his shoulder, "Man, lady, one of your friends has queer taste in flowers."

Puzzled, she headed for the door. She found them on the doorstep, neatly bunched with a crimson bow.

One dozen black roses.

Chapter 5

Dusk had already fallen by the time Thomas and Seth closed the last files in defeat. They had gone over each crime scene countless times, searching for any details they might have overlooked the first time around. The phone had been ringing off the hook, as well. When it had just been a prostitute killing, no one had known a thing. But the moment it looked like a serial murderer was on the loose, everyone seemed to have seen someone or something suspicious.

A task force had been assigned to follow up on the calls. Each and every last one was weighed, investigated and eventually dismissed. They did have one florist from the general area who had reported a thin man appearing twice, buying a single rose, paying cash and then disappearing. It was hardly breaking the law, but at this point, they'd take anything. No matter how small the information, perhaps it could make the pieces click.

But no such luck today.

They'd ended up pretty much where they'd begun—with two dead women, a few blue threads and two black roses.

Except, Thomas mentally corrected himself, now there were fourteen roses. *Fourteen.* He gripped the steering wheel of his car harder as he pulled out of the station's parking lot.

How had the killer known? Damn it, if he could just answer that one single question. He and Seth had combed their minds endlessly, both finally agreeing that the murderer had to have been watching at the crime scenes. They'd each made rough sketches of the people they'd noticed at the scenes. None of them looked or sounded even remotely like Sabrina's shadowy description. So had the man been watching from the window of a nearby building?

At this point there was no way of knowing, and that was almost more frustrating. When Sabrina had first called about the "gift" left on her doorstep, he'd felt as if the floor had dropped out beneath him. He'd known the inherent danger of being a witness, but that danger hadn't seemed a real possibility in this case. After all, how would the killer have known about her? But apparently he did, and now other pictures were rising, unbidden, to Thomas's mind. The look of fear on the young boy's face when he'd first come forth to testify in a gang-related killing. The riddled body when they had filled him with twelve lead bullets.

God, not Sabrina. Please, not Sabrina.

Funny, up until now he'd done a pretty good job of convincing himself he felt nothing for her. Oh, there was desire of course, but he'd convinced himself he could handle that. But now, now all he could think of were the times they'd shared. Short moments, yet, but moments that had made an impression on him nonetheless. Moments that came back to him again and again.

Perhaps he did care a little. Or, more likely, perhaps he had some errant noble knight complex that even after all these years just wouldn't quit. Either way, he didn't think he could stand to see her hurt. And he certainly wouldn't stand the thought of her being killed.

That battered body, those twelve red and ragged holes in a boy so young...

Damn it, he thought fiercely, and pounded his fist hard on the dash. He'd wanted to rush right over when he'd gotten the call. But that had been impossible. They'd needed people on the case too badly to spare him even for a day. They'd added an extra car to watch her house, but he'd known that wasn't the same as being there himself, watching her himself. He'd been relegated to the role of merely telling her to report the incident—and hand over the flowers, though he doubted they would yield any evidence—to the next patrol car to come around. Frustrated, he'd had to settle for racing to her house after work.

Running his long fingers through his hair, he felt the tension in every pore of his body. Time was running out. How long before the killer became tired of playing with Sabrina? How long before he decided to make his move?

They needed a break and they needed it now, Thomas thought grimly. Now, before it was too late. He drummed his fingers restlessly and glanced at the clock on the dash.

Ten more minutes and he'd be there. Silently he cursed the lines of slow-moving cars separating him from Sabrina's house. The sky was already pitch-black, night falling with deft quickness.

Somewhere in the darkness, in a rambling old house, was the woman he couldn't seem to stop thinking about. He gunned his motor, coming a bit too close to the car in front of him. Gritting his teeth, he forced himself to calm down. The strange urge to see her, to touch her, to make sure she was safe, was growing steadily by the second.

Damn it, why couldn't the cars go any faster?

Finally, at long last, he reached the turnoff to her street. If anything, the night was thicker here, shrouding the neighborhood in a dark cloak, relieved only by a few dim streetlights reflecting off the graffiti painted on old buildings.

Driving down to her block, he found himself gritting his teeth again. Somehow he couldn't stand the thought of her living here. He wanted, oddly enough, to sweep her away to a safe, warm haven, one where he could watch her constantly and reassure himself that she was truly safe.

Fat chance, he thought with a certain edge of self-directed cynicism, as he whipped into the cracked driveway. He'd probably have to drag her screaming before she went anywhere with him, or considered leaving her kids behind. He bounded up the worn walk. Automatically he reached for the knocker, then suddenly paused.

Something was wrong. Sabrina had promised him she wouldn't leave the house, yet all the lights were off. His eyes sharpened, instantly alert, and he strained his ears for a sound. Then he heard it. A muffled scream!

Without another thought he pulled his gun and lunged for the door. It gave easily under the force of his shoulder as he burst through. He came to a cautious halt, crouched in the doorway, his eyes adjusting to the darkness. At first he saw nothing.

Slowly, a blond head distinguished itself from the shadows. He had just made out the shape of someone tied to a chair, when a huge crash erupted overhead. With a curse, he raced for the stairs. He pounded up them, three at a time, gun in hand. Bursting onto the landing, he saw them across the way in a bedroom. Sabrina was valiantly trying to fight off a wiry man who was pummeling her with his fists. Her shirt was ripped and the man was grabbing for the waist of her jeans.

Realizing his gun was futile against the entwined pair, Thomas threw it aside and with an enraged war cry, sprang on the man. Through a red haze of anger, he saw the man's expression transform from one of triumph to terror as Thomas bore down upon him. His huge hands mercilessly fastened upon the smaller man's throat.

From a long way off, he could hear Sabrina shouting, "The knife, Thomas, the knife!"

But the warning was too late, and he felt the pain deep in his arm before he even saw the flashing blade. Backing off, holding his wounded arm with his other hand, he reevaluated his opponent and the situation. The other man was smaller, but his face held the snarl of a weasel and a bloody blade gleamed wickedly in his right hand.

Warily the two men circled, Thomas now unarmed but easily twice the size of the smaller man. He waited just one moment, until the man's eyes narrowed into sly, beady strips. Then, without warning, Thomas charged, arm outstretched to meet the knife. He contacted heavily with the small man, the momentum carrying them over onto the bed. He got a firm hold on the man's wrist. Ruthlessly his massive hand tightened, all the tendons standing out in brilliant relief as he squeezed, making his opponent drop the knife. It landed with a clatter on the floor, and Thomas deftly kicked it away. The pimp, once again robbed of his weapon and caught in an unshakable iron grip, crumpled before him, out cold.

Thomas looked down at the man in disgust. It was the same weasel from a couple of nights ago. He should have beaten the man then. When he thought of what the bastard had tried to do...

His fists still clenched, he moved over to where Sabrina lay huddled on the floor. Her eyes were open, but they were dilated with shock.

"Sabrina, honey," he called gently, but when she didn't react he crouched down and lightly touched her face, pulling her up from the floor. Slowly, he watched her eyes come into focus. He gathered her slight body close, relieved.

But she recoiled from his touch, urgently slapping his hands away. He pulled back, puzzled, to meet her wary eyes. She backed away from him, muscles still tense, her glance still suspicious. Her eyes darted back and forth between the two men.

"Sabrina," he began slowly, and took an easy step forward. She skittered further back, the shock in her eyes now completely replaced by a fierce wildness. With a start, he realized that she wasn't seeing him at all. *She didn't know who he was.*

She'd reached the doorway now, her hands feeling behind her for the open space. He stopped his steady advance and instead held out one hand.

"Sabrina, it's Thomas," he tried again, keeping his voice soft and level. "Everything's all right now. No one is going to hurt you."

But her eyes remained wary, panic still rimming the edges. Her hands found the emptiness they had been searching for. With a quick gasp of breath, she whirled and fled. Cursing, he bolted as well, but was too late. He made it onto the landing in time to see her door slam shut and hear the lock slide smoothly into place.

He looked down at his huge hands, cursing, long and hard. He wouldn't have hurt her. Didn't she know that?

Shaking off the urge to follow her and be sure she was all right, regardless of her emotional state, he turned back to Willy. He wondered idly how he was going to keep himself from killing the man. Coldly, Thomas hauled the man up, expertly twisting one arm behind his scrawny back as he shook him back to consciousness.

Briefly the small man tried to struggle, looking at Thomas over his shoulder through beady eyes. But Thomas simply returned the pimp's look with eyes that had grown so dark, they were nearly black.

"Keep trying," he said. "I wouldn't mind the excuse."

Practically snarling in frustration, Willy ceased his futile struggles. But his eyes remained calculating, and Thomas knew that at the first opportunity, the pimp wouldn't hesitate to move in for the kill.

Determined not to give him one, Thomas retrieved his gun and literally dragged him downstairs and into the living room. There he turned on a light with one hand and then called the station, giving a terse report on the situation and requesting a black and white. Hanging up, his eyes quickly flicked over the young girl who was tied to a chair, gagged. Conscious and, except for a few bruises, unharmed.

He eased his hold on Willy's wrist long enough to flatten him against the wall and search him. He found a switchblade in Willy's back pocket, but nothing else. He reached into his own back pocket for his handcuffs, then realized with chagrin that they must have fallen out sometime during the scuffle. Satisfied that the pimp was at least unarmed, he released the man and lounged against the wall opposite him.

"Untie her," he commanded, pointing toward the girl.

Willy hesitated, looking as if he might make a run for it. But one look at the huge man lounging opposite him, about as relaxed as a panther about to strike, and he changed his mind. Grudgingly, Willy moved over to the chair and started picking at the knots.

"Untie the gag first," Thomas ordered.

The man had no choice but to obey.

"Are you Suzie?" he asked the girl as soon as the gag was removed. She nodded her head slowly, giving him a quick look through terrified eyes.

"I'm Thomas Lain," he said, trying to soften his voice as much as possible.

"You're a cop," she said quietly.

Not knowing what to say, he nodded.

Her eyes roamed the room restlessly for a minute, like a bird too afraid to land on any one spot. Finally she risked another look at him.

"Are you going to arrest me?" she asked.

"I don't see any reason to do that. But I am going to put that weasel behind you in jail for as long as I can."

The weasel in question was beginning to look more daring again. Not wanting to take any chances, Thomas strode over and grabbed the loose rope from Suzie's wrists. Then, before the pimp realized what was happening, Thomas grabbed his wrists and wrapped the rope securely around them.

"No need to thank me," he said. "Really, it's been my pleasure."

Willy started cursing, but then a blue figure poked his head through the open door and he subsided. The cops had arrived.

Thomas turned over Willy after answering a few questions, drilling the uniforms on the whereabouts of the supposed watch car. It turned out that, since the two junior officers had been told to look for a tall thin man, they'd disregarded Willy's presence. Already frustrated, Thomas let them know in terse but graphic terms just what he thought of that. After this incident, they were to report in every visitor over the age of eighteen, regardless of shape, size, or gender. Feeling worn, Thomas returned to the living room to confront Suzie.

She sat in the worn blue easy chair now, her head down, her hands absently rubbing her wrists. A cascade of silky blond hair hid her eyes and he noticed for the first time that she was wearing the new sweater.

"All right, Suzie," he said as he swung himself into the chair across from her, "start talking."

She kept her head down, her shoulders hunched protectively forward. She flinched at the loudness of his voice and curled her shoulders even more.

"I'm sorry," she said, so softly he wondered if it wasn't merely his imagination.

He released his breath in a long sigh. "I know," he said, more quietly this time. "I know." It took a bit of patience, but eventually he got the picture.

It seemed that Sabrina had received an urgent call from another shelter about a kid she'd sent over. Thinking the patrol car would provide adequate protection for Suzie, and having made the young girl promise not to go near the door, she'd gone. She'd been gone for only ten minutes when Willy had knocked on the door.

"I didn't really want to let him in," Suzie said, her voice thick with anguish. "But he said he loved me, that he needed me. I've never been needed by anybody before." The girl shrugged miserably. "So I let him in."

Thomas nodded, knowing how easy it must have been for the weasel to dupe this uncertain girl.

"After you let him in, what did he do?"

"Well, he wanted me to come back to him and I agreed, but I said I had to finish my week here first. I mean, I *had* promised and Sabrina had been so nice to me." Her glance lingered on the sleeve of her sweater, one hand lightly stroking its softness. "But Willy got real mad. He kept screaming at me and calling Sabrina all these awful names. I tried to tell him he was wrong, that she wasn't anything like what he was saying at all, but he just kept getting madder. Then all of a sudden he grabbed me. I tried to struggle, but he's so much stronger..." Her voice trailed off, and Thomas could tell that she was trying very hard not to cry.

He didn't say anything, his own anger too strong. He suddenly wished the pimp was back just so he could land one good punch across all those gold teeth. Judging from the faint bruises that outlined Suzie's cheek, it was about time someone gave the man a taste of his own medicine.

His anger must have communicated itself to Suzie, for she cowered even lower in her chair. Realizing this, he immediately forced himself to relax, sitting there in the darkness with her as quietly as he could, waiting for her to continue. His hands fisted with rage, though, at the thought of what she'd been made to go through.

Eventually Suzie regained control and continued. "He tied me to the chair and gagged me so I couldn't warn Sabrina. Then he turned off all the lights and waited behind the door for her to return."

Thomas nodded, not needing to hear the rest, he could fill it in himself. Without any warning, Sabrina wouldn't have had time to defend herself at all. He was amazed she had lasted as long as she had.

"I'm sorry," Suzie said again. For the first time she looked up, and Thomas saw her eyes. The look in them stopped him cold.

They were filled with fear, nervously taking in his large size and his huge hands, which were still clenched into fists at his side. And they were filled with something else, something that shook him even more.

Acceptance.

She was waiting for him to punish her, he realized. Waiting and accepting.

Suddenly he couldn't swallow, couldn't breathe. He turned away, unable to bear looking at the huge blue eyes, filled with a defeat she didn't even understand. What kind of scum did that to a child? he wondered. What kind of sick bastard beat them so much that they believed they deserved it?

And then it dawned on him. For the first time, he began to realize just what life had been like for people like Sabrina and Suzie. And it wasn't the intellectual cold knowledge that came from reading books and case studies. It was the face-to-face, seeing-the-damage, seeing-the-scars kind of knowledge. These people didn't just live on the streets, they were destroyed by them, slowly eroded away until they came to accept the destruction. Looking at Suzie now, Thomas wasn't filled with disgust for her status as a young hooker. He was filled by the most amazing amount of pain and compassion. How could someone have done that to a girl so young? And why hadn't someone helped her sooner? Or any of them for that matter?

The seconds stretched on as he searched for what to say, what to do.

Finally he turned back, forcing his hands to relax by his sides.

"I understand why you did what you did," he said carefully. "You didn't mean any harm and everything's okay now. Let's just put it behind us."

She nodded slowly, her eyes still uncertain. "May I go to my room now?" she asked after a bit. "I'm kinda tired."

Thomas nodded, and, still keeping her huge, scared eyes on him, Suzie warily slipped from the living room and went down the hall. He watched her go, wondering if she was truly going to be all right. Not sure what else he could do for Suzie, a sudden image of the wild look in Sabrina's eyes flashed into his mind. Making a quick decision, he stood up. She'd had enough time alone. Ready or not, it was time he checked on her.

After a small search, Thomas helped himself to the first-aid kit and went to her room.

He knocked lightly on the closed door, and got no response. Tentatively he called out her name, but the other side of the door remained quiet.

Thomas reached for the handle, then hesitated. He felt like an intruder, just barging into her room. But then he purposely reminded himself of the wild look in her eyes. His face tight with worry, he grabbed the handle.

It turned smoothly, the lock having been undone at some point. He took that as an invitation and opened the door, entering a dark room.

At first he could see nothing, but then his eyes slowly adjusted until he could make out a slight form sitting cross-legged on a bed. She didn't stir or speak. Rather, she seemed to be a thousand miles away, like a person deep in meditation.

He whispered her name softly, as if soothing a frightened animal or a small child. If she heard him, she gave no reply.

Slowly he made his way to the edge of the bed and sat down, first-aid kit still in hand.

A silvery light escaped from the edge of the pulled blinds, streaking thinly over the bruises darkening her face. He had to swallow his rage at the sight. He should have bashed the man's brains in while he'd had the chance, he thought fiercely.

Taking a deep breath, he carefully reached a hand up to the gentle curve of her cheek. She flinched lightly at the first contact, but her expression didn't change. With tenderness bred of deep emotion, he slowly turned her head until it faced him.

The look in her eyes made him want to weep.

Had it been just moments ago that he'd seen the same dark cast in another pair of huge eyes? And here it was again. Acceptance.

But while he could see a trace of the fear that had also plagued Suzie, Sabrina's eyes were mostly empty, devoid of all emotion.

God help him, he wanted to kill *everyone,* all of the people who had done this to them.

His hands trembled as he tried to open the kit. When at last it gave way beneath his clumsy hands, he removed the antiseptic and bandages.

He knew that his huge hands weren't nearly as gentle as Suzie's would've been, but he forged on, cleansing the cuts and welts the best he could.

She didn't flinch again, even under the sting of the antiseptic. She simply looked through him with her age-old eyes, accepting the pain.

When long minutes passed without her saying a word, he felt his uneasiness grow. He tried to capture her gaze, to force her to acknowledge his presence, but she was far from him, fighting demons of another lifetime that had come and gone before he had ever known her.

Sick with worry, Thomas began to talk to her as he worked. He told her Suzie was okay and that she was a very special girl. Sabrina should be proud. He told her how important her work was, how her ability to reach out had touched even an old, burnt-out cop like himself.

On and on he went, cleaning, talking, and becoming increasingly scared.

Just when he was starting to become desperate, she spoke.

"You're hurt," she said quietly.

He looked at her in amazement for an instant, and then true to her words, he became aware of a sharp stinging in his shoulder. Oh, yeah, the pimp had had a knife. Dazed, he looked down at the long gash in his shoulder bleeding a deep red through his dress shirt, then back at her.

"Are you okay?" he asked again.

She still didn't say anything, just took the antiseptic from him. Lightly her fingers rested on the jagged cut, feeling out the damage. Then, with an abruptness that startled him, she ripped back the edges of shirt from the wound, and carefully began to cleanse it.

She still didn't say anything.

"You don't have to do that," he told her. "I can take care of it."

But she ignored him, tending the wound with hands that were amazingly gentle. Under the tender ministrations he felt the sting recede and settle. With deft movements she wrapped it up, applied a thick white bandage, taping it on.

"Thank you," he said softly. "It feels better now."

But still she didn't speak, only nodded her head. He leaned to the side to catch her eyes, but even then he only saw the emptiness.

"Sabrina," he said gently. "It's okay. It's over now."

"I need a shower," she told him.

He nodded, relieved to finally receive a response, and, only too happy to have something to do for her, he helped her to the bathroom. The minute she disappeared behind the closed door, he felt the helplessness set in. He roamed the room restlessly, running his hand over the empty bed, opening the blinds to combat the shadows with soft moonlight.

He wished he understood more about her. He wished he knew more about the demons she was fighting behind that painstakingly controlled exterior. And he wished he could understand by how many and for how long she must have been hurt before she'd stopped fighting the pain.

And he wondered if she realized just how strong she was.

The shower was still running, it had been for quite some time now. He remembered the look in her eyes and wondered if she was truly all right.

Well, there was only one way to find out. He strode over to the closed door. He knocked once, received no reply, and then walked straight in. The shower was on full force, so he didn't bother to call out, she wouldn't hear him. He almost choked on the thick steam wrapping tightly around the air. Pausing, he waited for it to clear out the open door, then reached for the shower curtain on the far end.

Taking a deep breath, he drew it back.

Sabrina didn't seem to notice him. She was scrubbing furiously on one leg, the other leg already a raw red from her heartbreaking task. He swallowed tightly and reached out a hand to capture her wrist.

"Don't," he said softly.

Her head jerked up, revealing eyes dulled with a pain he couldn't even begin to comprehend. Her breathing was shallow but fierce, as if she'd been running a marathon nonstop.

"Oh, God," he breathed, shaking his head in helplessness. "Sabrina, it's okay now. I promise you, everything will be all right. Please don't hurt yourself any more."

She started shaking, her eyes drowning in his, wordlessly pleading for his strength.

With a lump in his throat, Thomas knew he couldn't deny her, not now, not ever. He pulled her to him, enfolding her wet, raw body in his strong arms. He scooped her out of the shower, ignoring the pain that flared in his arm, ignoring the water that sprayed upon them both. He stopped only to turn off the shower and grab a thick towel.

Then he carried her into the bedroom, absorbing her shuddering into his own massive frame. Setting her down, he wrapped the big towel around her, tenderly drying her.

But even the bruises and bone-deep scrubbing didn't prepare him for her back.

Small, thin scars crisscrossed madly on the plane of her pale, otherwise smooth skin, each one white and ridged in the silvered moonlight.

"Oh, Sabrina," he breathed. "God, I am so sorry. How did...?" He found he couldn't speak, and tried again. "Did a man do that to you?"

She looked up then and met his eyes. The depth of bitter pain he saw there stunned him.

"It's okay," she said in a low detached voice. "As you said, it's over now, isn't it?"

Her words held a curious edge of sarcasm to them, and maybe she was right. How did you ever live through something like that, and get away from it completely? How could you ever be completely free, when even the physical scars were permanent? Overwhelmed by the tragedy and pain in her life, Thomas knew there was nothing he could say that would help.

So instead, he tucked the towel around her delicate frame, and drew her close. At first she was rigid in his arms, but then, with a long shuddered sigh, she pressed into the warmth he provided, burrowing her head against his shoulder. And he stroked her back as the first waves of the aftershock hit her in a long trembling deluge. He held her, his eyes fixed on the wall behind her, trying to still the unfamiliar emotions roiling within him.

She felt so fragile, so tiny in the circle of his arms. Suddenly he was struck with a surge of protectiveness and tenderness so strong that it was staggering. What was wrong with him? He'd never felt this way before. It was beyond his experience, his comprehension, and yet, at this moment, it didn't seem to matter. He only knew he *needed* to help her, wanted to make her feel safe, know that, as long as he was there, she need fear no one. Maybe it was because no one had helped her when she'd needed it before. Perhaps because the scars on her back were a permanent testimony to the failings of mankind.

Eventually, tucked in the warm security of his embrace, her breathing grew light and she passed into sleep. He untangled himself only long enough to find her an oversize T-shirt and to check the locks.

Satisfied that all was now well, he tucked her gently into the large bed. Then after a moment's thought, he removed his shirt, and, wearing his jeans, he quietly crawled into the bed himself, wrapping his arms around her softness, finally content that she was safe and with him. The sound of her deep even breathing soothed him and he drifted off to sleep under its calm reassurance.

Only to awaken to the hair-raising sound of her terrified screams.

The pain, the horrible excruciating pain of him driving into her body over and over again. And the smell, the gut-wrenching stench of dried urine and sweat. She fought to avoid him, but there was always more, coming over and over again. Too many, too much pain. The terror built and built and built—

"Sabrina, wake up!" a distant voice was commanding. "Sabrina!"

But it was the sound of her own screams that finally penetrated her sleep and sent her bolting upright in the bed. Her eyes were wide and frantic, her breathing harsh.

Thomas watched her, wanting to reach out but recognizing that look by now, he knew it was best that he not touch her. She was back to some world where he did not exist, fighting ghosts that he knew nothing of. Heart in his throat, he waited for her to come back to the world of reality, to come back to him. And eventually she did, as her breathing calmed and she realized that she was no longer in a small prison of an apartment, but her own bedroom.

Only then did she become aware of the man next to her.

Pain-filled eyes found Thomas's, and not needing any other sign, he drew her gently into his arms.

She relaxed against the protective strength of his broad chest, burying herself in its security. Thomas tightened his hold and hugged her closely, inhaling the fresh, soapy scent of her body. He could feel her trembling and began to lightly stroke her hair, trying to soothe her distress.

"You're safe now," he murmured to her over and over again. "You're safe now."

At last, in the shelter of his strength, her trembling subsided and she pulled back to look at him. There were no more shadows in her eyes tonight. Instead they were wide and vulnerable with fully remembered horrors. He crushed her to him again, unable to bear the sight of such pain or the knowledge he could do nothing to protect her from it now.

Gradually he relinquished his hold and turned to adjust the pillows behind them. Sabrina watched him, suddenly uncertain. She'd never woken up with a man in her bed before, she wasn't sure what to do, how to act. Then, for the first time, she became truly aware of the fact that his chest was warm and bare against her, that her own legs were just as naked and tangled with his. Embarrassment and a very real panic swept over her as the remnants of her nightmare, and three long years of abuse, clashed with reality.

Taking a deep breath, she forced herself to remember the tenderness of Thomas's touch as he'd dried her earlier, his soft whispers as he'd tucked her into bed. This was one man who would never hurt her, at least not physically. And with that realization came a flood of others: she liked the feel of his chest against her side and she liked the strength of his arms wrapped protectively around her. Unused to such feelings, to the knowledge that someone cared enough to make her feel secure, her fears took another turn. She remained tense and unbearably self-conscious, lying stiffly beside him even as he stroked her hair softly.

"Were you dreaming about tonight?" he asked after a short while.

Sabrina didn't answer, wouldn't answer. She didn't want to talk; she didn't want him to know of all the ugliness that had been her life and haunted her still.

"The past?" he prodded.

But she remained silent and rigid, feeling her own vulnerability overwhelm her. It felt so good to lie here with this man, so right to be in his arms. Yet he was Mr. All-American, and he could never understand a past such as hers. Better not to talk at all—she couldn't bear to see him turn away from her in disgust.

"Sabrina?" he asked finally. "Do you think that I'd ever do anything to intentionally hurt you?"

She couldn't stop the small, bitter laugh. "People do hurt people without intending to, you know."

"Yes," he said impatiently, "but you do understand, I wouldn't do it on purpose."

She did understand that. Already she knew he wasn't the type of person who could be cruel. Not to her, not to anyone. It simply wasn't his way. But she also knew he had trouble dealing with and accepting her former life.

"Talk to me, Sabrina," he said softly, and the words hammered gently against her resolve. "I really am trying to understand. Please, trust me enough to tell me."

"Is Suzie all right?" she asked instead, avoiding his gaze.

Thomas sighed. "Yes," he replied. "Suzie is just fine. I took care of Willy, had a patrol unit take him away, so everything is settled. Except I'm still worried about you Sabrina, *you*. Talk to me," he repeated urgently. "Trust me enough to let me in."

"Trust you?" she answered quietly, a trace of bitterness in her voice. "Thomas, you've already told me you have trouble dealing with my past. So why would I want to bring it up?"

"To explain it to me," he coaxed softly. "To get me to understand what you went through so that maybe I can see it the way you see it. I know I haven't always handled this the best way, but I'm trying, Sabrina. I'm honestly trying, so please, meet me halfway."

She hesitated a minute longer, torn between the desire to finally just get it all out, and the fear of the contempt she might see in his eyes. But his hand was still stroking her hair so tenderly, his arms tight around her. And it was tempting to give in to the desire, to believe for an instant that this man might really care, might, even with her past, accept her.

"I was dreaming of the night I came to the city," she said at last. Her voice was remarkably steady, despite the nervousness she felt inside. Even after all these years, the words were still difficult.

"How old were you?" he prodded gently, shifting her slightly until her head rested on his shoulder and he could feel the soft silk of her hair on his arm.

"Sixteen." She gave him a bittersweet smile. "A know-it-all sixteen," she said with a shrug, and the tears stung her eyes.

"I had just been removed from another foster home, my fourth in two years. It had been like that for... forever. In and out, in and out. In the beginning it was different. I'd look at each family with huge, shining eyes. I was always so sure that this would be the family that would love me, I was certain of it.

"But I was always wrong." She shrugged again and one trembling tear spilled over to roll slowly down. She ignored it and continued. "They all had reasons. Not enough money, not enough time, too many kids of their own, not enough energy. Whatever. For one reason or another, one day this official-looking woman with this sympathetic smile would appear at the door and that would be the end of it. Off I'd go. I never knew where, but after a while, I was pretty sure of the how long. It would be short, the stays were always short. After a while, I didn't bother to unpack anymore.

"Those things happen from time to time. Kids slip through the cracks. I just didn't understand that then. I just knew that I didn't belong, that I was the third wheel. See, I needed a home so badly, but no home needed me."

He nodded, having seen that happen one too many times himself. His heart went out to the lost child she must have been. Bringing up his hand, he rested it slightly against her cheek, holding her close, offering comfort. It was all he could do.

"I came to hate my age," she continued softly, her voice becoming thicker with the remembered pain. "I figured if I could just turn eighteen things would be different. Eighteen is the magical age if you're a foster kid. At eighteen you're automatically free. No more parade of homes, no more being part of an endless system. At eighteen I could make my own home and never have to leave. Only one day, eighteen just seemed too far away. So I left anyway. Just walked out the door with my little brown suitcase and didn't look back.

"I'd saved some money, so I checked the bus schedule to see how far away I could get. And here I am." She smiled at that. "Really, it wasn't a bad choice of a city. Portland's not a bad place at all. But," she said shakily, "it certainly has some bad people."

"I know," Thomas whispered soothingly. "I know."

"You have to understand," she explained earnestly, "that when I left, I never had any intentions of living on the streets. No one ever does. I just made all the mistakes everyone else does. I didn't realize that sixteen-year-olds can't legally rent rooms or sign contracts to buy things. I just figured I'd breeze in here, find some temporary job—either typing or fast food, it didn't matter—find myself a place to stay, save some money and be all set. I never imagined . . ." Her voice trailed off, and she shook her head sadly, unaware of the tears on her face. "I just didn't imagine."

An unfamiliar ache in his heart, Thomas swallowed and wished he'd stopped the conversation long ago. Instinctively, though, he knew he couldn't let her stop now; it was the only way she would ever be truly free. "Go on, Sabrina," he said coaxingly.

She took a deep breath and tried to calm the raging memories. Her voice was tremulous, but she managed to continue. "I fell for an old trick. It's a pretty good one, highly effective. A pimp sends two of his girls to a bus stop and has them check out the people getting off. They look for girls, lost unfortunates, and offer assistance. Since they're girls, too, most runaways will accept their help. They get into the car with their new friends and then the car takes them to a very bad area of town. There, they are raped and pumped full of drugs, and raped and pumped full of drugs again and again, until they simply don't care anymore. And, voilà, a prostitute is made."

She had switched to an impersonal third person for the explanation. He wondered if she even noticed. It hadn't softened the explanation for him, however. The images of what sick men could do to sixteen-year-olds were too vivid, too horrifying. He cursed silently, long and hard. He wanted to protect her from such horrors. He was eleven years too late.

"And your back?" he asked, his hand sliding down to caress it gently.

"The second time I tried to escape," she explained, her tone still carefully blank. "Pretty Boy—that's what everyone called him—only beat me the first time I tried, but since that hadn't been enough..." She let her voice trail off with another shrug.

"But eventually you did escape."

She gave him a small, bitter smile. "If only it had been that grand. I stayed with him for two years after that, Thomas. *Two years.* After the second time he caught me, I gave up hope. I hated him, I hated him like I'd never hated anyone, but I never thought I'd get away. I was watched like a hawk, forced to stay in the apartment unless I was outside...working. Those two years were the worst years of my life. People should never give up like that, never let the despair win."

He nodded, understanding her words more than she knew. Hope was definitely a sticking point these days. But then his thoughts veered back to her.

"So how did you end up in rehabilitation?"

"Pretty Boy met his match. One day he pushed one of his girls too far, and when he fell asleep that night, she took a knife to him. I arrived to see the ambulance taking him away. I didn't know if he was dead or alive, I just knew he was gone, so I ran. I hid for days, hunched in a small doorway without any food, or even a coat.

"Then one night, this bum came walking up out of the blue. At first I thought he was going to hurt me. But he didn't. He didn't." Even now, that fact amazed her. How had she ever gotten so lucky?

"He gave me his coat, and it was pouring rain outside. I mean, you should have seen this man. He was so tall and thin, with hunched shoulders and a ragged beard. His pants were two sizes too big, held up with a rope, and he was wearing the thinnest T-shirt that has ever been made. But he gave me his coat. His only coat. And never asked for a thing in return. He just wrapped the coat around my shoulders and told me that I should take better care of myself.

"And then he was gone. I never knew his name. I even tried to find him once, to show him that he hadn't wasted his coat that night. But I've never found him. He disappeared through the infamous cracks, as well." She gave Thomas a sad look. "I really wish I could have found him. I'm not even sure if he survived that night. Pretty Boy didn't. And for that, I am eternally grateful.

"And," she said, her voice picking up. "I checked into a rehabilitation clinic and after two more years of intense counseling, I became a human being. I started this shelter and since then I've helped reach quite a few kids."

"You've done an amazing job," he told her, a deep pride for her accomplishment settling within him, "an amazing one."

"See," she said earnestly, "one person really can make a difference. Even a caring bum. He helped me, I've helped them. It's the domino theory, really. All it takes is one person to get it rolling. And that's what I do." Her chin tilted up with that, and he saw a deep glow in her eyes. Pride. "You do that, too, you know," she said, and she smiled at him. "You make a difference, too."

So he had thought once, but even hearing it from her, hearing about her life, he wasn't so convinced. "Yeah, I suppose," he said with a shrug. "Sometimes I just wish I could make more of one."

"No," she said. "You can't know something like that. There's no sure way of measuring it. You deal with the people out there who have made another person's life go astray. But there are also people out there helping another person's life get back on track. It's just not always the same person being hurt and then helped. But I like to think that it works out in the end."

"Do you really believe that?"

"Yes."

Amazing. By any measurements, her life had been so much more tragic than his. What could he complain of? His parents had been happily married, his mother a rich but strong woman, his dad a self-made man with solid values and love for his family. The things Thomas had wanted in life, he had gotten. And yet it took this woman, this woman who had spent three years of her life in the gutter, to teach him of hope.

Sitting here, he had thought to protect her, to give her some of his strength, and in the end, she was the one who was the stronger. She was the one who still had faith.

He kissed her then, kissed her hungrily as if his actions could tell her what mere words couldn't. His kiss was an apology for all the things he hadn't been able to protect her from. His kiss was a thank-you for all the hope and faith she had shown him. His kiss was an ember to the fire that raged in both of them. It was need, desire, passion and something greater still.

She responded to all of it, tentatively, tenderly, as she would always respond to this one man she had fought so hard to find. But the kiss grew, spiraling out of control. What started out as spiritual need, became the need between a man and a woman, and she responded to that, too, as she never had before.

In the dark of the night, in the aftermath of the shadows, they came together.

Chapter 6

His lips were warm and soft as they touched hers. Her own were tentative, lightly responding to the gentle touch. It seemed she'd dreamed of this moment all her life. Now that it was here, she felt oddly afraid.

The way she'd survived made her an experienced woman, but the "experiences" she'd had were far too cold and harsh to ever compare with this moment. Technically she knew what went where, but with a sinking heart she realized that none of that mattered. For all her "experience" she was little more than a virgin. She knew the brutal side of sex. She knew of rape, she knew of the mechanical motions—the ones she'd long ago learned to disassociate her mind from—but she knew nothing of making love.

Biting back what would only have been a hysterical laugh, she fiercely concentrated on Thomas's lips. His lips were still gentle on hers, asking not demanding—so different from what she'd known that she found herself relaxing. She liked the way they felt, soft but firm, with a little bit of roughness added due to his end-of-the-day whiskers. And the way they moved—persuasively, almost coaxingly over hers—as if asking her to give in to the pleasure he could bring to her... She even liked the way they tasted. Hot and utterly, dangerously, masculine.

Then his hand suddenly came to rest on her breast. Startled, she jumped a little.

"I'm sorry," she whispered, turning her face abruptly from his. She could feel the low blush burning her cheeks, and was mortified. "I don't know what to do," she said softly.

"Sabrina," Thomas said quietly as his forefinger found her chin and gently turned her face back to his. "Sabrina, I know about your past. You don't have to lie to me."

For a minute she was confused, but then, like a cold shower, dawning washed over her.

"Do you really think it's the same?" she said sharply, her throat tightening at the reminder of what he thought of her. "Do you really think any part of my past was anything like this? Well, let me tell you something," she said intensely, starting to feel angry now, tears building hotly in her eyes. "It had nothing to do with making love. It was degrading and miserable and humiliating. It was something I endured because every time I tried to escape I was caught and beaten. Do you know how long it took me to realize sex didn't have to be like that? Do you have any idea?" She was openly upset now, unable to hide all the emotions that seethed within her. Her hands were rubbing her arms, as if suddenly chilled, her eyes darting around the room.

Thomas watched her for a long moment, berating himself inwardly, absorbing the impact of her words. He hadn't meant to upset her by bringing it up. He hadn't meant to spoil the easy warmth and trust that had slowly developed. Perhaps she was right. Maybe he *couldn't* understand. He had grown up with Mercedeses and white picket fences. Sure, he'd encountered the other side of life as a cop, but encountering it and *living* it were different things altogether.

"I'm sorry," he said at last. "I didn't mean to upset you. I guess maybe I'm not so sure what to do, either."

There was a sincerity to the words that managed to reach her through the agitation. He was sorry. She was sorry. The whole world seemed sorry. Sometimes she wished more than anything in the world that she could have a true second chance. Not starting over with a new life built on an old past, but starting *completely* over. Maybe this time her unknown parents would keep her. Maybe this time she would grow up in one good foster home. Maybe this time she wouldn't feel compelled to run away.

Maybe.

But there were no second chances, she realized. There was only this moment, only this man in front of her. And only the years that would yawn afterward, the years in which she would think back to this opportunity and wonder. In a moment of quick decision, Sabrina knew that she didn't want to wait eight more years to meet the right man. She wanted whatever small piece of happiness she could grab now. After all these years, she wanted just one night. Now, when death was delivering black roses to her doorstep. Now, when she might not even live long enough to have a future; let alone any second chances.

There was a long pause, a moment for second thoughts. But on this moonswept night, she found none. Slowly her violet eyes rose up to meet Thomas's deep emerald gaze. "Thomas," she said softly. "Please show me what's it's like. Show me what it's like to make love."

Those eyes were wide, wide and clear in the dark of the night. He took one look into their beautiful depths, and he drowned. How could he ever say no to eyes like that? How could he ever say no to *her?*

Then, in the back of his mind, the way he'd felt when she'd called in about the roses hit him once again, leaving him unaccountably breathless. God, what would it have been like if he'd lost her? And suddenly it didn't seem to matter what had gone on before in her life. What was important was the now. Taking what for both of them was so rare and yet felt so right. Taking her in his arms and proving, in the oldest and most basic of ways, that she was alive and safe.

Who knew if there would ever be another chance such as this one?

She felt the cool breeze as he slipped her light cotton shirt over her head. The soft chill of the night air sensitized her skin, tightening her nipples even as his warm breath lingered by her ear. Half for warmth, half to calm her nerves, she moved closer to him.

Her skin felt so soft against his, soft and curvy against all the hard planes of his own. And her hair slid like silk through his hands, he thought hazily as he combed through it with his fingers. It was so beautiful, nearly white-gold in the moonlight.

There was a moment of uncertainty. After all the waiting, all the anticipation, where to begin? Then the shadow of the curve of her neck called to him and he couldn't resist. He lowered his head, warm lips finding the tender hollow. He explored it slowly, languorously, savoring the wondrously soft feel of her skin, running his tongue lightly along the gentle curve, stopping to taste it with a tantalizing nip of his teeth.

She shivered beneath him, half in desire, half in fear. Unbidden, fragments of her nightmare came back to her, along with the pain and degradation she'd experienced. Fiercely she pressed herself closer to Thomas, trying to lose the images against the solid warmth of his body.

He felt her hesitation, and soothed her with gentle caresses and whispered words. Take it slow, he reminded himself. Take it real slow.

Gradually she relaxed again, calming under the soft strokings of his hands in her hair, on her face, down her arm. This time when his hand swept gently up to cup her breast again, she didn't flinch. A feeling of intense freedom had come over her, allowing her to give in to the deep waves of sensation growing in the pit of her stomach.

Reveling in the strong, callused feel of his large hands against her delicate frame, she moved restlessly. Moving closer to him, she rubbed her cheek against his chest, exploring the sensation of his bare skin against her face. Hesitant yet needing to touch him desperately, she brought her hand up, flattening it against the pounding of his heart.

Heated words of encouragement followed Thomas's moan as he eagerly guided her hand across his chest, showing her that it was okay to touch him. All the while he kept touching her, giving his hands free reign, stroking and massaging her languorously, keeping the pace slow and easy though each second made it more difficult. She was so soft, so damned soft... He had to grit his teeth against the overpowering urge to take her right then and there.

Lost in a haze of dizzying desire, Sabrina knew she was finding out exactly what it felt like to be cherished by a man. Thomas's touch was filled with passion yet tempered with patience, slowly building up the need in her to match his. She shifted restlessly, arching her back, pulling him closer.

Thomas groaned. Her sweet responsiveness to his touch was not helping any. Looking down at her, his eyes darkened to deepest deep emerald at the sight of the creamy skin of her breasts. Then, because he simply couldn't resist any longer, his head came down, his lips finding a nipple, suckling and teasing it with hot, wet kisses.

Sabrina gasped at the first heated touch of his mouth, tensing slightly, but he made no more sudden moves and she gradually relaxed, letting the swirling sensations overwhelm her. She cried out when his teeth lightly grazed at her nipple, playfully soothing it afterward with his tongue, wondering at the sudden yearning ache deep in her womb. It... he... felt so good, so very good, better than she ever thought anything could feel.

Her hips seemed to rise and surge of their own accord and she realized she wanted more, kissing and caressing were nowhere near enough any longer. Pulling Thomas's head to her, she kissed him frantically, all of her need and frustration in the long and burning kiss. "Please," she murmured huskily, fiercely. "Please, Thomas. Show me."

The soft husky plea nearly shattered his control and he took a deep breath to steady his desire. *Slow down, Lain,* he warned himself. Kissing her softly to distract her, he brought his hand lower and, murmuring heated words of passion, stroked down her legs, moving closer and closer to the juncture between her thighs.

She was uttering little cries from the back of her throat, but he doubted she was even aware of it. He was, though. And it was driving him crazy. She was so hot, so soft and silky... so wet. Lightly circling the core of her womanhood, he held her tighter as she cried out, shivering in his arms. Her uninhibited reaction was so powerfully arousing that he had to bury his head against her neck to control himself, had to clench his teeth from the pain of holding back. But when light and delicate fingers came to rest at the waistband of his slacks, it was his turn to shiver. He couldn't take much—

Her soft voice scattered his thoughts, making his pulse pound even more heavily. "May I?" she asked shyly.

"Oh, yes," he moaned huskily, kissing the pulse that beat in her throat. "Please, yes."

With a tentative smile and a catch of her breath at the marvelous sensations he was arousing in her, she allowed her fingers to continue. They found the button in the front and slid it smoothly from its hole. Slowly she dragged down the zipper. It rasped in the silence, a tantalizing sound that sent shivers up both of their spines. He groaned against the curve of her ear and it was all the encouragement she needed. She worked the pants over his hips and together they peeled them off.

He loomed over her, eyes a stormy green with passion. They drew her in, stripping her of all defenses, until her eyes were naked under his, vulnerable with desire and need.

She had never looked so beautiful. He leaned down and kissed her long and hungrily, moaning when she arched helplessly against him.

"Please, Thomas," she muttered, the sensations overwhelming her again. "Please."

The ragged sound of the word tore at him, and his loins tightened unbearably. With an effort he reminded himself to go slow. No way was this going to be anything but long, slow and very hot. He wanted it to last, he wanted it to linger. He wanted it to remain in her memory for a long time afterward.

Having regained his control, he allowed his hands to return to her breasts. They were white and pink against the dark tan of his skin he noted with fascination, molding them with his hands. The petal-skin warmth made him groan aloud. Giving in to his need, he took one tenderly into his mouth, rolling it seductively with his tongue, smiling wickedly when she gasped beneath him.

Fire was shooting up Sabrina's veins, only to settle low in her stomach, commanding her hips to move with pure instinct. Her body felt heavy and light all at once, enriched and yet needy. It was a breathless sensation, staggering her with its force. All of a sudden Thomas was the center of her world. She wanted him, needed him, waited for his touch. And he was there, touching her, making her gasp.

Never had she felt anything like this. The power of it dazzled her.

His touch was magic against her skin, sensitizing her to his heat, *to him,* awakening her to emotions she hadn't known she could feel. His warm tongue on her breast, his callused hands stroking her skin, sapped her of all will save that of touching him and being touched.

She lost all control, all sensible thought to his searing caresses. Of its own volition her leg came up, rubbing restlessly, sexily against his, and her hands moved down his back to caress the firm muscles of his buttocks.

And then he was there, positioning himself between her parted legs.

"Look at me," he whispered hoarsely, and even had she wanted to, she was powerless to do anything but obey. His eyes were everything, the center of her being, and she couldn't look away. He captured her lips in one last drugging kiss, and she felt as if she were drowning, watching the passion build in his eyes like a stormy sea. Her own violet eyes were filled with need, vulnerable with desire.

Body and soul, her mind whispered as he entered her with one smooth thrust. No matter what happens, you will always be a part of me. Body and soul. But then there was no room for thinking at all, just feeling, as the powerful surging of his body sent her soaring higher and higher to swirling worlds that she had only dreamed of. Eyes wide with wonder, she soared with him and watched the worlds shatter into mindless brilliance.

She awoke later to the soft moon still shining across the room. Lifting herself onto one elbow, she gazed at the man beside her.

In sleep his face was as innocent as a child's, his expression relaxed and peaceful. But his body belied his face, for even in slumber its ridged muscles and massive size maintained their powerful promise. He was easily twice her size, she mused, yet he had been an amazingly tender lover. A powerful man, but one who had learned control.

She wondered briefly how many lovers he'd had to learn such control, but discovered that she didn't want to know. A man like him certainly had known many women and she didn't want to think of any of them. He was hers now, if only for this one night, he was hers.

It was useless to ever count on there being more. There was an attraction between the two of them, an electricity that was startling in its intensity, but attraction would never be enough. Men like Thomas never married women like herself.

She should pull away. She should let him go now, while she still could. Now before she became too accustomed to the feel of his skin against hers, the warmth of his arms holding her close.

But she knew she wouldn't. Time was too short, these moments far too precious to throw away now that fate had at last chosen to throw her some happiness. Besides, her future was hardly certain. It was ironic. Somehow, after escaping the streets, after escaping Pretty Boy and his meaty fists and biting belt, she had thought that her life would be safe. That there would at last be security.

And now, eight years later, she was indirectly a witness to a murder, and the murderer had found her. There had been a queer, almost unreal sensation in finding the black roses on her doorstep. It was as if she was suddenly living somebody else's life, somebody else who should have been more accustomed to such things.

She wasn't. She was accustomed to actual threats, solid abuse. Not the chilling psychological tauntings of a serial murderer. Not the insidious promises of black roses.

Perhaps her future was shorter than even she'd envisioned, but she still had a hard time accepting such a thought. She had worked too hard for the promise of the future to imagine losing it now. But still, the roses had spoken. Still, the killer waited.

She shivered, feeling powerless.

The only thing that held her together was Thomas. Perhaps it had taken the shadow of death to help her find him. But now that she had, she was determined to keep him. Keep him for whatever desperate amount of time she could steal. Keep him for as long as he would have her. Keep him and store the memories, hoarding them carefully against a certain lonely future.

It *was* better this way, she assured herself fiercely. After all, he didn't understand her, perhaps never would. He still believed the past was like a chalkboard. What couldn't be erased, could simply be ignored. She wished it could be so, she thought bitterly, and her hand came to rest on her stomach. But the past followed, no matter how far one tried to run.

The shadows would never leave her. Three years was three years too long to wash it all clean. The price had to be paid, she knew that, too. And for her, the price would always be with her, a huge, yawning emptiness she would never be able to fill.

Inevitably Thomas would move on with his life and find some stable woman with a cream-colored Mercedes, have two-point-two children and retire to suburban bliss. It would suit him, she knew. She could see him, even now, in a sprawling house with two shrieking kids using him as a Jungle Gym while he laughed with them. And there would be some tall, beautiful woman there, too, laughing with them. She'd imagined it all before and knew it for the truth. It was the way some things were meant to be. She was meant to be alone and on the streets—she belonged there—and Thomas was meant to have a home and a family he could be proud of.

Once she had left the streets, she'd tried living on the other side of the river. But it hadn't been right for her, and eventually she had come back, back to the streets that were in her blood. She belonged in the shadows, she understood them. And she understood the children, too. *They* were her children and she loved them all.

Yes, when his duty was done and the case was over, Thomas would return to his world of light and sunshine. But she could never begrudge him that. He was a man with golden dreams, and she understood those all too well. Dreams were powerful. They shone like beacons at the end of dark tunnels, demanding the most from those who dared to reach for them. Fulfilling a dream was like being reborn, beginning anew on a clean, golden slate. Dreams had pulled her out of the gutter and started this shelter, so how could she possibly fault Thomas for his dreams of a family?

Along the way, she'd learned the pain of dreams that couldn't be realized. She'd had to learn to continue without them. But Thomas had every reason, every right, to fulfill his dreams. Even if they would take him from her arms.

Until then, she would give him all she could and savor the moments. She wasn't a lost sixteen-year-old anymore. She was a woman, making a woman's choices . . . and she would bear a woman's pain.

Resolved, she once again curled up against his side and placed her head on the firm expanse of his chest. His heart beat reassuringly against her ear. The sound was soothing and she relaxed fully.

"What are you thinking?"

She started, caught unaware, as he'd known she would be. Actually he had been awake for quite some time, watching her beneath shuttered eyelids even as she had examined him. While her body had glowed pure and welcoming in the moonlight, he'd been most intrigued by her face. So many emotions there, some bitter, some sweet . . .

"How many children do you want to have?" she asked suddenly, rolling onto her back and staring at the ceiling as she awaited the answer.

Thomas didn't answer immediately, looking at her in bewilderment. Traditionally he took it as a bad sign if he went to bed with a woman and she woke up asking about children. But he doubted Sabrina was thinking along traditional lines. Her mind was much too complex and he wished he could tell where her thoughts had begun this time and where they would lead.

She waited expectantly. Not knowing what else to do, he answered, trying to keep his voice as casual as possible.

"I know I want kids," he said carefully, "but I'm not too clear on how many. Three isn't a bad number. I got along well enough with my older brother and younger sister. Most families have two kids. That makes for a more well-rounded family. I could go for that. Two or three, then."

She nodded, moving back onto her side, resting her head against his chest.

There was silence for a bit as she listened to the rhythmic sound of his chest rising and falling. Absently she doodled with one fingertip on his chest. She liked the crispy feel of the scattered hairs. She flattened out her palm and ran it lightly along the impressive muscles. Warm, hard, wonderful. She was suddenly awed by what it felt like to sleep with a man like Thomas, a man she cared for. After all these years, this was what it was like.

"Sabrina," Thomas said at last into the silence, feeling suddenly awkward. "Sabrina, I didn't take any precautions..."

Her finger stilled for an instant, then she purposely shrugged casually against him. "It's okay," she told him. "I...I already took care of it." It was perhaps not the truest of statements, not in the way he would assume, but it covered the basics—and would allow her some illusions for now. She paused again, feeling him relax slightly, and was unsure whether she should continue. But then she figured that he had the right to know, given the situation. Besides, if he didn't think of it now, he was bound to wonder about it sooner or later.

Shifting herself more comfortably against his muscled expanse, she searched for the right words. There didn't seem to be any polite or socially correct way of saying this. Just the raw words, needing to be said. With a sigh, she closed her eyes, and quickly said what she had to say.

"You don't need to worry about anything else, either," she said slowly. "I mean, with my...past...and everything. I've been tested for AIDS and other diseases. I'm clean. And as long as it's six months after any exposure to the virus, the tests are considered over ninety-nine percent accurate. It's been, well, eight years since I've been with...a man, and I'm still testing negative."

He nodded slightly but remained tense. He hated these questions, but knew she was right. For both their sakes, embarrassment had to take a back seat. Unexpectedly a warmth settled deep within him, at the way she'd approached the topic. He could feel himself relaxing again.

"Why did you become a cop?"

The question startled him, coming out of the blue the way it did, but he tried to come up with a good response. For some reason—one he didn't care to examine too closely right now—her interest in his reasons for becoming a cop warmed him.

"I wanted a job with action," he told her at last. "Something other than pencil-pushing from nine to five. And I wanted a job with meaning, where I could come home at the end of the day and feel like I had made a difference."

"Do you like it?" she prodded.

He sighed and ran his hand through his hair. At one time the answer would have been easy, basic. The world was filled with good guys and bad guys, right? There was the Lone Ranger and the evil rancher. Superman and Lex Luthor. There were the heroes and then the bullies. Hadn't he always been the good guy? Hadn't he always followed the rules? But the good guys just weren't winning anymore. These days...these days he just wasn't so sure.

"I don't always know," he told her honestly. "I used to see it in terms of riding off into the sunset. They'd put Thomas on the case and the bad guys would run. But it just isn't that simple. Sometimes, I'm not even sure who the bad guys are. Half of the people I catch are off the hook with pleas of mental insanity. Society makes them out to be another victim, not a villain. Some are beaten men who've lost more jobs than most Americans will ever have and just can't take it anymore. Then I have the privilege of arresting street punks who were probably born to be busted and have never had a chance to make anything else out of themselves. Things just aren't that simple anymore."

"But doesn't it all seem worth it once you've solved a case?" she insisted. "Doesn't finding the guilty person give you some satisfaction?"

"Yes," he agreed, "but even that's becoming frustrating. You know, when I started working, maybe eight percent of the cases went unsolved. Nowadays, it's closer to thirty percent. That's almost a third of the cases. The stacks of files are just getting thicker and it's a hard responsibility to bear. Take this case. We know this is going to be a serial killer, everything just points that way. But we have virtually nothing to go on. And every day we go without solving this case, another woman's life is in jeopardy. How many more will die before we catch him? And how do we live with ourselves, knowing that, if we could have just been a little quicker, one or two or three more women could still be alive?" He gave another helpless shrug, his desolate tone echoing in the night. "How?"

"One day at a time," she told him with certainty. "Bit by bit, knowing that if you had caught the criminal even later, even more people would have suffered."

"It's not enough, Sabrina," he said softly, a grim undertone to his voice. "When you're at the scene, looking down at a dead body, it just isn't enough."

"I know it's hard," she told him. "Do you think I save every kid who comes through these doors? I had a kid walk out on me just this morning. His need for acid is still stronger than his need for love. And do you think I don't still think about it? Do you think I don't wonder what I could have said or done differently? But I can't spend all of my time wondering about the ones that got away, and neither can you. You have to have a bit of yourself for the ones who are still out there, the ones who still need you."

"Maybe you're right," he told her, refusing to argue a point he was so certain of.

There was another long pause when neither spoke, a pause where her fingers restlessly moved along his chest.

"Thomas," she said after a bit. "I just wanted to say thank you for... this evening. It was nice."

"Nice?" he repeated, half teasingly. "It was *nice?* Somehow I was hoping for a higher rating than that. I must be losing my touch."

She laughed shyly.

"All right," she finally admitted. "It was better than nice. I...I had my doubts," she said softly. "I thought maybe I might disappoint you. Tell me, honestly, did I?"

"No," he told her sincerely, brushing his hand softly against her cheek. "You were right the first time. It was nice."

She smiled then, a bright smile of relief. And by the soft glow of moonlight, with her shining eyes and flushed cheeks, she looked young and fresh to him. With a start, he realized that she'd never had a chance to be young, to be sweet sixteen. She'd never flirted, had never gone out on a first date, or planned for a prom. Then it came to him. Maybe, just maybe, he could give some of those moments back to her. After all that she had done for him, all the hope and trust she was willing to share with him, it seemed the least he could do.

"There's going to be a reception and a dance in a few weeks," he said suddenly. "A captain is retiring and they're bringing out the whole nine yards. Come with me."

She smiled at him, but it wasn't the slow smile of acceptance. It was a sad smile of regret.

"No," she said, and shook her head softly. "It just wouldn't work."

"What do you mean, it wouldn't work?" he challenged gently. "There's no 'work' about it. You simply dress up as ravishing as ever—*I'll* even dress up, too—and then we go out. We eat too much food, drink too much wine, I step on your toes, and we have a good time."

She had to smile at his description. He was innocent in so many ways.

"Thomas," she said, just as gently. "I tried living in that world once. I went to all the state functions, wore the right clothes, met the right people, gave the right speeches. And it just didn't work. No matter how fancy the dress, no matter how glittery the jewels, I'm still a former prostitute and those people know it. And I'm always either snubbed entirely or swamped by the men who figure I'm 'easy.' I'm something exotic to them, a temptation. I'm the bad girl good boys like them shouldn't play with. Either way, I refuse to put up with it. I worked too hard to get out of the gutter, to go back to feeling so cheap, to having men mentally stripping off my clothes and degrading me with their thoughts and dirty comments. I won't do it.

"Besides—" And here she stopped, taking a big breath, rushing the words out so she wouldn't chicken out. *It had to be said.* "How would you like to introduce me as your date to some guy who knew me back when. You don't really want other men smirking behind your back, elbowing each other with glee. There is a good chance some of them will know me, or say they do. I wouldn't know the difference, they were all the same to me."

She finished with a matter-of-fact shrug, explaining facts that she had long ago come to terms with. None of it was romantic, or sexy, or very pretty. It was brutally raw and she deliberately kept it so, challenging him to accept it and her. She would never be the princess in an ivory tower, or the girl next door, or the perfect woman. She would always simply be Sabrina, a woman who had at one time done desperate things and lived a desperate life. A life that she knew he wasn't able to accept yet, perhaps never would. It was the reason she was being so honest. She would never, not even for him, sugarcoat the truth.

He heard the bluntness of the words, and through it all, heard the slight challenge, as well. He had doubts about her, too, hadn't he? Even now, after all the wonderful things she had done for him, he, too, could not quite see clear of her past. And what kind of man did that make him? Surely a better man would simply see, and accept, the wonderful woman she was now, and let go of the rest. And if he couldn't do that, wouldn't it be better if he got up and ended this now, so she would be free to find a man who could?

But he found he wasn't ready to do that. Selfish it might be, but she needed him as much as he needed her right now. And deep within himself he sensed that the dance would be good for her. In fact the more he thought about it, the more important it seemed. He would do this for her. He would take her out, take her to the dance. It was the least she deserved. If he couldn't do the rest, at least he could do this for her.

"Come on," he cajoled softly. "It's really not a major affair, Sabrina. But it could be a great time, and I promise you I'll try to make it even better."

She didn't understand why he wanted her to go. Didn't understand why he didn't just let the matter drop. She wasn't ready for this yet, she told herself. And more important, she didn't think he was. But for some reason, she just couldn't find the strength to say no.

"I don't have anything to wear," she said instead. "Honest! When I chose to get out of talking and start doing, I got rid of the dresses. You have to admit, they wouldn't go with the neighborhood."

"Buy something, then. If you're not certain, you can ask my mother. Trust me, she'd an expert on these things."

She froze at the mention of his "mother." Her being an expert was exactly what Sabrina was afraid of. She was having enough problems with just the son, she had no intention of meeting some aristocrat of a mother. She'd learned the hard way that no one considered her take-home-to-mother material.

"So what do you say?" he prodded. "Will you come?"

"I'll think about it," she said finally, more to avoid further discussion than anything else. "Honest, I'll think about it."

"You know, Sabrina," Thomas said softly. "After everything you've been through, I wouldn't think something like a dance would scare you."

"It's different," she told him bluntly. "And I wouldn't say I'm that brave a person. The things I've done in my life I've done because there really wasn't any other choice. You see, you can only be a coward if you have the choice. You should see the kids I work with every day. They have more courage in their little finger than most adults have in their entire bodies. Mainly because they're going to need that courage. It's their only way out. And it's the same for me."

He nodded, fully understanding her point. "I've seen that too, you know. There's a man at the station who positively hates violence. Won't go to violent movies, watch the news, or read the paper. But in a shootout, he's the best man around. No one can shoot better. And when it's over, he puts his gun away, takes a long shower, and just sits and shakes all over. You'd think he was falling apart."

"That's why you do what you do," she said quietly. "Because of guys like him and kids like the ones I work with. It's the same reason I keep going. With people as courageous as that in the world, how can we simply give up?"

"We can't," he said, but inwardly he knew that didn't mean do-gooders like him—or even like Sabrina—would always succeed. The odds were stacked against them, he thought grimly.

Dismissing it from his thoughts he shifted slightly until her light frame rested more comfortably against him. Almost absently he ran his fingers through the short strands of her hair, stroking the silky curls. She felt so good in his arms. So *right*.

"How did you get started in this?" he asked finally, breaking the small silence between them. "How did you go from getting off the streets and making speeches to running this rickety old house?"

She gave him a slanted look. "It is *not* a rickety house," she corrected him archly. "It's a wonderful house, one of the best."

"Whatever."

"Besides, I thought of buying this house before I even got into making speeches. As part of the counseling I was undergoing, I was visiting and helping at a shelter, *that's* where I got the idea. The speeches were totally by accident."

He frowned at her in the darkness, his hand stilling momentarily. "That's not common, is it? The going to shelters."

"No," she agreed, "it is an unusual practice, but my counselor thought it would help. I'd been on the streets too long. I had gotten so good at disassociating myself from what I felt or thought, that, even after two years of being off the streets, I was still cold inside. Once my counselor held up a lighted match and kept bringing it closer and closer to my hand, telling me to say when it got too hot. I never did. Too much had been locked up inside of me. And they were worried that I would never be healed until I dragged everything back up and learned to deal with it.

"So they sent me to work at a shelter, completely surrounded by everything I'd been so good at avoiding. At first it didn't get to me. I did what I was told, pretty much ignored the kids around me. I was good at keeping myself distant. Then one day I stumbled across this seventeen-year-old boy sitting with a girl in a corner. He was wearing a short-sleeve shirt and you could see the needle tracks running up and down his arms like a train gone berserk. He was bragging to this girl about all the drugs he'd done. He said he'd once been so desperate that he'd injected window cleaner into his veins. He managed to live, but his veins had collapsed soon after. And he said it all so casually, so proudly, that even I was shocked. I'll never forget what he said after that, either. He told her that it wasn't a problem since he could always inject it into the whites of his eyes. In fact, it was better that way. Left no tracks and had an immediate effect.

"That was the first time I ever really saw just how bad 'the life' could get. I mean, even though Pretty Boy used drugs to keep me in line in the beginning, I never really got into them, though I think if I'd stayed on the streets much longer, I might have. And then I might have been sitting there like that boy. It was like staring destiny in the face and realizing that, through some strange quirk of fate, I had managed to survive. It completely floored me.

"Then two days later, when I came back, the boy was gone. And one week after that, he finally succeeded in killing himself. Overdosed in some alley. We found his parents, though. We told them their son had died and they told us he had died the day he'd decided that drugs were more important than his family. And then they hung up. We closed the file and that was the end of it.

"Except for me. That day I went home and I started shaking, and I just couldn't stop. I curled up into a ball and shook for two entire days. And then I got up and started really learning how to live again."

"And," he continued for her, "started this shelter to save the kids."

"No," she said. "You don't understand yet, do you? I started this shelter so these kids could save *me*. The county wanted me to give speeches to help them, but it just never worked out. I was left feeling out of contact with those who needed me and understood me, while cheapened by some of the people I met.

"So I came back here, to this house. The one I'd chosen a long time ago. By then I had met two very wonderful and wealthy people who wanted to do more. By then I also had a college degree and a savings account from traveling the talk circuit. Mrs. Jacquobi and Major Price helped with the down payment. Then I bought basic supplies, furnished the house with my savings. Now I support the whole shelter by balancing the books for a lot of small businesses. I can work here, there's a computer in the room across the hall. So it's perfect. This is what I need. Each time I reach a child, I renew myself. They give me a reason to get up each morning, a reason to keep going when I'm so lonely and tired I just don't want to care anymore.

"You have to work with them. You have to see them come in, angry or sad, tough or defeated, but always needing you, even if they can't admit it. You have to see their faces, watch them grow and change as they learn to start demanding things of themselves and life. You have to have them come back a year later, glowing with news of their new jobs and sometimes, new families. They're everything to me, Thomas. They're the family I never had."

He saw the glow in her eyes as she talked, heard the ringing clarity in her voice, and felt pride in her, then shame in himself. This was a woman who deserved the best, so why was it that he couldn't, when all was said and done, reconcile with her past? Feeling guilty, and needing to feel her close, he kissed her.

Hard lips met soft and he savored the sweetness of her lips. But it wasn't enough. He wanted to absorb her conviction and hope and strength. He wanted to touch her deeply, just as somehow, she had managed to touch him. He kissed her again and again, becoming hungrier rather than satiated.

He wanted her, wanted her with an intensity that was almost frightening. He didn't know where such desire would lead, to what places it would take him. But he was lost to it anyway, caught up in the raging tide, wanting, needing, desiring. With a groan, he succumbed completely, sweeping her up into his arms and immersing her in his passion.

Her skin was soft and pale in the moonlight. His fingers smoothed over it, tracing the delicate outline of her cheekbone down to the warm hollow of her throat. He found the rapid beat of her pulse, and felt the gentle whisper of her breath. It beckoned to him and he bent his head down again, finding the soft, supple curve of her lips.

Warm, inviting, and oh-so-feminine.

Lightly, hesitantly, the tip of her tongue crept out to slowly trace his lips. He groaned, clutching her closer, and kissed her even harder, fiercer.

"Please," she whispered finally. "Please, Thomas. Touch me, make me feel again. Show me..."

He couldn't refuse her. His hand found her hand, guiding it to his chest, pressing it against him. It was such a small hand, delicate and fragile. And its tentative, silky strokings were going to drive him mad. He shifted, rolling above her, propping himself up with one arm while the other slid long and lingeringly down her body then back, finding her breast, gently teasing its rounded form. And then his hand drifted lower, whispering between her thighs until he found her warm and moist, ready for him. His eyes darkened to deepest emerald and he watched with male satisfaction as she gasped, arching against him.

He tried to hold out a little longer, wanting to make it last for her, wanting to drag out the pure wonder of it. But then her own hand drifted down, wrapping around his velvet hardness. It was too much and with his face buried in the silken pillow of her hair he moved urgently into position, murmuring her name throatily and plunging into her, hearing her gasp, feeling her hands clutch at his back.

Desire. It sent them soaring. Passion. It toppled them over the edge. Until they cried out each other's name and found each other's eyes, wide and vulnerable and filled with wonder. They couldn't look away.

The sensations they'd evoked were almost unbearable in their depth and intensity. They sank down slowly, clinging together desperately. Sleep came, and enfolded them softly, together.

He woke up abruptly, arm flying out and finding emptiness.

"Over here," came the soft voice.

Groggy with sleep, he peered through dim light. The clock now read four. Dawn would come soon. Eyes still searching, he finally found her.

She was silhouetted starkly against the window, the streetlight casting her face and white T-shirt into a myriad of harsh whites and deep grays.

"What are you doing?" he asked sleepily.

"Searching," she told him.

With a long sigh, he tiredly rubbed his eyes and sat up. "What are you talking about?"

"I don't know," she said. "I can't pinpoint it yet. It's just an eerie feeling, from somewhere out there. Do you think he's watching?"

He didn't have to ask who "he" was.

"I don't know," Thomas told her honestly. "We haven't been able to come up with much yet."

"It's strange, you know," she said softly. "It's strange to know that there's someone out there who wants you dead." Absently she rubbed her arms. "And it's stranger still to know that I don't even know one thing about him. I know he's tall, I know he's thin. But I don't know his name. And I don't know where he is, or what he's planning to do."

Thomas could hear the low quiver in her voice. Concerned, he swung himself out of the bed and walked over to her. "It's okay," he told her. "I'll protect you."

"Will you?" she asked intently, turning her head until she could stare deeply into his eyes. "You're only human, Thomas. And I'm sure there are some types of evil you can't protect against."

"Sabrina," he said sharply. "Don't lose perspective. This psycho's only human, too, and sooner or later he's going to make a mistake. In fact he already has. He let someone see him. We'll get him, Sabrina. I promise you, we'll get him."

He wasn't sure if he'd totally convinced her, but before he could speak again, her eyes slid back out to the cold dark night behind the window.

"Why does he do it?" she asked suddenly.

"I don't know," Thomas said grimly. "I'm not sure I care. I just want him caught, one way or the other."

"Do you think he's simply lost control? I saw that happen once. I saw this pimp get mad and hit this girl. Nothing unusual about that, but the more he hit her, the madder he got. Until pretty soon he just couldn't stop. I think every raw deal, every bad minute, every bad thing that had ever happened to him converged on that one poor girl and he was determined to make her pay. I think he would have killed her, except that two guys finally pulled him off. He just couldn't stop.

"It's like all of us live on the edge of the darker part of life—where all the passions run so deep and so intense you could just drown in them—and he did. He fell over that edge, Thomas, and he drowned in all the hatred he'd ever felt. It was the scariest thing I'd ever seen."

"Yeah," said Thomas, "I've seen it, too. But I don't think that's what's going on here."

"Mentally ill?"

"The department psychiatrist who did up a profile on the killer after the second murder, certainly seems to think so. No sexual assault, you see. That makes things more interesting. The doctor's theory is that the killer's mother might have been a prostitute. That's why he kills old ones. Right now, we're busy cross-referencing files with some of the psychiatric wards around. Then we get to track down all the patients who have been released that have that kind of background. But we're going back as far as patients released ten years ago, so it's not exactly going very fast. Lots of legwork."

"Do you think you can catch him?" she asked softly.

"I don't know," he told her honestly.

They remained standing there a few minutes more, both of them staring out into the cold dawn, searching, but not finding.

Finally Thomas reached out and took Sabrina's hand. "Come on," he said quietly. "I have two hours left. Let's get some sleep."

She nodded, letting him lead her away. Her one night was ending now. After eight years it had come, and now it would leave. She didn't say anything. There were no words to say.

Another dawn, another new day. She was strong, she could take it. She waited for the alarm clock in silence. And beside her, Thomas slept.

Then at last it came, the sharp ring. Time was up, the night over, the day beginning. Had it been worth it? she thought as she wrapped the robe around her. Had it?

Short-term pleasure versus long-term pain. If the nights had seemed lonely before, she had a feeling they would only be lonelier in the future. Especially now that she knew what it was like to sleep in a warm embrace, to share a lingering kiss with someone she cared for, to burn in sweet passion.

And she found, quite suddenly, that she wouldn't trade in this last evening for the world.

No matter what happened next, even if Thomas walked out and never came back, even if the killer decided he was tired of games and moved in for the real thing, no matter what, at least now she had a memory or two to carry with her.

"I'm not much of a cook," she told Thomas as he slowly crawled out of bed and fumbled for his clothing, "but for you, today, I might get lucky."

It wasn't too bad. The bacon was burnt and fried eggs became scrambled, but Thomas assured her that was just the way he liked them. She had a feeling he was saying it just to be nice, but she didn't question him. Awkwardness had settled all too quickly between them. What did you say the morning after? How did you act, particularly when the previous night had been the most wonderful experience of your life?

He would leave her now, of that she was fairly sure. Already she could feel the distance between them growing. It had been a beautiful night, they'd shared more than many married couples did. But it was the cold light of morning, and Thomas was once again Thomas the cop, Thomas the All-American. And she was just Sabrina. Sabrina with the past.

Yet already, after a mere few days, her mind was filled with Thomas in a million different poses: eyes soft as he talked of his father; laughing as he threw whipped cream onto her face and she retaliated with hot fudge. She could even easily remember the way his face tightened with worry whenever he searched for answers that eluded him. And she could clearly see his face, dark with passion, as it was when he'd brought her pleasure she'd never known could exist between a man and a woman.

How was it possible that she'd gotten to know him so well, in such a short span of time? How was it that she knew that, no matter where she looked from now on, there would always be memories of him? In her own kitchen and in her bedroom. He was everywhere.

Finally she acknowledged the truth. She had searched forever for this man. He was, for her, the ultimate dream, the dream of a lifetime. A part of the dreams that were the hardest to fulfill, yet were the sweetest to savor. And the hardest to let go.

She cleared the dishes in silence while he disappeared to take a shower. Then not fifteen minutes later he reappeared, combing his wet hair with one hand while trying to button his wrinkled and torn shirt with the other.

"Your shirt needs a good washing and ironing, not to mention a little mending," she informed him.

"Are you volunteering?"

"Only if you want it back with big black holes."

He gave her a quick uncertain smile. He lingered for a moment, as if he wasn't quite sure what to do with himself, then he turned and headed for the door.

"Just one thing," he told her on his way out the door already. "Promise me, *swear* to me, that you will not leave this house—" he held up a hand just as she was about to answer "—it's not safe, Sabrina. I just lost my last witness.

I have no intention of losing another. So please promise me that you'll be careful."

Witness? the word washed over her coldly. He was worried about losing his *witness*. They had just spent the night together, they had made *love'* and come the morning light he wasn't worried about *her,* but was worried about his witness? Anger filled her, only to be quickly replaced by a deep sorrow. So it had happened already. He had withdrawn, pushing them back onto the distant, formal level of before. Fine, she told herself fiercely, she would not let it hurt her. She would not!

"All right," she said finally, keeping her voice cool and pointedly polite. "I'll make sure someone comes with me. How does that sound?"

He frowned for a moment, startled by the sudden change in her voice.

"Not good enough, but I suppose it will have to do."

Seconds passed, neither of them sure what to say. Finally, Thomas bent down and kissed her softly, not noticing the confusion in her eyes when he drew away.

At that moment something gave way inside him and something warm took its place. Looking down at Sabrina, he suddenly found it hard to remember why he couldn't become involved with her. Having her cook breakfast for him—burned though it had been—and having her see him to the door somehow felt too right to be wrong.

Then he remembered. Sabrina was a witness in a murder investigation—ethically he could not risk compromising the case and her testimony by taking their relationship to a level other than detective/witness. Besides that, Sabrina had been a prostitute. He understood how it had happened. He understood that she had been the victim. But still, the thought of her with other men—

Refusing to think about it, he squared his shoulders and walked away. He had a job to do.

Sabrina watched the light go out of Thomas's eyes and saw him stiffen slightly, as if bracing himself against something, before he moved away from her. Her heart ached. She knew what had made him draw away and what she normally would have dismissed in anyone else, not caring what they thought of her, labeling them too ignorant to know better, suddenly pained her as never before. With Thomas there was no denying it. She cared what he thought of her, maybe too much.

Chapter 7

"Thomas?" asked the voice on the other end of the phone. He had answered the phone without immediately responding, his mind a thousand miles away, reliving scenes, interviews and reports. But at the sound of the voice, *her* voice, it snapped back to attention instantaneously. Not just because it was Sabrina, but because she didn't sound all right.

"What is it?" he asked urgently, a dozen dangerous scenarios already flashing through his mind. The killer had sent her more roses; the killer had gotten Suzie; the killer was standing right there, forcing her to call as he held a knife to her throat. "Talk to me, Sabrina."

"Suzie's gone," she said softly. "I just went to her room, and she's disappeared."

"Do you think she was forcibly taken?" he asked, all police instincts sharpening. Across from him, Seth looked up from a pile of reports in sudden attention.

"No, no," she said quickly. "The bed's made. She even folded the sweater I gave her and placed it at the end of the bed."

He could barely contain his sigh of relief. He nodded assurance at Seth, and the other man returned to his reports.

"Look, Sabrina," Thomas began, "I understand that you're worried, but I thought this kind of thing happened all the time."

"It does. But this is different, Thomas. She promised me she would stay a week. And frankly, as strange as this sounds, with Willy in jail, she'll have no place to go. She doesn't even have decent clothes for this weather. Thomas, I'm seriously worried about her."

With a sigh Thomas forced his mind back to his first impressions of Suzie. Timid, shy; a child, really. Sabrina was right, they should be worried.

On the other hand, if Suzie had left, she'd probably done so because she needed the space, the time to take everything in. God knows, after the past forty-eight hours, he needed some of that himself. The situation with Sabrina had intensified so quickly that it startled him. And frankly, he wasn't sure how he felt about any of it. He was becoming involved with a woman who was not only his witness, but had a past that twisted his gut every time he thought about it. All logic told him to stay away. The only problem was that every time he saw her, logic seemed to go by the wayside in favor of instinct . . . and desire.

"Sabrina," he tried again. "Look, Sabrina, I understand you're worried. I really do. But I'm pretty much grounded here and I can't go look for her right now. As it is, Seth and I will be lucky to leave at all tonight. And frankly, finding this killer before he claims another victim has got to take priority. How about you give her some time? Maybe she'll come around. She'll see that she doesn't have anyplace to go, and she'll come back."

"I don't think it's that simple," Sabrina said stubbornly. "I think she left because of last night. I think she left because she feels like she failed by letting Willy into the house. If that's the case, coming back is the last thing she's going to do. She'll go back to prostitution before she'll do that. It's what she knows, Thomas. She understands punishment better than she understands hope."

For a moment the words brought back the look in Suzie's eyes when she'd glanced up at him last night. That look of total acceptance, of waiting. Sabrina was right. Even last night Suzie had been expecting to be punished, and violently, brutally so. Perhaps because he hadn't punished her, she'd decided to punish herself. Oh, God.

"Give her until nightfall," he said tersely, cursing silently at the entire situation. If only he had the time.

"Thomas," Sabrina's voice came again, calmer now, more even in tone. That alone should have warned him. "Thomas, if she isn't back by nightfall, I'm going after her."

"The hell you are," he exploded this time, and he must have been louder than he thought because Seth looked up with avid interest again. "Look, lady, in case you've forgotten, someone is trying to *kill* you. You're also the only witness in an ongoing murder investigation. As a cop, I *forbid* you to leave that house. Is that understood?"

"Am I under arrest?" she asked him evenly.

"No—"

"Then I intend to do my job to the best of my ability. And if that means I have to go looking for Suzie, then I will."

"Damn it, Sabrina," he exploded again. "You're being unreasonable. You don't do this kind of thing for the other kids that leave. Didn't you tell me that?"

"I know, I know. But this is different. She didn't leave because she isn't ready to be helped. She left because she thought she screwed up too badly. If I don't find her, she won't ever come back, and, Thomas, I can help her. I know I can. I can't just turn away from that. I *won't* turn away from that."

He sighed heavily. "I don't suppose you'll allow two officers to escort you?" As if he even had the manpower for that. Hell, they didn't even have enough officers to handle burglaries, let alone baby-sit a grown woman. Increasing the patrols in her area had been stretching himself to the limit as it was. No way could he get any extra detail for something like this.

It didn't matter. She wouldn't accept it, anyway. He knew just what she would say: It would scare all the kids away. He was left without a choice.

"Okay, Sabrina," he said at last. "I'll try to get back there to help you. Just promise me you won't leave before calling first. And if I don't answer, wait. I'm probably on my way over. And for God's sake, make sure all the doors are locked and the windows, too. I have enough headaches right now as it is."

He was angry when he hung up the phone, angry and mad. But not just at the pressures that seemed to tear at him, demanding more than he could possibly ever give. He was mad at himself, mad at what he was feeling. If she had been any other witness, he knew it wouldn't have mattered. He would have been concerned, he would have tried to convince her not to go. But if she had, he would have lived with it. Not like now. Not like this moment when his guts were all twisted in knots with his fear.

He was scared, damn it. Scared for her in that rickety old house the killer already knew too much about. Scared for her on account of her stubborn streak, which got her into more trouble than it kept her out of. Scared for her and her good intentions that would most likely get her killed.

Somewhere out there was a man who wanted her dead, and Thomas wasn't any closer to catching him now than he had been the week before.

And it scared him.

It shouldn't. It shouldn't matter. She was just a witness, just a woman he was attracted to, that was all. At least, he wished that were the case.

It was a worried man who went back to the reports in front of him. A worried man with a furrowed brow and a heavy heart. The clock was ticking away, and in the silence, it sounded ominous to him.

He wasn't able to pull away until nine, and by then it had been dark for hours. But to her credit Sabrina had not left. Even though it went against her grain, against her very nature to act immediately, for him she had waited.

Yet the moment his battered blue work car pulled into the driveway, she was out the door and sliding into the other side. She handed him a paper bag as soon as she closed the door.

"Dinner," she announced. "Nothing fancy, but at least I didn't burn it."

Looking tired and worn he opened the bag to find two ham sandwiches and an apple. He smiled. Exactly what he needed. He hadn't had time to pick something up after rushing home to check on Woof. Luckily he'd been able to get a neighbor to dog-sit. It only took about five bites to take care of the sandwiches. He decided to eat the apple while he drove.

"Where to?"

"Hollywood Boulevard. Are you still mad?"

"No," he said with a long sigh. "Just tired." And worried, too, but he wasn't about to admit that to her. "Let's just go and see what we can find."

It was a long night for them both.

They must have searched for hours. Hours of simply walking up and down the streets, in and out of bars and restaurants. Sabrina seemed to know her way well, a little too well, Thomas thought uneasily. It was hard for him to see her here, he admitted. Hard to watch the way she moved, the easy way she spoke to the other prostitutes. In a way, it explained why she was so good at her job. Out here on these streets with all their glitter, all their grime, she belonged.

He wasn't sure if he could handle that yet, even as he appreciated her deft skill in handling the people they met. Answers they would have refused him, they gave her. By the time Sabrina and he had passed the second hour, he was halfway ready to recruit her for the police force.

But still Suzie eluded them.

It was Thomas and his raging appetite that finally lured them back to the restaurants. As far as he was concerned, it was bad enough he was walking his feet to the bone, he shouldn't have to starve doing it.

Sabrina spotted her first.

"Over there," she said suddenly. "Look, at that table. There's a golden-haired girl. What do you think?"

He maneuvered them a little closer, gaining a better angle. From here she certainly did look like Suzie. She seemed to be talking to a man sitting across from her, and whatever he was saying must have upset her for she began to push her chair back, inch by inch. The man noticed, too, his hand flying across the table to catch her wrist.

Thomas never hesitated. In three long strides he was pushing his way across the floor, but the place was crowded and he had to fight his way through, losing precious time and alerting the man to his presence with the commotion he had to make. He looked up, caught Thomas heading toward him, and grew wild. A second later, in the masses of bodies, the man had disappeared. Two seconds later, Thomas was at the table.

"Are you all right?" he asked Suzie immediately. She nodded her head slowly, then her eyes clouded over and she lowered her head.

"Are you okay?" Sabrina echoed as she at last made it to the table. "Suzie, please. Talk to me."

The girl nodded again. "I'm okay, I guess," she said finally.

"Suzie," Sabrina began. "Suzie, why did you leave?"

"I changed my mind," the girl said softly.

"I don't believe you," Sabrina replied evenly. "I think you left because of last night. But, Suzie, it doesn't matter. We *both* made mistakes last night. I shouldn't have left you alone. I had promised I would protect you, I should have been more careful. It's not all your fault. It's mine, too. And maybe, if we work together, we can make sure it never happens again."

Suzie didn't look convinced.

"Suzie, there's nothing out here for you anymore. Just cheapness, degradation. You deserve better that."

"He said you ran a white slavery ring," the girl blurted out suddenly.

"Who said that?"

"The man. The man that was here. He said you were evil. That I should stay away. But then he said you were in the mafia, and I was confused. But I think so was he because then he told me he had lied the first time. Not lied really, but had forgotten. Or mixed it up. Or something like that."

"Who was the man?" Thomas asked gently. "Did he give you his name?"

"Johnny," she said softly. "His name was Johnny and he said he used to be a go-go dancer here. I don't know what he does now."

"Do you believe him?" Sabrina asked. "Do you think I want to sell you or hurt you?"

There was a long pause. "No," she said at last. "I guess not."

"Do you think Johnny was telling the truth?"

Again, Suzie shook her head. "I think Johnny's sick," she said softly. "He said he forgot to take his medication, or maybe he just doesn't have it anymore. He said something about going back to look but that his lover was trying to kill him, just like he killed the cat. I think Johnny's sick," she said again. "Very sick."

Then there was another small pause, and she suddenly rushed out. "I want to go back. I really do. It's just that... It's just that I always screw up."

"It's okay," Sabrina told her. "You're only human. You're allowed to make mistakes. To tell you the truth, I make them myself."

"And so do I," Thomas assured Suzie.

"Let's get out of here," Sabrina said, and offered Suzie her arm. "Let's go home."

The girl paused one more time, one last time, then with a long sigh, she took the arm and allowed them to lead her back. Back to hope.

It was so late when they got back, nearly three in the morning, that it seemed silly for Thomas to leave. He had to be up by six as it was. So by unspoken agreement he simply crawled into the bed with her and, curling her up next to him, drifted quickly off to sleep. Three hours later he was gone.

But a little after noon, she received a phone call.

"Sabrina, I'm coming over tonight, and I'm bringing my clothes," Thomas said. He rushed on, forestalling the protest before it could even be voiced. "The killer knows where you live and the bastard's been a step ahead of us all the way. The safest course of action here is to have someone in your house, at least during the night hours. And don't worry about sleeping arrangements. I can make do with the couch." He stopped abruptly, willing her not to argue. The department hadn't been able to give him the added manpower necessary to increase overall surveillance on her house. The only way to ensure her safety, as far as he was concerned, was to take matters in his own hands. Safety for the only person who could finger the psycho terrorizing the city, he assured himself briskly. He refused to listen to the small voice in his heart that said his need to stay at Sabrina's, to be close to her, was anything more than that of a cop doing his job.

Sabrina wasn't quite sure what she was hearing. On the one hand, he sounded so cold, she was almost hurt. Somehow, after the past two nights, she had thought . . . well, she had thought that maybe he would want to stay.

But the attraction must already be fading. Just two nights and he was offering to sleep on the couch. Just two nights. She had known this would come, she reminded herself, straightening her spine. She had known that sooner or later it would end. A part of her ached at his rejection. It had come earlier than she'd expected. And yet perhaps this was better. They didn't know each other well yet, she was less accustomed to having him in her life, in her bed.

Let him go, she told herself. You know where he's from, you know his background. *Let him go.*

"That will be fine," she replied at last, keeping her own voice professional and brisk. "I'll be sure to find the blankets and sheets for the couch."

The couch? It took him a moment to remember that he'd been the one to mention it. Oh, yeah, the couch. The idea was beginning to appeal to him even less now. But at least he would be there, in her home. Watching and waiting. If anything happened, if—when—the killer came again, he would be there.

"I'll be a little late," he said after a moment. "Probably around nine. So I'll see you then."

"Would . . . would you like some dinner?" she managed to ask. "I could burn something for you."

She heard his small laugh on the other end.

"No," he assured her, some of the tension dissipating. "Seth and I will send out for a pizza, I'm sure."

"Okay."

"Okay."

"Goodbye?"

"Goodbye."

But that had been at one, and it was already well past nine. She was beginning to feel worried. Not to mention that Maria had called from the other shelter. The temperature was dropping, and the shelter there was at capacity. They would start sending kids her way soon.

So she and Suzie sat together and waited. And played cards, and waited.

But then at last, the knock came. Not quite sure who to expect, Sabrina looked through the peephole, then rapidly undid the locks to open the door.

Standing in the doorway was a group of five kids. They all looked to be around sixteen or seventeen, all decked out in black, one smoking a cigarette.

The one who was smoking took a step forward and Sabrina inhaled the scent of tobacco with something akin to envy.

"Hey, man," he said as the lights on the porch caught his flaming red hair and crystal-blue eyes, "we were sent here by the shelter. You're Sabrina, right?"

She nodded.

"That's cool," he informed her, and without waiting for further invitation, sauntered on in. He glanced around briefly, his eyes quickly settling on the kitchen. Nodding to himself, he turned back around and stuck out his hand.

"I'm Ricko," he told her with a flourish, and flashed her a wide grin. "Pretty neat name, isn't it?" He didn't seem to need a reply, continuing on without a pause.

"This is Rachel," he said, and pointed to a petite girl with long dark hair and eyes so blue they were almost black. Sabrina flashed her a smile, but the girl merely nodded, caution rimming her exotic eyes.

The other three were all boys. She had to concentrate to remember the names correctly. The one with long blond hair tumbling across his forehead called himself Steve. The one with dark hair and a nose that had been broken at least three times, went by Eric. The last boy was smaller, with a wiry build and hunched shoulders. He squirmed uncomfortably under her look and peered back from under a mop of hair with bloodshot eyes and flushed cheeks. Ricko introduced him as Shaun, and Sabrina gave the small boy more than one worried look.

Introductions made, Ricko led the way into the kitchen. "Don't worry," he called back over his shoulder, "we know the routine."

They certainly seemed to. Working as a small but efficient group, they sorted through the cupboards until they had collected the materials for sandwiches and, working assembly-line style, rapidly made a plateful.

In no time at all, they fixed their dinner and then proceeded to devour it.

"There are a few simple rules," Sabrina began as they all sat around the table, but Ricko cut her off.

"Yeah, yeah, yeah. We know. No drugs, no stealing. Treat each other with respect. Don't worry. We won't be a problem. Here today, gone tomorrow. That's our policy. Don't sweat about it."

Sabrina could only nod. She felt somehow that she had lost control of her own house and wasn't completely sure how to get it back. She certainly hoped Thomas would get home soon. There was power in numbers. As if in answer to her prayers, a sudden knock on the front door sounded. The kids looked up in immediate suspicious attention.

"It's okay," she told them. "It's just Thomas. He. . . he works here, too." That explanation seemed safe enough as she quickly moved across the room to let him in. But suddenly she felt nervous, unsure of herself. Wiping damp palms on her sides, she swallowed. She'd been excited about seeing him again, but now that the moment was here, she didn't know what to say or do. And, to make matters worse, she and Thomas had a six-person audience! Taking a deep breath, she opened the door.

There was one small instant of contact, one small moment where her eyes searched his anxiously, then she realized that his gaze, while on the weary side, held only warmth for her. She relaxed a fraction, watching silently as Thomas's eyes slowly drifted past hers to find six more pairs scrutinizing him.

Ricko met the older man's gaze levelly, even as he nodded at Shaun to start clearing the dishes. Introductions had just started when with a clatter of falling glass, the boy collapsed.

In an instant Sabrina was at his side. Placing the back of her hand on his flushed cheeks, she felt the blaze of his fever.

"He's burning up," she told Thomas. "We've got to get him cooled down."

With a quick, efficient nod Thomas assessed the situation and gently picked up the boy. "Bathroom?" He looked enquiringly at Sabrina.

"Yes, please. I'll get a few washcloths and the first-aid kit." She spared a quick look at Ricko, who seemed a little pale in spite of himself. "He's going to be all right," she assured him. "We'll take care of him."

Or at least, so she hoped.

Upstairs, without words or conscious thought, Sabrina and Thomas began working together as a team. Between the two of them, they got the boy out of his filthy clothes and into the bath. At first it didn't seem like they were getting anywhere; the child thrashed and bucked beneath Thomas's grip. But then Sabrina saw it—a long, thin gash in the child's hip that had turned a sickly green.

Further investigation revealed a wicked sliver, which Thomas, with his large but steady hands, proceeded to fish out. It was a long and nerve-wracking process. By the time they got the wound completely clean and bandaged, they were both drenched and exhausted.

Sabrina set up the bed in the room not far from hers and Thomas brought the boy in, laying him down gently. Together they turned to leave.

She touched his arm in the doorway.

"Thank you," she said softly.

He didn't say anything, but suddenly he grabbed her arms and pulled her against him in a long embrace, burying his face into the thick gold of her hair, inhaling her warm scent.

She was soft and wonderful in his arms, he thought dimly. She was so small, so delicate. It seemed impossible to him that his big hands didn't break the very curves he wanted to caress. But though tiny in stature, she was firm, solid, giving. He couldn't seem to hold her close enough. God, it had been a long day. Long and exhausting and tiring. And in the back of his mind through it all, had been the desire to do just this. To simply take a break and hold this woman in his arms.

He shouldn't, he told himself. He should remember that he'd been relegated to the couch. But he didn't let go. He *couldn't* let go. After the grueling harshness of his job, he needed this moment of softness. This moment when he could almost pretend that only they existed in the world. No pasts, no murderers.

As abruptly as he grabbed her, he let her go.

"I'm sorry," he said. "I shouldn't have done that."

She looked at him warily, feeling at once lost and confused. One moment he touched her, the next he withdrew. One night he spent in her bed, the next he asked for the couch. She would never understand him. The gulf between them had never seemed as wide as it did now. He was here now, but would he be tomorrow?

There was a price to be paid.

"Oh," she said suddenly, turning her thoughts to a safer topic. "Don't tell them you're a cop."

Thomas nodded, fully understanding. From their perspective he represented the enforcement of a judicial system that, more often than not, left them out as losers. For them the law was an extension of parents that claimed the right to beat them, while breaking the law—by stealing, selling drugs, or themselves—was often the key to survival. It would only be natural for his profession to scare them away from the shelter.

But he'd barely taken two steps when the beeper fastened to his belt sounded its annoying tune. Thomas looked down at the offensive box with a groan.

"Can I use the phone in your room?"

"Of course. It's to the right of the bed."

He nodded and she saw the tiredness pulling at him, wearing him down. And suddenly it was she who was struck with the sudden urge to draw him into her arms. At this moment, more than anything in the world, he looked like a man who needed a break. Like a man who needed a woman to hold him. But that wasn't her place, she reminded herself sternly.

So instead she watched him go, and did nothing. As soon as he disappeared into the bedroom, she turned and went back downstairs.

She found all the kids gathered in the living room in front of the TV. Ricko seemed intent on assessing Suzie, his blue eyes showing his appreciation as they skimmed over her delicate countenance.

But he managed to tear himself away as Sabrina entered. "Will Shaun be okay?" he asked.

"I'm not sure," she told him honestly. "We'll have to keep checking on him every half hour, just in case. I think we've taken care of the problem, but I'm not an expert. If his fever goes up for any reason, I'll have to take him to the doctor."

Ricko nodded his understanding. "So even in the best case scenario it's gonna take a few days, huh?"

"Yes," she replied with a nod. "Even if everything goes very well, he'll need at least four days to rest and recover, probably more."

"Yeah, yeah." Ricko gave a sigh, seeming none too pleased. But then he brightened and flashed her his wicked grin. "So then, it seems like we'll be sticking around, too. All right, what kind of beds do you have in this joint?"

"There are two rooms left open, both downstairs."

He nodded. "Okay, Rachel, you take one room, Eric and Steve can share the other. I'll do the couch. That works? Cool."

And that seemed to be the end of the matter for him as his attention turned to the TV. But just then Thomas came bounding down the stairs, trying to get an arm in his coat. His face looked grim, but there was a light in his eyes that she'd never seen before.

Sabrina caught him at the entrance.

"What is it?" she asked in hushed tones.

"We've got a tip about the murderer. We haven't had time to check it out completely, but it looks like we may have come up with the location he'll strike tonight. This is it," he said excitedly. "This is the break we've been needing all along."

She nodded, resting a hand on his rough cheek. "Be careful," she said.

He nodded once, kissed her quickly on the cheek, and was gone. She should be excited she knew, happy. But instead she had a very bad feeling in the pit of her stomach. Tonight was going to be a long night.

Thomas was thinking the same thing himself just two hours later. He was hunched down in a faded blue sedan with Seth. Both had their parkas zipped to their chins, but the chill was incredible.

Every few minutes they debated whether to turn on the engine to heat the car, but each time they decided it would call too much attention to the vehicle. Their own body heat was enough to fog up the windows. Thomas kept himself busy trying to clear a small hole above the dash to peer through.

A few blocks down they could make out the outline of another dim car. All in all there were four of them on this street and two more a block over. On that block was where the real action was. Tightly dressed hookers, neon signs, flashy cars. They figured that was where the guy would pick up his girl. What they were concerned with were the small alleyways running from that street to this one.

This street was long and gray, rimmed by tired buildings with sagging windows and boarded-up doors. Here and there were bright flashes of color as girls brought their "johns" to the deserted doorways. They kept their eyes peeled on each man that wandered through, but they had yet to see a tall, thin man with a blue scarf.

It's just a matter of time, Thomas thought. Be patient. But his patience was starting to wear thin. There was a tenseness in his muscles and a knot in his gut that he didn't completely understand yet. Above all, there was a sense of urgency. And then, they saw the man. Tall, slender, in the shadows, an obscure woman in a short, tight skirt on his arm....

"This is it," Seth said suddenly. "Go."

They were out of the car in a flash, pounding down the pavement. While Thomas was bigger, Seth was quicker, and he reached the man first, whirling him around. Young, frightened eyes met his and Seth swore vehemently.

Thomas swore with him, as he took in the young man and his equally young but furious counterpart. He wanted to hit something, slam his fist through a wall, feel the plaster crumble. Gritting his teeth, he struggled for control. He was not going to lose his grip now.

"Let's book 'em." But inwardly he kept cursing. All this time, all this waiting and all they had done was catch a hooker and a regular customer. *Great.* If the murderer had any brains, he would have spotted this little scene, and, by now, be high tailing it out of here.

But still, they had to keep trying. Without much hope they pawned the two off onto another squad car and once again returned to their car.

They'd been sitting there, fuming in their seats for not more than five minutes when the call crackled from the CB. Thomas felt his face turn gray and his heart plummet to his knees.

A body had been found, with another black rose. And it was only one block away from Sabrina's house.

Thomas whipped out the red light, Seth gunned the motor, and off they went, tearing into the night.

Seth had barely stopped the car when Thomas was swinging the door open and jumping out. With long, running strides he was across the street in seconds, leaping over the crime tape and kneeling over the body. Taking a deep breath, he pulled up the sheet.

The relief staggered him, even bringing tears into his eyes as he took in the brown hair and thick mascara of another aging prostitute. But hard on the heels of the relief was anger. They had been tricked. That goddamn...

"Easy," came Seth's voice. "We'll get him, you know we will."

But Thomas was shaking his head, anger tightening his voice. "I don't want to just get him, I want to nail him to the wall. I want to make him pay, Seth. Can't you see what he's doing? He's playing with us. I'll bet you twenty to one he made that call tonight, that tip. He knew we'd be watching her now, so he lured us away. He's playing, damn it." Thomas's voice was low and burning. "I'll make him pay."

"No," said Seth firmly. "You'll act like a cop, because you are not personally involved with this case, remember?"

Thomas looked into his partner's warning eyes and took a deep breath. "Yeah," he said at last. "I'll remember."

"All right," said Seth and slapped Thomas on the back. "Now, where the hell are the two officers who were supposed to be patroling this beat?"

They weren't of much help. They had circled in a pattern, they admitted. Coming around each spot in fifteen minute intervals. All the killer had to do was watch and time. Just as he'd done when delivering the roses to Sabrina's.

The thought brought Thomas up cold again.

"My God," he said. "Sabrina! What if this is another diversion!"

He didn't wait for the car or for Seth. He took off at a run, fear giving him speed as his blood pulsed fiercely through his body.

"Please," he begged as her old house loomed in front of him. A light flickered on the front porch, but all the windows were dark. He grabbed the door handle, but found it locked. He wasn't sure if he should be relieved or not.

He pounded on the door. "Come on, Sabrina," he whispered urgently. "Answer the damn door!"

He was about to crash through it, when he heard the sound of the first lock being drawn back. She had no sooner cracked the door open than he whipped it open and grabbed her close.

"Oh, thank God, thank God."

"Thomas," she protested as he smothered her, "you're hurting me."

He immediately released her, his eyes still wild. "I'm sorry, are you okay? Honest, I didn't mean to hurt you."

"I'm fine," she told him, still looking puzzled. "Everything is fine." Then she saw a man jogging up the path and tightened her robe self-consciously. She took another step forward, shutting the door behind her so they wouldn't disturb Ricko. The intense chill of the night made her shiver and she unconsciously moved closer to Thomas's solid warmth. "What's going on?" she asked against his chest.

Seth stopped on the edge of the driveway, panting heavily from his run as he waited to see Thomas's signal. Catching sight of him, Thomas nodded over Sabrina's head. There was a secondary hesitation, a small lingering, but Seth was a man of tact. It was very clear that his partner wanted privacy. The forms, the questions, could wait until morning. After the long hours they both had been putting in, Thomas deserved at least that much.

As Seth turned and walked away, Thomas explained the evening to Sabrina. She just nodded through most of it, but he saw something flash behind her eyes. Something assessing and final. When he asked, she denied anything was amiss, but he didn't believe her.

Somehow he got the feeling that a decision had just been made. And it terrified him.

Suddenly he felt all the frustration and fear of the past few days boil up inside him. Frustration toward the man who eluded him still, the man who was threatening this tiny golden woman before him. And fear, such a deep, deep fear that the next time it wouldn't be a game. Next time the killer wouldn't settle for a block away. And the next body Thomas would be forced to identify would be hers.

And deep down, it was only now that he was beginning to realize just how much that would cost him. When he had seen that body, heard that call of a murder just a block away from Sabrina's house, he hadn't been thinking of her past. He hadn't been thinking of her as a former prostitute. He had been remembering her warmth. Remembering her faith. Remembering how good she could make him feel. All the way to her old house, the only thing he could think was that he couldn't lose her now. Not now, when he had just found her.

Right this second, though, the swirling mass of emotions within him refused to be sorted out. He only knew that at this moment he had to have her. He had to touch her, to feel that warmth, to have her in his arms, vibrant, sexy, alive. His.

He didn't wait. Before she had time to react, he was scooping her up in his arms, carrying her through the doorway, stopping only to lock the bolts behind them, then they were heading up the stairs. With one foot he closed the bedroom door behind him.

There was a moment when she thought to protest, but then she saw his eyes. They were dark, almost black in the darkened room, and burning into hers with such an intense desperation it took her breath away. Then there was no more time for thinking, as his lips swooped down and claimed her own.

His kiss was burning and bruising. It demanded with an arrogance that sent her reeling and retaliating with equal fierceness.

He did not ask, he took; stripping off her robe, ripping off her T-shirt until his hand could greedily roam the body that tortured him so, that he needed so. Her own hands came to life, responding to the passion he had taught her, dragging off his own shirt and pants until he, too, was naked beneath her touch.

Growling low in his throat, his lips founds hers again, devouring. His hands seemed to be everywhere, claiming her curves, reveling in her softness. She could only surrender, moaning low as he stoked the fires that flamed hotly in her blood.

The more he touched, the more she wanted, demanding the pleasure that only he could bring her. And then he was there, fiercely driving into her. Forcing her to brilliant heights as she clawed his back in pleasure so intense it was almost agony.

But it was a shared agony, as he threw back his head and gritted his teeth in the shadowed darkness.

"Sabrina," he gasped, and then they were both there, shattering apart, plunging through brilliance.

He collapsed and she welcomed the weight, gathering him close with limbs now heavy with contentment.

He moved only once, to roll off her and draw her closer to him.

"You're mine," he murmured sleepily. Snuggled contentedly against him, she didn't protest.

Chapter 8

In the week that followed all of the inhabitants of the shelter—including Thomas—settled into a routine. The kids stayed for the simple reason that Sabrina had no other place to send them to; the other shelters, including Maria's, were filled to capacity. And while Sabrina worried about their safety, what with a serial killer delivering black roses to her doorstep, so far there had been no indication that the killer was the slightest bit interested in them. It helped that the police remained on watch with unmarked patrol cars, keeping a tight surveillance on the neighborhood as well as Sabrina's house.

Thomas remained with her, sleeping in her bed each night, since Ricko had the couch. There was no passionate lovemaking, though Thomas would sometimes reach for her with an almost fevered desperation, not saying a word, just holding on to her tightly. She never questioned him, but held onto him just as tightly. When her heart ached for more, she simply reminded herself brutally that the time they had together was very limited. He was here because it was his job and once the case was over, he would leave. She would take what she could get, and survive the pain of his loss when it happened, not before.

On the seventh day of Thomas's stay, Sabrina awoke with a start in the early morning hours, her head jerking up suddenly, her nerves strung tight. She lay there for a long moment, totally rigid, trying to pinpoint whatever noise, whatever movement had disturbed her slumber.

Just inches away she could hear the even breathing of Thomas deep in sleep. Some ways off, the soft tick-tock of the old clock pattered out its ancient rhythm. For all intents and purposes the house and its inhabitants were asleep.

But Sabrina did not relax. After three years of living on the streets, where waking up in time was the difference between being robbed or remaining safe, she trusted her instincts. They might have become slightly duller in the last eight years, but they were still sharper than most people's. And in the past few days, since the third prostitute had been murdered just a block from her house, they had had every reason to become even sharper.

Softly now, not wanting to disturb Thomas and the rare few hours of sleep he had managed to steal, she crept out of the bed and padded her way softly to the window in her old T-shirt. Peering out, she still saw nothing, detected no one. But she stayed anyway. Instinct told her that she was closer to the source of her nervousness now.

It was a strange feeling to know that someone wanted you dead. And even more frightening to know that they were so confident of their eventual success, they weren't in a hurry to get you. Instead, the killer continued his onslaught of psychological games until her nerves felt so tightly strung they twanged when she walked.

Thomas and Seth had investigated the tip that had had them waiting at the one spot that night while the killer struck at another. Sure enough, with a little legwork, it had been tracked down to having been placed from a phone booth only two blocks from her house. It seemed that the killer had decided to distract the police for a little bit so he could have more fun. For this week's fun and games he had continued the "presents" of black roses, only he mailed them now, one each day, all received from different drop boxes. None had included writing, and her address on the front of the sinister missives had been cut from one of the very pamphlets she so often distributed to street kids. Sabrina let Thomas collect the mail now. After that first hideous morning of opening the door and seeing those perfect black roses with their bloodred bows, she didn't want to know.

It filled her with anger, though. Anger that slowly superceded the fear. She had fought too hard, worked too long to obtain control of her life only to lose it now to some whacked-out psycho. She was angry at him for infringing upon the new world she had spent so long in building. And angrier still for the threat he posed not just to herself, but to every kid living in the shelter right now, kids with nowhere else to go.

Damn it, she had sworn to protect these kids, promised that she would keep them safe. How could she do that when she couldn't even find a sick man who seemed bent on destruction? How long before his warnings got to be more personal? How much longer until he went from killing old prostitutes just a block away, to killing someone like Suzie or Ricko? Shadow had come back for one night, and for the first time, she had been forced to wonder if it wouldn't be safer for him to simply stay away.

This was her life. Not perfect, not even close to any fairy tale, but her life nonetheless. And she didn't want to lose it. Not now. Certainly not now.

Unbidden, her eyes returned to the bed and Thomas's slumbering form. In some ways it was painfully ironic. At last, after all these years, she had finally found someone she really trusted. Someone she cared a great deal about. And some psychopath she didn't even know was threatening to take it all away from her.

She didn't want it to end, she thought vehemently. She wasn't ready yet. On its own, killer or no killer, the relationship she had would die, she knew that. But by what right did this man threaten the only piece of happiness she'd had in all her life? Sooner or later, Thomas would leave her. She understood this already, understood it probably even better than he did.

Silently, leaning against the cold glass of the windowpane, her hand drifted to her stomach. She wished sometimes, with the greatest intensity, that she could go back. If only so she could change one thing. Just one thing. She would suffer through being a prostitute again, she would suffer through the beatings, the despair, if only fate would let her change one thing. One little bit of knowledge that would have saved her so much.

And maybe even bought her a future with the slumbering man just a room's length away.

With a long sigh she turned away from the window. Whatever had woken her, whoever it had been, had left now. Now it was just herself in the early morning dawn, herself and this man who shared her bed.

Time was running out, slipping away like sand through her fingers. She couldn't slow it down. Couldn't catch it and freeze it for one long instant, if only to prepare herself, if only to learn how to let Thomas go.

So it rushed on by, leaving her floundering in its wake, wanting what she couldn't have. Mourning the loss even before it occurred.

She had to come to terms with it. All things must end. All things must come to pass. *Even love.* Perhaps there would come a time when she would meet another. Someone else who warmed her heart and soul as this man did. But she didn't think so. She really didn't think so.

So that was the way of things, she repeated to herself over and over. Only she found she didn't have a choice at all, not anymore. The killer was too close, threatening everything she had worked so hard for, threatening the very shelter she had dedicated her life to protecting. Suddenly it was very clear to her. Something had to be done. No more games, no more black roses in the mail. It was time for action now. Time to resolve things once and for all.

She believed she knew just how to do it. She could bring it all to an end. She'd learned a few things on the street. Things one never forgot.

Only one thing held her back. One little thing.

The man in her bed.

If she went through with her plan, then, either way, it would be over. She would either be killed or she would catch the killer, and Thomas would have no more reason to stay.

Lightly her hand came up and gently stroked the rough feel of his chest, the muscled plane of his arm. He stirred slightly, but he did not awaken. God, he felt so good to her. There was nothing quite like curling up with him, and awakening to arms warm and secure around her each morning. Nothing quite like the way he would sweetly stroke her hair, her arm.

He made her feel alive. He made her feel safe. He even made her feel loved.

If only...

She lay back down, resting her cheek against his shoulder as she settled against him, absorbing his rich warmth. There was one hour left before the alarm would ring. One hour left in the hourglass of time, one hour left to slip so fast through her fingers, falling, falling, until nothing would be left at all.

Nothing but memories framed in moonlight. Nothing but deep impressions tucked deeply in her heart.

"You're beautiful," she told him softly, shielded by the cover of the night. "You are so beautiful to me." But the words weren't quite enough, perhaps because she was still afraid of the words that would be. So instead she leaned over again, and placed a gentle kiss on warm lips that parted easily beneath hers.

Finally leaning back, the words crept into her throat, threatening to choke her with their intensity. And still, she held back, knew she would always hold back. She placed her arm carefully around him, once again resting her head against the gentle curve of his shoulder.

Content now, in a way she would never be content again, she lay with the man she had spent a lifetime trying to find, and awaited the dawn.

And time rushed on. Faster and faster, dwindling to nothing.

The doorbell rang sharply at ten o'clock, and not wanting to look too eager—though she was—Sabrina walked slowly to the door. Calmly she peered out the peephole, expecting to see Thomas's huge frame. She didn't see anything. For a moment icy fear swept over her. There would be more roses, she thought, and her heart leapt and accelerated in her chest. The killer had grown so bold he was delivering them to her in person.

Taking a deep breath, she told herself to stop acting like a fool and forced herself to glance downward as far as she could. And suddenly came across what looked very much like the tip of a furry ear.

Puzzled now and intrigued, she drew back the bolt lock and cautiously peeked out with the chain still in place. There, sure enough, sat a huge mongrel with a laughing doggy grin and a red ribbon around his neck. He was by far the ugliest creature she had ever seen. He had a gray and brown mottled coat, with a dark chest and paws. One eye was a clear blue, while the other, circled with a huge patch of black, was a deep brown. Part everything, Sabrina figured. But in spite of his looks, he politely offered her his paw.

Baffled, she released the chain, cautiously opened the door and accepted the handshake. Bending slightly down to grasp the huge paw, she saw a slip of paper buried within the red folds of his ribbon.

"So you come with a note," she said to the dog. He just grinned.

"Easy, boy," she murmured, reaching over to carefully lift the square from its protective hold. So far, the mongrel didn't seem to have any aggressive inclinations. He simply panted at her, grinning away.

She gave him an exasperated look, and unfolded the note.

"Cute, lovable mutt in need of warm, loving home," she read out loud. "I am housebroken and I love kids. P.S. Owner is included."

"Ohh, she thought, so that's what's going on.

"All right, Thomas," she called out. "It was cute, very cute. You can come out now."

The shadow to her right shifted, and Thomas magically materialized next to her. "His name is Woof," he supplied. "And honest, I've been meaning to bring him over. He's been all alone in a huge loft with only the neighbor boy to watch him for days now." At the skeptical look on her face he rushed on. "Have a heart. Besides, I would feel better if he was around during the day. He may look homely, but he's one of the best guard dogs you'll ever find.''

She wasn't so sure about that. The dog grinned so much about the only danger he seemed to pose would be sliming someone to death. But still, perhaps having the huge mutt around would settle her own nerves a little. With a nod she stood back and let them both inside.

Ricko whistled as he watched the huge dog stroll into the room. ''Man, oh, man,'' he breathed in appreciation. ''How much does that thing eat?''

''More than I do,'' Thomas assured him.

''How'd you get him?''

''Moral conscience. I found him at the pound when he was still a cute and little puppy.''

Just then Suzie walked out from her room. Her eyes lit up, huge as saucers, and the next thing anyone knew, she was on her knees, throwing her arms around the massive neck. Woof panted obligingly and licked the side of her face.

''He's wonderful,'' she exclaimed. ''What's his name? How long is he staying? Can he sleep with me?''

Sabrina stared at the girl in amazement. She had never seen Suzie glow so brightly, nor talk so loud. Perhaps they had hit on something.

Ricko wasn't as impressed. He'd been trying all afternoon to get Suzie to glow like that. He failed to see what the dog had that he didn't.

''Keep him for as long as you'd like,'' Thomas said, dismissing the matter altogether. ''Just don't feed him too much junk food. He loves junk food.''

Now that the matter was resolved, Thomas tugged on Sabrina's hand and led her upstairs. It had been a long and grueling day. Seth and he had put in a good ten hours of solid legwork, trying to track down the killer from the post office drops he was using. They had only come up with a weak lead, and frankly, Thomas was becoming more worried with each passing day. It had been a week now, but his instincts told him that the killer was due to strike at any moment. And somewhere, deep in his heart, he was terrified that this time the target wouldn't be another aging prostitute. That this time, it would be Sabrina.

No, he swore vehemently. He couldn't let that happen. He *wouldn't* let that happen. Still, he felt the desperation build within him.

Now he didn't stop to give an explanation to her, barely even waited for the door to shut behind them before he grabbed her, pulling her into his arms. He didn't say a word, he simply buried his head in the soft curve of her neck.

It was like coming home, each and every time, he thought dimly as she relaxed against him, returning the embrace. He could smell the fresh scent of her hair, and feel its silkiness against the roughness of his cheek. She felt delicate and wonderful, feminine and soft.

He didn't want it to end, never wanted it to end, but forced himself to finally pull away.

"I missed you," he said suddenly, surprising them both with the words. But he didn't take them back.

She tried to laugh lightly. "You were only away ten hours," she told him.

"I know," he said evenly.

There was an intensity in his gaze that left her throat dry, and her pulse heated. "I missed you, too," she found herself saying against her better instincts. "I really did."

He didn't say anything more. Instead, his eyes never leaving hers, he drew her back in, leaning his head down, down, until his lips touched hers, sweet, strong, heady. He moved his lips against hers seductively, nipping at her bottom lip, slowly licking at the pretend hurt. Then he deepened the kiss, taking them further and further until she was sighing into his arms, giving everything he had ever wanted and demanding it all back.

"Thomas," she managed to gasp before she lost all sanity, "Thomas . . . I've really got to . . . get back downstairs."

"Do you really want me to stop?" he whispered as he nibbled on a particularly sensitive spot on her fragrant neck.

"No," she said, and her eyes shut with the fierceness of her longing for him. She had to moisten her lips to continue. "But I think you'd better."

"Yes," he sighed against her mouth, kissing her one last time. "I suppose you're right."

Then he simply buried his face in the curve of her neck, bringing her nearer into a long embrace.

They held each other a minute longer, giving the fires a chance to cool before returning to the teenagers below. Then, together, they descended the stairs.

For the rest of the evening, Sabrina was careful not to touch Thomas. When they both volunteered to do the dishes, she was careful to keep a towel between them at all times. When they all sat down to watch television, she maneuvered Suzie between them.

But the physical distance didn't keep his words from her mind.

"Do you really want me to stop?"

No, she didn't want him to stop. Not now, not ever. But she was letting him get too close. Worse still, she didn't want to stop that, either. She wanted to spend eternity with him, sharing the joy and sharing the pain that was life.

Step back, Sabrina, she warned herself. Don't hang on just when you have to let go. Remember, he's not yours forever. Just for the moment. Just for the few precious moments framed in moonlight.

I can do it. *I can,* she promised herself. She'd allowed their relationship—such as it was—because she so needed the happiness he brought into her life. Because he'd been what she'd dreamed about for years. But the deal had been that she would accept what was, not ask or expect more. When the time came she was to let go, with no tears and no regrets. And that was exactly what she would do, no matter what the cost to her heart.... *No regrets. I will let go.*

The thought helped her get through the evening. At almost midnight Shadow appeared on the doorstep. He and Ricko exchanged long, assessing glances. Somewhere in the silence they seemed to reach an agreement, and each settled down to one side of the room, Shadow taking the floor.

Sabrina tried to ask Shadow about Mike, but he just shrugged, so she finally let the matter drop. All she could do was wait.

Finally, at half-past midnight, Sabrina commanded lights out, and with a bit of grumbling, everyone settled down. She and Thomas checked the locks, then waited at the foot of the stairs for the last sleeping bag to be rolled out, and the last light to be turned off.

They lingered there, gazing at a room now cloaked in mysterious shadows. Beneath the plains of darkness and the slivers of light, lay the quiet forms of Ricko and Shadow. Almost her children, she thought as she leaned against Thomas's solid build. At least, in the ways that mattered, they were.

She smiled softly into the silky night. *Her children.* As close as she would ever get. And suddenly a wave of protectiveness swept over her so intense that it was almost overwhelming. What she was going to do was right, she thought fiercely. It was the only way.

She would lose Thomas. Once again, the price had to be paid.

Let go of him now, she advised herself. Just let him go. But in that instant, she knew she wouldn't. She couldn't turn away from him, not just yet. Like a moth dancing with the flickering flame, she couldn't move away. This was her time, and for the only time in her life, she would be greedy, taking everything the night had to offer. There would be time enough later for regrets.

Deep down, though, she knew there wouldn't be any. Not now, not ever. No matter the pain, some things were worth it. *This* was worth it. She turned in his arms, taking his hand. Slowly, with sure steps, she led him up to the bedroom.

Dim light cascaded through the window, casting the room into myriad shades of light and darkness. It darkened her eyes, giving them a mysterious hue, even as it accented the delicate perfection of her cheekbones. Her lips were a sensual slash of shadows, shifting restlessly as she moved.

Unaware of the magic the night worked on her face, Sabrina closed the door and turned fully to face Thomas. She found him staring at her with eyes burning with dark need.

"You're so beautiful," he told her, his voice husky with awe.

"Do you really think so?" Her own voice was soft, breathless. Suddenly it was urgently important to her that he did find her beautiful, desirable.

He didn't answer, instead watching her with hotly gleaming eyes as he reached over and slowly slid the top button of her shirt from its hole. And then the next, and the next, until he could slide the shirt from her, exposing beautiful white shoulders, to the hunger in his gaze.

"Make love to me," she whispered, and he saw something deep in her eyes that twisted his heart until he couldn't breathe or think. Reaching up, he peeled his shirt off smoothly. His chest was magnificent in the night, a smooth maze of glowing planes and plunging shadows.

Tentatively she reached out a hand, opening it onto the sheer expanse of his chest. So smooth, so broad, so hard. Muscles rippled under her exploring fingertips, sending chills up her spine.

She raised her head to find his eyes, dark and intense upon her. Blind passion, burning need, consuming her in their endless depths.

"Love me," she whispered again, the words husky with need, soft with longing.

Slowly he reached down to caress tender flesh. The clasp of her bra gave smoothly, the lace falling before his skilled hands. Holding his breath in heart-wrenching need, he gently cupped the swell of her breast. His hands were rough and warm against her skin, tantalizing and teasing. She couldn't stop the moan as she arched up, giving herself to his wonderful hands, magical hands. Giving herself to the sensations as his fingers lightly pinched her coral nipples.

She was delicate but firm under his hands. And so beautiful. God, she was so beautiful. Unable to hold back any longer, he gave in to the desire, the need. His lips swooped down, capturing a pert nipple, rolling it luxuriously in his mouth. She tasted like fine wine and steeped passion. He smiled with male triumph as her hands buried themselves deep in his hair and she pulled him closer, firing his desire with her unconditional response.

His hands drifted lower, finding the clasp of her jeans even as her hands settled upon his own. But he caught her hands, kissing each fingertip in long, sucking kisses. Eyes dark with need, she watched him stand and peel away the rest of his clothes.

He stood arrogant and magnificent before her, his rippling body awash in the night's gentle light. He looked like a sculpture, powerful and awe-inspiring. And then he moved, reaching down to find the snap of her jeans, sliding them firmly down her hips. All that remained was the thin lace of her panties. He scooped her up then, easily carrying her gentle weight in his arms as he brought her to the bed and placed her on it.

His hands caressed her legs, his touch tantalizing, teasing against her thighs. His fingertips whispered down one leg, slowing around the areas that burned for his touch. Finally, unable to stand it, she arched up, whimpering low in her throat. And then his fingers slid under the elastic, finding her warm and moist with desire. But still it wasn't enough, wasn't the total consummation that they both burned for.

He touched her again, slowly, seductively. She arched up once more, instinctively lifting her hips, and beckoning him closer.

"Oh, please."

The softly uttered plea was more than he could stand. The wisp of her panties floated away, leaving her completely open to his touch, open to the night, open to the glory. No longer able to wait, he rose up and slid smoothly, firmly, into her wonderful warmth.

He moaned fiercely as she arched to take him deeper, to take all of him, needing everything he had to give.

"Yes." A sigh of delight, of need being fulfilled. But it was only the beginning as with sure strokes he drove them higher and higher. Until they were beings of only feeling, needing only each other, wanting only what the other could give.

"Yes."

As he swept her up into swirling desire.

"Yes."

As he plunged into silky warmth.

"Yes."

As they climbed to the highest pinnacle, beyond all reality, beyond even moonlight, to explode in each other's arms.

"Yes."

The alarm finally roused them from their warm cocoon. Groggy with sleep, Thomas reached over to slap the alarm away, then rolled over and pulled Sabrina closer. He snuggled down, burying his face in her hair, his arms protectively wrapping around her waist.

Still half asleep herself, Sabrina murmured softly, then sighed against him. But eventually consciousness began to weasel itself into her mind, penetrating the wondrous warmth and languor.

"Thomas?" she murmured softly.

"Mmm?"

"Time to get up," she managed to mumble as she cuddled closer to his warmth.

"Okay," he told her, and arranged himself more securely around her.

It was enough effort for both of them, and they drifted off for a few more minutes. But then Sabrina's conscience began to nag at her again, forcing sleepy eyes to open and blink owlishly.

"Thomas," she tried again. "You have to get up."

"Don't remind me," he informed her, and snuggled down deeper into the folds of the bed.

But the sleep was starting to clear from her mind, and she ruthlessly pulled away from the circle of his arms.

"No. You have to get up now."

"Now?"

"Now."

With a huge groan, he opened one eye and peered at her from under the covers. "Are you sure?"

"Yes. Definitely now."

Sighing heavily, he managed to peel open the other eye, then reached out to stretch his arms over his head. It was too much of an opportunity to resist, and she planted a kiss squarely on his chest.

"Hmm," he said, and stretched again. She obliged with another kiss.

"Definitely better than my dog," he mumbled.

"What?"

"Never mind," he informed her. "You had to be there."

She simply nodded, not quite awake enough to ask what he meant yet. She patted him on the shoulder. "Go hit the shower. I'll start the cereal."

"Deal," he agreed, and managed to roll out of bed.

After he left, she sat for a moment, alone in the pile of blankets. The coziness of sleep was fading fast, leaving her vulnerable to the sharpness of reality. She wasn't sure what was going to be the hardest to make it through once he was gone. The long nights, or the lonely mornings.

Refusing to dwell on the thought, she bravely set a foot onto the freezing floor. Shivers raced through her entire body and she almost gave in and crawled back under the covers. But the mornings, like all things, had to be faced sooner or later.

She gritted her teeth and set both feet firmly on the floor. It may be cold now, she thought, but it was only going to get colder.

The cereal wasn't too soggy by the time Thomas crept down the stairs. As quietly as possible, he pulled out the chair next to Sabrina's, wincing as it gave a protesting screech. He peered back to the sleeping forms in the living room. So far, nobody had moved.

He gave Sabrina a weak smile as she looked sharply up at the sound.

"Sorry," he whispered.

She nodded, and motioned to the cereal. "Hurry, before it drowns," she whispered back.

He obliged, and for several moments they ate in companionable silence, staring out the front window into the grayness of the day. They had settled into the pattern after a week. He slept in her bed every night and they rose together each morning. It was deceptively domestic. Deceptively settled.

As if it wasn't all strictly temporary. As if there wasn't a man waiting out there, somewhere, to kill her. As if they really belonged together.

She shook the thoughts from her mind, concentrating instead on the view from the window.

At this time of the morning the street in front of her house was eerily quiet. Gone were the neon-coated pimps and pushers that periodically strutted by during the night. The panhandlers had settled down to abandoned doorways and fire escapes, leaving the streets deserted and barren. The buildings looked even more tired, robbed of the players that gave them life. They seemed to sag on their foundations, windows hanging morosely down.

"Who owns all those old buildings?" Thomas asked Sabrina quietly.

She shook her head. "I don't know. Probably a bank repossessed them, or the city, maybe. I'm not sure. Most of them are condemned, anyway."

"But could they be fixed up?" he prodded.

"It depends on how badly damaged they are. Some probably have cracked foundations by now. You'd have to tear down the whole building before you could get it to pass an inspection. With enough money, one or two may be salvageable. But no one wants to invest that kind of money in this kind of neighborhood. Property values are going down here, not up."

Thomas nodded, chewing thoughtfully as he looked at the buildings in a new light.

"I bet one of those is big enough to make a wonderful shelter," he said. "It would just need a lot of fixing up."

She gave him a wan smile. "Thomas, to build a shelter of that size, even starting out with *one* of those buildings, would still run into millions of dollars. The county just doesn't have that kind of money."

"Then who does?" he wanted to know.

She shrugged. "Last year the Salvation Army bought out one of the homeless shelters and fund-raised around a million dollars to overhaul it. Before, the place was infested with rats, and there was one shower for something like every fifty men. It was really a disgrace."

"If the money could be raised once, couldn't it be raised again?"

"Through what organization? I barely keep this shelter running by acting as an accountant on the side. One of my friends, Maria, has a shelter that was started with some county assistance but mostly through volunteers and donations. We're both very small, with relatively little monthly expenses. It would take a huge organization to start a shelter on the type of scale you're talking about."

Thomas nodded again. "You know, my mom heads a big charity organization. They sponsor a wide variety of causes, help with fund-raising and give donations. Maybe they could help."

"Just how rich is your family?" she asked finally, her breath catching in her throat as she waited for his reply.

"My mom comes from a long line of wealth. She inherited huge trust funds from her parents as well as from my dad. And my dad made his fortune in the construction business. He did so well, my brother, sister and I are all comfortably well off. We wouldn't have to work if we didn't want to."

"But all of you do?"

He shrugged again. "We can't help it," he said. "My brother went from being a pro football player to coaching. I became a cop, and my little sister went on to become a doctor. It's my father's fault, blame it on him."

"But your father had a heart attack when he was still fairly young. Didn't that make an impression on any of you?"

"Yes, but it was the wrong one. See, my father always believed in doing fifty things at once, since time was too short. His death seemed to prove his point. He died at fifty, but man, the things he had accomplished by then. I really wish you could have met him, Sabrina. He was such an incredible man."

"I would have liked to have known him," she agreed softly. She glanced up at the wall and saw the time. "Hey—" she pointed up to the clock "—it's time for you to be hitting the road."

He agreed with a sigh, gulping down the last bit of his coffee as he was rising. He grabbed his coat and his gun, then reached over and gave her a lingering kiss. His eyes grew serious.

"Promise me you'll be careful, Sabrina. It's been days since the last killing. In all honesty, the way the profile we got on him reads, he's due to strike again very soon. So please, please be careful."

She nodded, and lifted up a hand to brush his cheek. "I will do my best," she promised carefully.

He nodded, realizing that was as good as he was going to get. He bent down and gave her one last kiss, and then he was gone.

The rest of the week continued in the same pattern. Thomas left for work each day, coming back late, and frustrated, each night. Two more roses arrived by mail, and on three separate nights, Woof brought the house down with his barking. The second night Thomas turned him loose from the house, but the huge mongrel came back empty-handed. Whatever was out there, not even he could catch it.

Sabrina dealt with it the best she could. She threw herself into the shelter and the kids there, anything to keep her mind off the permanent shadow that seemed to have cast itself over her life. One more week, she promised herself. She just wanted one more week, before she did what she knew she had to do.

Shaun slowly began to heal, and the restlessness of the group grew. Suzie's face cleared up completely, and slowly but surely, she began to move around with more confidence. Occasionally, she could even look a person in the eye while she talked.

As part of her campaign to have the kids help out around the shelter, Sabrina bought gallons of white paint. She let Ricko organize the painting project and they spent one afternoon painting the rooms.

Sabrina was very impressed by Ricko's management skills. He overlooked only a detail or two, which she subtly took care of herself. But with a little more experience, she had a feeling he would make an excellent manager.

Mrs. Jacquobi had been open to the idea of hiring teenagers to help with a lot of the heavier spring cleaning she couldn't do herself in her own home. Even Ricko had nodded thoughtfully at the idea, but had yet to give his final approval.

Shadow faded in and out, not much caring for the three-ring circus the house had become. Especially when Woof, in his exuberance, managed to take out the table with a wild jump. Shadow had fixed the leg himself, throwing the grinning Woof dark glances the entire time. Sabrina had come up with a list of odd jobs for him and under the guise of payment had been able to get him to accept some new jeans, a jacket and a blanket. Shadow was a difficult problem because as much as he liked to work, he was still underage for employment.

What she really wanted was to get him back to school. Once, she'd left a book on Westerns sitting around to see what would happen. It had disappeared for a few days, then magically reappeared. After that she'd bought a more difficult version, one without pictures, and had handed it directly to him. Shadow had returned it a week later, clearly expecting another.

After this, they fell into a pattern, and she was able to determine that his reading ability was extraordinarily high for his age. That established, she proceeded to ask him to help her one day with balancing the books for Maria's shelter. She had wanted to test his ability with numbers, but he had declined and she had been unable to make contact since.

On Friday night, Thomas didn't return to the house at all, as a drunk driving accident kept him out all night. When he returned, early Saturday morning, his face was so pale she was afraid he was going to faint.

But he made it up to the bed, where he collapsed into her arms and she held him as he talked out the horrific images he didn't want to remember but was unable to forget. It was strange, some time ago he'd looked at the body of a murdered prostitute and felt absolutely nothing. He'd been cold, burned-out. Now, after being with Sabrina, witnessing her faith and the value she held on all life, he was learning how to hope. After years, he was learning how to feel again. The way this drunk driving incident was affecting him was certain proof of that.

Eventually he drifted off into a badly needed sleep, still in Sabrina's arms. He didn't awaken again until Sunday morning.

When he finally returned to the land of the living, the color had returned to his face, but there was a grim set to his mouth that Sabrina had never seen before. He couldn't seem to unclench his fists, until finally, he headed out the door for a long jog. He was gone for two hours, and when he finally returned, the sweat was rolling off him in big drops to land in puddles in his shoes.

But somewhere during the run, he had managed to sweat out the bad images along with the frustration. Sabrina completed the task with a long massage that worked the last of the kinks out. Grateful beyond words, he simply held her close.

For dinner, he did his part by ordering in seven large pepperoni pizzas. He then proceeded to earn Ricko's never-ending respect by polishing one whole pizza on his own. Shaun even joined them for the meal, looking pale and tired, but doing his best to smile. He still limped slightly when he walked, but was doing well.

Looking at the faces around her, Sabrina knew it was only a matter of time. Ricko still refused to commit his group to staying or to working for Mrs. Jacquobi, and Sabrina could feel his restlessness growing. Precious things came and went in her life—that was the way of it—but it would be hard to let this group go, just as it would be hard to let Thomas go. But that was the way things were, she reminded herself sternly. Concentrating on enjoying her pizza, she tried to use it to block the pain that would soon take over. Somehow, it just didn't work.

Sunday was a slow, languorous evening. They all watched late movies on television, then retired for the evening.

Upstairs, the night continued its easy pace. Sabrina slipped the clothes gently from Thomas, kneading the strained muscles on the back of his neck as she did so. And slowly, she stripped the pants from his long, powerful legs. But her touch was soothing, a gentle caress absorbing the rest of his tension.

Taking his hand, she guided him to the bed, and there enfolded him into her comforting arms, resting his head upon her breast. Her hands stroked his back, a tender caress that moved them both.

It was a novel experience, one that touched her beyond anything she had never experienced. To hold his head upon her breast, to offer comfort to the man that meant more to her than anything in the world. To absorb the tension of his muscles into the strength of her fingertips. To feel him relax against her, accepting the solace she was so willing to give.

At long last, she spoke. "Is it getting any easier?"

He sighed against her, inhaling the warmth of her skin, so soft against his own. "Yes," he said at last. "I just wish I could kill that bastard. I wish I could force him to see those children, to see the look on the parents' faces when I had to tell them...God, Sabrina, it was such a waste. And the worst part is, he'll probably never face it. He'll just keep drowning himself in booze to numb the pain. So his life is pretty much over with, anyway. Maybe it would seem more worth it to me if it did sober him up, if he got his life back on track so he could make up for what he's done.

"But he won't. Not this guy. He was so far gone I don't know how he even managed to start the car. He had enough booze absorbed into his system he could probably go a week without a drink and never sober up. So two lives are gone, and there's nothing I can do about it. Nothing."

She continued to stroke his back, searching for the right words to say. "You can't be everyone's keeper," she said at last. "You can do your job, and do it the best you can, but you can't make up for an entire system. You can't blame yourself for the leniency of some laws, or the lack of jail space. You can only do your best. Just remember one thing—you're protecting the future victims."

"Yeah, maybe."

"Come on, Thomas. You can't punish yourself for things you can't control. You simply can't quit because of a reason like that. What would happen if each officer felt like that? We'd end up with no police force at all, and then that accident really would be a waste. All right, it took two lives.

So what are you doing, throwing in your life as a bonus? You don't reward waste with waste."

He was quiet for a moment, then he rolled back onto one elbow until he could see her. "That's what I've been doing, isn't it?"

She nodded softly. "I think so."

He peered down at her, hard and long. "Damn," he said at last. "I've been such a fool."

"No," she told him. "Just tired and frustrated. It happens to all of us."

"I've never seen you frustrated."

She gave him a small smile. "That doesn't mean I'm not. I've also done my fair share of stupid things, too."

"Then we've both done stupid things," he said, and drew her into his arms. "But in spite of ourselves, we've managed to get one thing right."

"And what is that?"

"Us," he said softly.

The words were tentative, yet his tone challenged her to deny them. She shied away from analyzing them. There was a part of her that wanted to believe the hope they offered. This was, after all, the second time he'd opened up to her. The second time he had implied that maybe his feelings for her were beginning to change after all. Did he really care? Did he see them as a couple?

But then her mind veered sharply away. No. It simply wouldn't work. And why should he be attracted to her that way? He didn't belong with a former prostitute. He never would. He probably just thought that they made a good working team.

She didn't question it. She didn't have the heart.

She simply lay next to him, listening to the even sound of his breathing as he faded off to sleep.

But even then, with all her denial, the word lingered in her mind. Us.

Us.

A few more days, she promised herself as she felt her eyes begin to fill with moisture. Just a few more days.

Chapter 9

Monday morning dawned gray and drizzly. It suited Sabrina's mood and she stared out the window with a dismal sigh. Last night, after a lot of intense debate, she'd allowed Thomas to persuade her to attend the dance with him. Now, by the cold light of day, she was beginning to think she must have been insane. Something like this would never work out, she was certain. Not to mention that now she had to buy a dress. And if the dance itself didn't terrify her enough, that alone certainly did.

Last night she had also arranged for Gord to come and stay at the house so she could at least try to find something suitable. And arranging for the volunteer had been a delicate matter. She didn't want the youths to feel like they had to have a baby-sitter, but neither did she want to tempt them with an overabundance of freedom.

Shaun was almost perfectly healed, and Ricko was already eyeing the door with an anxious gleam. The rain might keep them around for now, but she didn't think they would stay much longer. Ricko still refused Mrs. Jacquobi's offer of work, and when Sabrina had approached him about staying, he'd simply shrugged and given her his crooked grin.

"We do just fine on our own," he had informed her.

"But don't you want to do better than fine?" she had insisted.

"We are. We've formed a group, a family. One we can always count on. You can't give us that in one of your shelters."

"But what about a job, what about some security for your 'family,' " she'd continued.

But he had shaken his head firmly. "Look," he'd said. "You've been pretty good at not feeding me a lot of bull, so don't start now. The shelter you're talking about would change things and you know it. They would insist on individual counseling, individual this, individual that. We take care of each other. Shaun needed help, we brought him here and we've stuck by him. A shelter won't give us that, either, okay?"

"If your group is really that strong, Ricko, a future shouldn't threaten it."

But he hadn't wanted to listen, and eventually she'd run out of words. So here she was, staring at the rain that was buying her the time she couldn't seem to manage on her own. Well, they had come and gone so many times before. Chances were, they'd come back again.

She'd tried a desperate call to Maria, to see if she had any ideas. But Maria said that Ricko had given her the exact same lines, as well. Through some bizarre twist, the streets had given the group freedom and family. They weren't ready for anything else yet.

At the moment Sabrina couldn't blame them for wanting to run. She wanted to run, as well. Shopping just wasn't her idea of a good time, she thought with a sigh. And buying a dress made the dance on Friday night a concrete reality, one she wasn't sure she could deal with yet.

She wondered if Thomas had any idea what he was getting himself into, taking her to a policeman's formal. Oh please, don't let anything dreadful happen, she pleaded silently. But in her heart, she knew it was useless. Someone always had to say something, that was just the way it was.

There would be nice people who would have the intelligence to look deeper. And there would be the petty people who needed to make others feel low to make themselves feel big. For them, she was a wonderful target, virtually made to order.

She had learned how to handle it, with cool looks and biting comebacks. But she wondered how Thomas, of the perfect family and perfect background, would handle some of the things he would inevitably hear. He seemed to think that he could handle it. She wasn't sure, though, if he even realized what "it" was.

But there was no way around it. He was determined that she should accompany him. It was the noble thing for the former Boy Scout to do. And she, who should have at least had the sense to say no, somehow just couldn't seem to manage it.

Because, deep in her heart, she really wanted to go. She wanted one night out with him, one night of magic. One night when maybe she really could pretend that they had a normal, wonderful relationship. The type where people went on dates. The type where people might eventually marry.

It was a pipedream. One that would end shortly. She would give herself Friday night. Then, on Saturday, she would end it. It was the only way.

She glanced at her watch, and realized that she should be leaving soon. A knock sounded and she left the kitchen to let Gord in. A firm believer in punctuality, he was right on time. He was also big enough to make everyone else punctual, as well.

He wasn't any taller than Thomas, but easily fifty pounds heavier. An ex-marine, he still sported buzzed hair and a grizzly face. Today he wore faded jeans and a famous beer on his T-shirt. His brown hair was streaked with gray, but his blue eyes were crisp and penetrating.

"Long time no see," he said gruffly, and ruffled her hair with a heavy hand. That was one thing about Gord. In his eyes, she would always be about sixteen.

"Didn't you take the hint?" she responded tartly, and was rewarded by the deep rumble of his laugh.

"So what do you have for me today?" he asked.

"Six. Suzie has the blond hair, she's very helpful. I've talked to Maria and arranged counseling for her, which should actually begin soon. The other five are all part of an efficient self-made group, not prone to taking help or advice. The redhead is the leader, calls himself Ricko. You'll have your hands full there. He's been getting tired of running rings around the rest of us. He'll love the new challenge. The dog's name is Woof. He's my supposed guard dog, but I think he's fallen in love with Suzie. He won't give you any trouble, but he'll most likely eat all of lunch if you're not careful. Don't worry, once they hear you can cook, they ought to be happy. Ricko's been trying to have me sued for child abuse on the grounds that I can't. So see, you have it made."

He chuckled again, and lumbered into the living room to check out his new charges. Sabrina watched him go with deep affection. Gord had become a volunteer when his own son had run away a decade ago. By the time he'd found his son, the boy had been too far into drugs to ever reach. He had eventually overdosed, but Gord had stuck around anyway. He was a natural with the kids. He specialized in coming up with activities for them to do that helped draw many to Maria's shelter, and kept others out of trouble for another afternoon.

Knowing the kids were in good hands, Sabrina took a deep breath and headed out the door. Like a prisoner going to execution, she headed for Nordstroms.

Shopping for formal wear was not easy for someone of her size. At barely five feet, most dresses made her look like a little girl playing dress up. In pink she looked like a bonbon. In green, she was Tinkerbell revisited. It seemed like she could never win.

Finally, after hours of thumbing her way through sales rack after sales rack, she hit upon something. It was a very simple dress, made of black velvet with a rounded collar and long sleeves. It came to just above her knees, and, frankly, she wasn't sure if that was formal enough for a formal. But the back sold it to her anyway. Elegant and seductive, it was tailored to perfection, with a discreetly plunging V that stopped just above her waist.

With her blond hair and trim figure, it suited her well enough. Or so she hoped. After spending so much time in faded jeans and plaid shirts, she wasn't sure if she remembered what elegant was.

Had she ever had a formal evening out with a man? None came to mind. Before, she'd simply dressed up, given her speech, mingled a bit, fended off a few advances, and then returned to her house as alone as when she'd left it.

This would be another first after Thomas. Taking a deep breath, she paid for the dress and just hoped nothing went wrong. Just this once, she prayed.

The shopping had taken her much longer than she'd anticipated. Outside it was already growing dark, and she waited impatiently for the bus. Thomas had only agreed to let her go out on her own on the condition that it was during the day and that she stuck to well populated areas like the shopping mall. Her returning this late would probably make him mad as a hatter.

She didn't entirely blame him. These past few days no new roses had arrived, but she had been continually plagued with a deep uneasy feeling that worried her even more. She would have sworn that, somewhere out there, that man was watching. Watching and waiting.

With a low hiss, the bus finally arrived, and after giving one last worried glance at the darkening sky, she boarded.

Suddenly she felt anxious to get back to the house. She missed Thomas, she realized, missed him intensely. They really hadn't had much time alone together lately. It seemed he was always working, coming home only after he was thoroughly exhausted. But then, she had to remind herself, what did she expect? He was only coming over at all because he felt bound both by his protective nature and his job to watch over her. That was all. Still, maybe Friday night wouldn't be so bad after all. It would be their first night out since going to the mall and the Rose Gardens.

She imagined that going out with Thomas on a real date would be something special. He knew how to make her feel cherished, opening the door for her, lightly touching her cheek or her hair. At odd moments he would catch her eye and just smile with a warmth that made her heart turn over. How had she ever gotten so lucky as to meet him? And how was she ever going to let him go?

Soon, she promised herself with a sigh. She would let him go soon. But not until after Friday night. She deserved one magical moment. Just one.

Sabrina pulled herself out of her thoughts long enough to feel the dim, uneasy feeling she'd been feeling all day grow stronger. The tingling started at the base of her spine, working its way slowly up until the small hairs on the back of her neck stood up in rigid attention.

Trying to appear unconcerned, she glanced at the passengers around her. They seemed to be the usual assortment. A few people in business suits, finishing up a late night at work. There were two women seated to her left, both hunched over a fashion magazine. An elderly lady sat in the handicapped section, knee stockings slowly rolling down to expose blue veins through translucent skin. She was staring out into the darkness of the evening, her lips moving soundlessly as she mumbled to herself.

Then, further over, Sabrina saw him. He was a thin man, hunched low in the seat. A raincoat was pulled close around him, a wide-brimmed hat pulled low over his face.

Don't be silly, she admonished herself. Lots of people who are tall and thin ride the bus. But she watched him carefully anyway.

The bus came to its first rolling stop and the two women with the magazine gathered up their bags and departed. The next stop claimed the old woman and a well-dressed young lady.

The bus was rolling along again, lumbering through dark streets lit only by streetlamps reflecting off puddles. There were seven people left now. Among them, the man with the wide-brimmed hat.

Another hiss, and the bus stopped. It opened its door to reveal huge pools of blackness. Three more people stepped off and were swallowed up. Four people to go. The hat still winked boldly at her.

They were nearing her street now. The road was becoming worse, the bus creaking and groaning as it hit the deep potholes. Now the darkness was broken up by white, red and orange graffiti, glaring its messages of rage and defiance.

Just two more stops.

The bus slowed laboriously, swaying lightly as it rounded the corner. Then once again the doors slid open. Now, two youths in dangling chains and red bandannas strutted forth with defiant stares. One flashed her a bold white grin, and tipped his head forward in mockery.

It didn't bother her, didn't affect her in the least. But the remaining passenger did. He still slouched down, head tilted back as if he was sleeping. But she could feel the awareness, it radiated off him like an electric charge. He was awake. He was waiting.

The last stop approached, the darkness looming outside. She would be fine, Sabrina promised herself as she rose. She gave the man one last quick glance, but he didn't move. Somehow, it didn't surprise her. She walked out the open door, welcoming the night with its dark protection.

The bus hissed off, but she didn't move. She watched it go, waiting for it to fade out of sight. Instead, red brake lights glowed fiercely like dragon's eyes as it came to an unexpected stop. The doors rolled open, and the man stepped off.

She could see him, silhouetted eerily against the glow of the streetlights. The hat was tipped back now, and she could feel his eyes piercing her through the shadows. Even from this distance, she could see the white glint of his smile.

Without another thought, she turned and headed straight back to her house. At first she limited herself to a brisk walk, feeling the garment bag slap rapidly against her legs. But over the sound of flapping fabric, she heard the telltale clipping of dress shoes. She risked a hasty glance over her shoulder.

The man was following briskly, easily keeping pace. Fear pricked at her, sending sharp jolts through her veins. Her breath came in small gasps as she quickened her steps. The sidewalk seemed to fade before her as she rapidly devoured the weed-choked cracks with quick strides.

But another glance revealed that the man was gaining, his longer legs effortlessly eating away at the distance between them.

Don't show your fear, she told herself firmly. Never show your fear.

Her house was only two blocks away now. If she could just keep ahead for a little bit more! But the clip-clop behind her quickened its beat, rapping out a loud rhythm into the quiet night. She quickened her steps again, but it was no use. The sharp noise seemed to be all around her, surrounding her with its ominous tone.

She took one last deep breath, then exploded into a mad dash. Half a block down, she raced across the deserted street, dress bag flailing wildly against her knees. Forty feet. Thirty feet. Loud steps pounded out behind her, drawing closer and closer.

"No!" she gasped out and poured on more speed, stretching her short legs beyond all previous ability. Fear gave her an edge, forcing the blood through her pounding veins in terrific bursts. But still she could hear him, gaining, gaining.

Twenty feet. Ten feet. She burst into the clearing with a scream.

"Thomas!"

She raced up the lighted steps, breath heaving and sweat pouring down her face. The door slammed open, barely missing her as Thomas came barreling out.

She flung herself forward, into the solid muscle of his chest and arms. Automatically his arms came up to enfold her, stroking her hair in soothing movements, as his eyes searched the darkness around them.

"I'm sorry," came a voice in the shadows. Sabrina whirled around, her heart still beating rapidly.

There, on the edge of the darkness, stood the man in the wide-brimmed hat.

"Honest, Thomas," he was saying. "I didn't mean to scare her like that."

Eyes now growing huge with outrage as comprehension struck, Sabrina pushed herself out of Thomas's arms.

"Would you like to tell me what's going on here?" she demanded. The fear was fading fast, but anger easily took its place, increasing the flush in her cheeks and the shine in her eyes.

Her hands were planted firmly on her hips and she was glaring at him with a poisonous look that spelled trouble. He didn't know where to begin. He gave the other man a pleading look, but the man just shrugged his shoulders helplessly.

"Now, Sabrina," he began carefully. "You know how worried I've been about you. There are the roses that keep arriving, the murder this creep committed just a block away. And we both know Woof wasn't up barking all those nights at the mailman. He's out there, Sabrina. Out there waiting for you. And I don't have any intention of giving him a chance at that. Not a one."

"So you took it upon yourself to have me followed," she finished for him, her eyes growing even brighter with outrage. "Of all the low down...I would like to remind you, Lieutenant," she bit out, feeling the rage spiral even higher, "that I have been doing just fine on my own. I certainly don't need some overgrown thug to come into my house and take over my life, nor arrange to have me followed—"

"Now just a minute," Thomas interrupted, his own countenance growing red with anger. "I don't recall it ever being a crime to want to keep a person safe. Look, maybe I don't know all the right words to say. Maybe I don't know all the right things to do. And in the beginning, yes I did have my doubts, but I'm beginning to care about you, Sabrina. And I don't want you getting yourself killed."

The man on the sidewalk was still watching, his head going from side to side as he followed the verbal war. But things were beginning to heat up. Still unnoticed, he edged away, before their anger could become focused upon him.

But Thomas and Sabrina had already dismissed him from their minds. Thomas was too intent on trying to explain himself, and Sabrina was too intent on trying to understand what he was saying. It seemed unreal to her, unreal and almost scary. Thomas cared? Thomas cared about her?

It was impossible. Inconceivable. He couldn't care about her. They were from two different worlds. He was Mr. All-American. She was a former prostitute. It just couldn't happen.

Confused now, she abruptly turned away from him, struggling to make some sense of this madness. And it did seem that the whole world had suddenly tipped upside-down. Some deranged killer was playing games with her, messing with her life, and she was unable to stop him. And then there was Shadow and Ricko's group, kids she'd come to care a great deal about, but seemed unable to quite reach. Unable to pin down.

And now here was this man, the man who had stepped out of her dreams and into her life. The man she cared about way more than she would ever tell him. The man she wanted to keep, but knew she had to let go. Care about her? He couldn't care about her. It wasn't right, couldn't be right. It was hard enough to let him go as it was, how could she do it knowing that he might care?

No, she told herself. He might think he cared, but he didn't, not really. How could he, when he didn't understand, didn't see the differences between them? He was a man who'd come from white picket fences, a product of suburbia. He would go back to that world. And she couldn't follow him there, wouldn't follow him there. This was her world, this was where she belonged.

Here in the madness.

"Sabrina," Thomas said softly. "Sabrina, did you hear what I said?"

Dimly she shook her head. "You don't know what you're saying," she whispered, more to herself than him. "You just don't understand."

"Then help me understand, Sabrina. Help me."

Again, she shook her head. "It just wouldn't work," she said abruptly, turning back to him now with withdrawal in her eyes. "It just wouldn't."

He wanted to argue, to force her to explain, but he recognized the look in her eyes and it stopped him cold. It was the same glance she'd given him almost three weeks before, that very first day when she'd come into the police station. It had intrigued him then. It frustrated him now.

Damn it, he knew she had reasons to doubt him. He still wasn't so sure of his feelings himself, still wasn't so sure of just what it was he wanted. All he knew was that the last few weeks had been among the best of his life. She, who had spent so much of her life in darkness, was helping him find the light. Last night alone she had taken the weight of the last year off his shoulders, making him feel something besides utter exhaustion for the first time in months. When he'd gone back to the station this morning, he'd felt almost reborn. The determination had been so sharp, the desire so fresh. And it had showed. Even Seth had commented on it.

And she had given him that. When he was with her, he felt he could do almost anything. More than that, he felt at peace. For the first time in his life, after forty years of searching without quite knowing that he was searching, he felt content.

She had done that for him, as well.

Looking at her now, remembering how his heart had turned cold in his chest when he had heard her scream for him, he simply knew that he didn't want to lose her. He didn't want to let her go. Not now, not ever.

There was only one hitch. He wasn't sure he knew the words to make her stay by his side.

But he would try. Thomas Lain could be a very persuasive man when he wanted to be.

"Come inside," he said finally. "You've had a long day, we're both tense. Just come inside for now."

Nodding dimly, still feeling as if she was half in a dream, she followed him into the welcoming warmth of the old house. Her house, she thought fiercely. Her house.

But it wasn't enough, she knew suddenly. She didn't want to just run a shelter anymore. She wanted a man to share it all with. Only the one she wanted was the one she could never have.

She wanted Thomas.

Chapter 10

By Thursday night Sabrina was feeling so nervous she thought she would be sick. About twenty times she was tempted to call it off altogether. About twenty times the words simply froze in her throat. The dance terrified her, and yet at the same time, she couldn't bring herself *not* to go.

A part of her knew that it was her last night. Her last night with Thomas, and then it would be over.

Perhaps that scared her even more. He had been in her life for barely three weeks. And yet he fit in it so well and in so many ways, that she was already beginning to wonder how she would manage without him. But perhaps manage wasn't the right word for it, since she knew that, either way, she would manage. She would always manage. But she didn't want to just "manage" any more. She wanted love and laughter. She wanted someone to share her life with, someone to hold at night, someone to grow old with. She wanted Thomas . . . forever.

There was no use dwelling on it, she thought abruptly. They did not belong together in the long run. He wanted things, needed things, she could never give him. And so she would end the case, and he would leave her life. Saturday night.

And that was an odd feeling as well. In all of her years on the street, and all of her years off it, she'd never done what she was doing now. Planning to catch a killer.

But she had to do it. He was threatening her life, threatening the very shelter she'd worked so hard to build. And he wasn't going away. She had a garbage can full of dead roses to prove that. Just last night, he had been back. She had awakened once again, abruptly—wide-eyed awake—and known. He was out there. Watching. Waiting.

And she had a feeling he wouldn't wait much longer.

In a way it was the logical thing to do. Meet the killer on her own terms before he forced her to meet him on his. She had a feeling she wouldn't like it his way. She had a feeling she wouldn't live through it, either.

This way she had a better chance, she told herself. Her eyes crept to the small end table with its locked drawer sitting not far from the door. The drawer with the gun.

So by all intents and purposes, she was a woman with the weight of the world on her shoulders this Thursday afternoon. She was a woman trying to let the man she cared very deeply for go free, and a woman plotting a confrontation with a serial killer, before he murdered her. And while Sabrina had learned to deal with many pressures in her life, the stress of these was definitely showing. Her hands were shaking, her face was chalk-pale and she was dreaming of cigarettes.

It was Ricko who finally took pity on her. With a deep sigh, he reached into his jacket pocket and took out a crushed pack of Marlboros.

"Hell, man, you need this worse than I do," he said, and offered her the pack.

Sabrina turned her attention from the window she had been staring out of, eyeing the red and white box. You shouldn't, she told herself. But the nicotine pull was too strong. Feeling almost mesmerized, she reached out, selecting one precious cigarette. For a minute she just rolled it between her fingers, then lifted it to her nose and inhaled the sharp sting of tobacco, as one might do with a fine cigar.

Her hands were still shaking, but Ricko, having taken his pity this far, held out the lighter to catch the wavering cigarette.

She inhaled deeply, waiting for the welcomed taste. But instead the nicotine stung her throat, bringing tears to her eyes. The second puff was little better, tasting like pure tar. By the third puff, she was feeling dizzy and beginning to wonder why she had ever wanted the filthy thing.

But the fourth drag was the charm, and she felt the nicotine work its wonderful magic. It flowed through her like a forbidden dream, easing her shaking hands, soothing her raw nerves.

She leaned back against the wall, savoring the sensations. Her eyes drifted half closed as she watched the smoke rise in a soft haze.

"Need any more?" Ricko prompted impatiently.

Heck, she thought. She'd take the whole pack. But unfortunately, or perhaps fortunately, her conscience was working overtime. On the heels of the nicotine came the guilt, pricking the very nerves she had just calmed.

With a sigh, she refused his offer. Better to quit before she'd done too much damage. Still, she was impressed that Ricko had even offered her a cigarette. Normally he kept to himself. Things were starting to change, she mused, though she wondered if he realized by just how much. Shaun had been in perfect health for days now. And each morning she watched Ricko stare out the window with longing.

She had approached him once again on the subject of staying at the shelter, and once again he had turned her down. Soon afterward, he had taken off one afternoon, only to squeeze back in as the clock struck the curfew hour of midnight.

Since that time, the group had taken to wandering in and out during the daylight hours. But they always managed to leave something behind, a piece of jewelry or clothing. Anything. And by midnight, they would always return. In their own way, they were taking the first step. They just couldn't seem to admit it.

As of Tuesday Suzie had started going for counseling, making the past week especially difficult for her. Wednesday afternoon she had come back shaking all over and unable to stop. It was a common stage that most of the kids went through. Counseling meant facing all the horrors they had done and seen. It was a traumatic step, but one that had to be completed before the healing could begin.

Sabrina and Thomas had sat with her most of the evening, just holding her hand and talking in soft tones, trying to ease her through it. Around midnight her shaking had begun to abate, though the nervousness was back in her eyes in full force. Woof had kept a tight guard, his worried face perched upon her knee.

After Sabrina and Thomas had retired for the night, Sabrina had heard Ricko and Suzie talking for hours. When she and Thomas had come down the next morning, both had been asleep on the couch, Suzie's head resting on Ricko's shoulder, where it must have fallen sometime during the night. Woof was still watching over the pair earnestly.

They had stood in the doorway for a long while, watching the sleeping pair. Suzie's long hair had fallen forward to cover most of her face. She had curled her legs under her, fitting neatly into the notch between Ricko's arm and body. Her head rested easily on his shoulder, her body still at last. As for Ricko, his feet were still propped up on the coffee table, his arm flung across the back of the couch. His head rested above Suzie's, his mouth slightly ajar as he slept.

It was a peaceful picture, a rare moment of comfort between two people who knew little about such things. It had brought a warm smile to Sabrina's lips, and she'd leaned back against Thomas. Automatically his arms had come up to embrace her, and together they'd shared the view.

But then Ricko had opened his eye and given them a wink. The picture had been ruined, but Sabrina's smile had remained. She understood now why he'd stayed. Slowly but surely, he had become attached to them, just as he was attached to his group. Though he would never admit it, there were bonds now that held him here.

Bonds of love, she hoped.

She finished the last of her cigarette, eyeing the remaining stub with a sigh. That's all folks, she told herself. Time to get back on the wagon.

Smoking was her only vice after all. Not a mean feat for someone the psychiatrists had once called "obsessive compulsive."

Looking at her watch, Sabrina realized that it was now six o'clock, and if all was going well, Thomas would be home soon. Somewhat guiltily she went to brush her teeth.

It didn't do her any good. Thomas came home around six thirty, grabbed her in a quick kiss and then immediately frowned.

"You've been smoking again," he said.

"Just one," she said quickly. "Honest."

"You don't have to defend yourself to me," he informed her. "You are your own worst critic. If you can keep smoking and still have no problem facing yourself in the mirror, then more power to you."

"In other words, I'd better stop."

"I think it sounded better the way I phrased it," he said. "But sure, the idea's the same." He shrugged, giving her an easy smile and another kiss. "So," he said, switching topics. "Whose turn is it to fix dinner, or should I ask?"

"Dinner," she informed him, "is being prepared even as we speak, by a special chef of honor."

The chef of honor turned out to be Shadow, who had materialized at dusk and had headed straight for the kitchen. Of all the talents he had picked up along the way, cooking was definitely one of his best. He moved around the kitchen with smooth efficiency, lightly tasting and stirring until rich aromas floated out to tantalize them all.

In the end dinner surpassed even their expectations, the taste even richer than the smell. It was a rare person that could make spaghetti into an art, and Sabrina wondered if there wasn't a little bit of Italian in Shadow somewhere. They devoured it to the last drop, Shadow and Ricko going head to head over the last piece of garlic bread. But even Ricko, with all his brash humor, couldn't withstand Shadow's chilling stare.

The confrontation left Ricko quiet and thoughtful. Sometime later when they were still sitting at the table, too full to move, he spoke.

"You know, man," he told Shadow, "you really aren't a bad dude. I mean, you never talk back to me. Your cooking is awesome. All in all, I'd say you were cool. But, man, you've really got to lighten up."

Shadow merely shrugged, giving him a dispassionate stare. Sabrina took that as their cue.

"Come on," she told Thomas. "It's our turn to do the dishes. I'll rinse, you just keep kicking the dishwasher until it works."

The system was actually fairly amazing, one that they had carefully tested with time. If the truth were known, these quiet moments in the kitchen were some of her favorites with Thomas. Normally the kids returned to the living room to find a decent television program, leaving them alone to talk. And there was something wonderfully domestic about doing the dishes together. It tugged on her heartstrings in ways she'd rather not think about.

"You're nervous about the dance," Thomas was saying now as he started loading the dishes she handed him.

"A little," she admitted.

"A lot," he corrected.

"All right. So a lot. I'll get over it."

"You make it sound like it's the flu. Come on, Sabrina." He took the dish from her hands, setting it aside so he could hold her hands. "I wouldn't have asked you to go if I didn't think both of us could handle it. You deserve a night out, Sabrina. Something special and different, just the two of us. Besides," he said, turning back to the dishes and attempting to sound casual, "there isn't anyone else I'd rather go with."

He let the words hang in the air, watching her carefully. It wasn't the first time he'd found himself hinting slightly with words, then waiting like some eager schoolboy for her reaction. And frankly, he wasn't quite sure where it was all going. He just knew that when he was away from her, he felt oddly restless, even afraid. What if the killer came when he was gone? Perhaps one day he would return to the house too late, finding her already dead... It was one scenario he knew he wouldn't survive.

He didn't want to lose her, he had come to the sudden realization just a few nights ago. Not to the killer, not to anyone or anything else. He didn't want to lose her period. And deep down inside, former prostitute or not, Thomas was beginning to think that there was only one woman in the world for him.

But so far the initial probes hadn't gone well. So far she had reacted mostly by ignoring his comments or simply brushing them aside. He was afraid it was what she would do right now, and he wasn't far off.

Sabrina simply disregarded the last statement, giving him a small smile instead. "Do we get to take the Mustang?" she asked.

For a moment he was afraid the disappointment would show on his face, but then, grimly, he swallowed it. He'd made it hard on her in the beginning, he reminded himself for what seemed to be the fiftieth time. He had hesitated about giving in to his feelings about her because of her past, and even now, he still didn't like to think about it. But now it was more a question of his liking the thought of losing her, a hell of a lot less.

So he forced himself to relax, forced himself to set aside his own fears.

"Sure," he said calmly enough. "We can take the Mustang."

"All right," Sabrina said. "Then everything's fine."

Somehow, neither of them quite believed her.

And later that night, when Sabrina jerked awake, the sense of being watched was so strong, she couldn't bring herself to move because she was afraid, so desperately afraid that all she had to do was turn her head, just a little, just a fraction of an inch toward the window, and the killer would be there.

So she lay there, rigid, feeling her heart hammer so loud in her chest it should have woken up the entire house. And for the first time since that long night eight years ago, she was so afraid that she simply couldn't have moved even if she'd tried. And long after Woof's hair-raising barks had erupted in the house, jerking Thomas into immediate action as he awoke and slid out of bed all in one breathless second, she still didn't move.

But it wouldn't be fast enough, Sabrina thought as she waited for Thomas to return. Not even Woof could catch him. And she was right. Thomas was back an hour later, empty-handed, the fear even rimming his eyes.

He took her into his arms for the rest of the night, holding her like a drowning man, like a man desperately afraid of letting go for fear of losing the one thing most important to him.

Neither of them slept, but neither of them spoke. They lay there in the silence, and their own fears kept them apart.

But by Friday afternoon, Sabrina's nerves were reaching the breaking point. She didn't want to go to the dance. She had to go to the dance. She wanted Thomas to stay with her forever, she had to let him go. She wanted tonight to last forever, she had to face the killer once and for all.

Round and round went her head. Tighter and tighter wound her nerves. Thomas had told her to be ready at seven, he would pick her up then. That was still four hours away, and she was sure she would be sick.

Her hands were shaking again, and she had taken to wandering into the living room on the off chance someone else would be smoking so she could bribe a cigarette from them. Shadow had already disappeared again after spending the night, but she thought she might get lucky with Ricko. But he simply gave her one of his disgusted glances and shook his head to himself.

Finally she became sane enough to realize she had to do something or she truly would make herself sick. So with a long and determined sigh, she threw herself into her chores. She filled up a bucket with soapy water and scrubbed the inside of the fireplace until she thought her arms would fall off. It was two hours of backbreaking labor, the kind that should have worn her out and left her feeling relaxed.

Instead she was even more tense than before. So, with two hours left and already streaked from head to toe in black soot, she mopped and waxed the kitchen floor. Unfortunately the tiled area was pitifully small. Six o'clock found her, still coated in grime, sitting in the middle of the kitchen floor, staring morosely at the dirty water.

"Sabrina!" came Suzie's horrified voice. "You have to get ready! There's only an hour left."

"I know," Sabrina mumbled to the water. "I can't go, Suzie. I just can't."

But Suzie, with her newfound authority, wasn't buying it. She put both fists on her hips, and looking for all the world like a cheerleader drill sergeant, commanded Sabrina to get up to her room and into the shower. Now.

Sabrina didn't have much choice. Sometime during the week Suzie had discovered that Sabrina was a pushover, so she refused to relent.

At 6:10, Sabrina found herself in a steaming hot shower, reciting every litany, every calming mantra, she could think of.

"You will look wonderful," she told herself. "You will smile and chat inanely and have a good time," she continued. "You will be the perfect date, and you will make Thomas proud. And," she threw in for good measure, "you will have fun."

But then she paused, and with a deep sigh, leaned her aching head against the shower wall. "Come on, Sabrina," she said softly to herself, "This is it. One last night to hold close for later. One last night to remember when he's gone. Enjoy it now. There will be all the time in the world to mourn it later."

So that was it. Time, in its infinite speed, was catching up with her, winding down even as she wished she could grab for more. But it didn't matter. She had known from the beginning it would be temporary. Known from the beginning that this night would come. The last night.

With that realization, things went smoother. Suzie helped her into the form-fitting dress, her eyes glowing in admiration.

"It's so beautiful," Suzie breathed, entranced by the soft velvet folds. "I hope I can wear something this beautiful someday," she said wistfully.

"You will," Sabrina replied confidently, and gave Suzie a quick hug that took the girl by surprise. "I'm sure of it."

Slowly, Suzie gave Sabrina a dazzling smile. "Thank you," she said softly. "For everything."

"Nonsense," said Sabrina as she felt her eyes growing moist. "You've had to do the hard part on your own. If anyone deserves a pat on the back, it's you."

Suzie just shrugged, her cheeks growing pink. Then she perked up. "Can I do your makeup?" she asked impulsively.

"Sure," said Sabrina with a shrug. "At the rate my hands are going, I'd probably end up with lipstick on my nose."

Suzie showed a surprisingly delicate hand with the makeup. She chose soft colors that highlighted Sabrina's pale coloring without overwhelming. When, at long last, she was done, Suzie stepped back and smiled with the first faint traces of pride that Sabrina had ever seen in her eyes.

"Look!" Suzie said eagerly. "You're beautiful."

Turning, Sabrina caught her reflection in the mirror, and had to admit that Suzie had worked wonders. The face staring back at her was soft and radiant. Her eyes seemed to have grown, leaping out in rich color and depth. Her hair was shiny and full, one side flirtatiously half covering one eye, the other swept back to reveal the glittering yet simple crystal earrings she wore. For the first time in her life, she really was beautiful.

"Thank you," she told Suzie, clasping her hands. "Thank you so much."

Looking at the reflection, she felt the last of her nerves flee and her stomach settle. This was her night, and she would make Thomas proud, she vowed.

Tonight, she would be Cinderella.

When the doorbell rang promptly at seven, Suzie gave her one last reassuring look, then bundled her off to the door with a dark woolen wrap for warmth. Taking a deep breath, Sabrina opened the door.

Thomas looked incredible. Standing before her in a black tuxedo with a black bow tie and a vibrant green cummerbund, he commanded attention, especially hers. A delicate white rosebud was pinned to his lapel, gleaming a snowy white against the shiny black edging on his collar. His bow tie matched the cummerbund and drew attention to his vibrant green eyes.

A slow smile was spreading across his face as he looked at her.

"You're beautiful," he told her, and looking into the shiny depths of his eyes, she felt that she was.

She smiled slowly back. "Thank you."

The words seemed to jar him, and hastily he brought his hand forward. "For you," he said. He felt, oddly enough, nervous, more like some lanky kid on his first date than a man in his early forties. But somehow he knew that this was one of the most important dates of his life. It was the *only* date he had to somehow convince Sabrina to stay with him.

Like Sabrina, Thomas was aware that time was running out, the clock winding down. Sooner or later the killer would make his move, and when he did, the case would be over and Thomas wouldn't have an excuse to stay in her home anymore.

He couldn't let that happen. So here he was, trying to impress a woman he had known only three weeks—but felt like he had known forever—into wanting to stay with him.

Taking another deep breath, he held out a clear plastic box filled with delicate tissue paper. Upon the crinkly pink paper, rested three perfect white rosebuds tied together with lavender ribbon to form a beautiful wrist corsage. Shaking only a little, his large hands carefully opened the container and, setting it down, he lifted the roses from their bed.

"May I?" he asked softly.

She nodded, unable to speak as he slowly slid the elastic band over her hand. He brought it securely into place, his warm fingers brushing over her skin in a tantalizing caress. She looked down at the roses, now resting against the pale canvas of her skin.

"They're beautiful," she told him, and her eyes were once again beginning to shine with moisture. He grinned back, his eyes still devouring her delicate form, so elegantly wrapped in black velvet. Her eyes were wide and glowing, filling him with wonder and awe.

For a minute he forgot where he was, and he wanted to fall to his knees and beg her never to leave him. He wanted to crush her to him, in all her beauty, and kiss her with a passion that would brand her as his own forever. But then it came back to him, the tired porch, the six teenagers standing in attendance.

So instead he flashed her another deep look and offered her his arm. She accepted it, placing her small white hand on the black sleeve of his coat. And then they were off.

The magical night had begun.

They sped smoothly down the long streets, snaking in and out of traffic with gliding ease. Watching the lights blur on by into one long white streak, Sabrina felt a glorious sense of freedom. She was wearing a gorgeous dress and sitting with the man of her dreams in a red sports car. Moments like this came along only once in a lifetime.

They crossed the river in a blur of colored lights. And then the northeast section of town was behind them altogether. They were at the good end of town now, and the riverside glowed before them.

Thomas glided down Front Avenue, then turned into the parking lots by a cluster of hotels, restaurants and small shops.

"I thought dinner might be nice first," he said, and once again offered her his arm. He led her to the Waterfront Restaurant, which overlooked the lights of the river. A tuxedoed waiter led them to a discreet table that allowed a generous view of the waterfront. From there, Sabrina could see the riverboats, outlined in sparkling white lights, float by on midnight cruises.

"This is perfect," she told him. "Thank you."

"This is only the beginning," he told her quietly.

The waiter returned then, and Thomas ordered a bottle of wine. It came well chilled in a silver ice urn. The waiter offered the first taste to Thomas, then at his nod of satisfaction, poured them both glasses.

"I propose a toast," Thomas said, raising his glass high.

"To what?" she asked, also raising her glass.

"To the most beautiful woman I've ever seen," he said, and while his grin was mischievous, his eyes were serious.

But she refused him lightly.

"No," she said. "I know a better toast. To the most commanding man in the city."

"Just the city?" he asked with an arched brow, then smiled. "How about to us?" The words came out even more serious than he'd intended, and for a moment he held his breath, waiting for what she would say.

But she simply nodded, smiling easily at him. "To us."

The white wine was cool and fruity on her tongue. It brought a warm flush to her cheeks and a glow to her eyes. She sipped it slowly, savoring the rare taste and texture. How long had it been since she'd had wine with dinner? Better yet, how many times had she even drunk wine in her life? She found she could count the occasions on one hand.

Thomas, on the other hand, was in his element. He spoke with the waiter in a courteous voice that was accustomed to being obeyed. He seemed at home with the wine list, linen napkins and fine crystal. She liked watching him, seeing the natural elegance in his movements, seeing how he relaxed against the fine upholstery of his chair.

She was still sitting rigidly forward, reminding herself that the smaller fork was for the salads and that the thin stem of the wineglass would hardly break in her hand. But Thomas's own confidence soon conveyed itself to her, making her feel more comfortable as the evening progressed.

Thomas didn't seem to mind her nervousness, chatting smoothly, putting her at ease. By the time their dinners arrived, she found that she was sitting comfortably back, even enjoying herself. She had ordered the sautéed prawns, while Thomas received the filet mignon.

The prawns were buttery and succulent, bursting in her mouth until she smiled with pleasure. It certainly was a long way from roast beef sandwiches.

Captured by the warmth of her smile and the lights dancing in her eyes, Thomas leaned forward lazily, capturing her hand in his.

She couldn't stop smiling.

Thomas released her hand once to finish slicing the rare piece of steak on his plate. Then he once again leaned forward and, oblivious to the other diners, offered her a small piece on the tip of his fork. She took the fork lightly beneath her lips, removing the piece of steak with her teeth under the heated gaze of his eyes.

There was something unbelievably intimate about the gesture. It brought another flush of color to her cheeks and feeling suddenly flustered once again, her eyes darted back down to her plate. But then, feeling a bit more daring, she managed to spear one of her shrimp to return the favor. His gaze never wavered as he accepted her offering, his lips closing softly yet firmly over the prawn, his eyes still dark and burning. Slowly, he licked his lips, savoring the butter left behind.

"Delicious," he said softly, and for a minute, she couldn't remember what he was referring to. Her attention remained transfixed on his mouth. She barely registered the waiter taking away their plates or glasses. She had eyes only for the man before her with his burning green gaze and dark blond hair that looked like blond fire under the lights.

She memorized each detail of his face, from the rugged tanness of his skin to the silky pale lashes that framed his eyes. There were crinkles in the corner of his eyes, lines of laughter and worry. About his temple, the hair thinned a bit, and in places it was growing suspiciously pale. But he looked wonderful to her, from the high arches of his cheekbones to the stubborn square of his chin.

She would remember him like this always, framed in elegance and magic.

"It's time to go," he whispered, and she could only nod.

She linked her arm firmly in his as they left, unaware that her hair was caught in a golden halo under the lights, making him reach up and touch it in wonder. They walked out together, their attention so focused upon each other that they didn't notice all the heads that turned in admiration upon the commanding couple.

The night air was chilly, causing her to pull the wrap a little tighter around her body, but the sky was clear, stars twinkling like a jeweled carpet above. The hotel hosting the retirement party was only a few blocks away, and they walked there briskly and in silence.

This night was like nothing Sabrina had ever experienced, a shiny moment that stood out like fire against the backdrop of her life. There were no words for such things. So she paid Thomas the highest tribute that she could. She simply smiled and enjoyed.

Before she was quite ready, they were at the hotel. But standing before the circular drive, watching the limousines and Mercedes pull sleekly up, she squared her shoulders and tilted her chin in determination.

"All right," she told him. "Let's do it."

Giving her a reassuring hug, he led her inside.

Cinderella's ball had begun.

The banquet room was a glittering sea of brilliant silks and satins. A huge chandelier glistened like a waterfall forever frozen in time. The tear-shaped crystals caught the shimmering colors below, reflecting them back in an endless display of sparkling rainbows. The laughter floated across the air like a fine spring breeze, and the champagne flowed as easily as a river.

They had barely entered the room when a man was clapping Thomas firmly on the back.

"Looking fine, looking fine," the man was saying. Then he saw Sabrina and let out a low whistle that brought a flush to her cheeks.

"So you're Sabrina Duncan," he said at last. "Now I understand everything."

At her confused look, Thomas intervened.

"This rude fellow," he said with a pointed look, "happens to be my partner Seth Stein. You talked to him on the phone before you came in to the station, but unfortunately, he just wasn't around when you came in. Sorry, guy," he told Seth. "But it was your loss."

Seth was nodding vigorously. "Well I can see that. We have met once before, but you were in your bathrobe then and a certain person wouldn't let me proceed up the walk. Tell me, Sabrina, is he treating you well? Because if he isn't, you just let me know and I'll set him straight."

She was saved from a reply by Thomas's laughter. "Stein, you can't even straighten out your own life, let alone anybody else's. Where's your date, anyway?"

"She's still mesmerized by the ice sculpture at the buffet," Seth said humorously. "She's an aspiring chef, so..." He shrugged. "I have a feeling I'm about to lose her to the pâté."

Sabrina couldn't help smiling. "It was nice meeting you," she said to Seth. "And good luck with the chef."

Seth nodded, then disappeared back into the sea of people to find his date. And Sabrina soon discovered that they didn't have to go anywhere to meet anyone. An endless stream of people seemed to keep coming up to them. Soon she felt lost in the onslaught of names and faces. They all flowed into one another, until she was left with only one impression: they all seemed sincerely friendly.

Sabrina didn't know how much—if anything—the guests here tonight knew about her. It was certainly possible that those who weren't policemen themselves had heard her speak once, or that perhaps they'd simply heard rumors about her from those who had. Whatever the case, she caught one man, another lieutenant, giving her a leering once-over, and another woman narrowed her eyes upon hearing Sabrina's name, looking at her thoughtfully. Sabrina could also have sworn that someone had pinched her derriere, but in the swarming mass of people, she doubted that it was anything personal.

Finally they started to make headway as people began to look for seats at the round, white-cloaked tables. Thomas led her confidently through the crowds, his hand protective on the curve of her back. They'd barely sat down before the drumroll started and the ceremony began. It was a good-natured event. To honor his retirement, they toasted the captain good and long. Then, as soon as the laughter died down, they presented him with gift after gift, some of which were even humorous, such as a hearing aid and four dozen doughnuts.

The gift-giving lasted for more than an hour, then with a barreling yell, the captain himself stood up and issued his last order.

"Quit bothering an old man and get back to the party," he barked out.

Even Sabrina couldn't help laughing as Thomas swept her out of her chair and spirited her away to the area cleared for dancing. The music was wonderful and intoxicating, going to her head like a fine wine. Her hips seemed to sway on their own, her hands automatically finding Thomas's shoulders. He smiled roguishly down at her, his eyes twinkling like the chandelier overhead. His arms came around her, his hands warm and firm upon the curve of her spine and hip.

He danced superbly, guiding her easily through the music until she felt as if she were floating. There were no set steps, which was fine because Sabrina never would have known them. Instead they simply moved together, allowing the music to guide and direct them.

Heaven was in his arms. It was his warm breath against the curve of her cheek, his hands upon her waist, his legs solid against her own. It was the feel of his tuxedo pressed against her, his eyes sparkling like bubbling champagne.

Soon she was breathless and her cheeks were flushed, but she wouldn't have stopped for the world. The green depths of his eyes beguiled her, drawing her in until she felt certain she could never pull away. They became her world, and it was a swirling world of green passion, whirling wonder, and never-ending awe.

She couldn't release her hold on the sleeves of his jacket, couldn't tear her eyes from his. Excitement quivered through her, a tingling river that electrified her. She could feel the current in the air, his mouth was so close, slightly parted. She could feel his breath, lightly caressing just inches away from her own lips, parted and ready.

Unconsciously her eyes drifted closed and she arched her neck back, straining up to meet him. And then his lips were there, warm and firm upon hers as he kissed her in the middle of the dance floor for all the world to see.

By the time he pulled back, her eyes were glazed and she swayed slightly on her feet. Maybe it was the one glass of wine, or maybe it was the wonder of the evening, but she felt drunk with passion, heady with desire.

"I think . . . I think I'd better go freshen up," she said at last. Her lips still seemed to tingle, and her hands still clutched his arms.

"All right," he breathed against her ear, then dipped his head slightly to place a soft kiss next to the delicate curve of her neck.

She had a hard time tearing herself away; a hard time leaving the green world of his eyes. But somehow she managed, only tripping once as she made her way across the dance floor.

It took her a while to find the women's room, but the walk was good, clearing her head and calming her blood. She was beginning to feel more in control and less like a girl in the heat of her first romance by the time she found the right door.

She opened it to a plush waiting room, one wall completely covered in mirrors while a velvet sofa rested against the other wall. A huge vase filled with long flowers decorated one corner, and a wicker table resided in the other. She was surrounded in a sea of soft rose, making the room look pampered and feminine.

It was a beautiful room, but looking at it, Sabrina suddenly felt some of the excitement of the past few hours dim. Like heady wine wearing off, her sense of reality set in.

Perhaps because just looking at this room, this lavishly decorated *bathroom* of all things, she once more felt the differences rise up. It was a matter of perspective, she thought dully. Some people saw this room and saw beauty. Some people saw this room and thought that they would do the same thing with their bathroom when they got home. She saw this room and simply thought of all the clothes, food and blankets that could have been bought with the thousands of dollars spent here.

Indifferently she looked at the woman reflected in the mirror. The image still looked radiant, cheeks flushed, eyes bright, hair golden. The diamond-cut crystal winked at one ear, scattering the light of the room. For this moment in time, she looked elegant. She looked like a woman, who would frequent a thousand-dollar ladies' room.

But she wasn't. Deep in her heart, she wasn't. She was a woman who wore faded jeans and walked the gutters of the city at night to see what souls she could save. She was a woman who spent her time worrying about whether Shadow would ever return, Ricko ever stay, Suzie ever recover. She wasn't a woman of glitter. She was a woman of the streets.

It was ending, she thought. Because when it came right down to it, this was Thomas's world. She recalled how well he moved in these circles, always knowing what kind of wine to order, what kind of things to say, what steps to dance. He belonged here. And he belonged with a woman of this world, too.

A woman who could give him his laughing children, his suburban dreams. A woman who could give him a future.

It was a much more subdued and quieter woman that left the rest room and walked back to the dance floor. The glitter was gone, but an ethereal quality had taken its place, a quality that caused more than a few heads to turn. But Sabrina did not notice.

Instead, her eyes were upon Thomas. He was standing across the banquet room and next to him stood a tall, willowy blond. She had rich hair that cascaded down her back like a silk waterfall. Her dress was a Grecian style that outlined her form in a tantalizing white caress. Her hand was resting lightly, casually, on Thomas's arm, and she was leaning forward to catch something that he said.

Red lips moved silently, then parted to reveal perfect white teeth as Thomas threw back his head and laughed.

They looked beautiful together, Sabrina realized and a dull ache settled somewhere in her stomach. She could see them, floating elegantly through the Rose Gardens, golden-haired children in tow. And she could see Thomas playing catch with a toddling blond boy, while the woman shouted her encouragement with laughing red lips.

She had forgotten her own advice, Sabrina thought abruptly. She'd disregarded her own warning. She had let him in, let him touch her heart, let him grow inside. So now she forced herself to keep looking at the pair, to see how well they moved and laughed together. They fit, she saw, in ways she never would. That woman was a part of Thomas's world. She would always know what to wear, what to say, what to do.

It's over, Sabrina told herself. You wanted Friday night, and now you've had it. Let him go, like you should have done so long ago. You were greedy, wanting more than you should have. Now you have to let go.

She looked over one last time, and his green gaze caught hers. She smiled at him, one last smile, and then she turned and left.

She walked out of the hotel with firm steps, not looking back, not even bothering to stop for her wrap. What was done, was done. She concentrated on keeping her head up and her stride steady.

The night was cold, hitting her in a clear gust. She looked up to see the stars swimming above her in crystal wonder. It was a beautiful night, she told herself and the stars blurred before her gaze.

"No," she said out loud and kept walking. But now her legs were shaking. "It's just the cold," she whispered. "Just the cold."

She made it one more block before he caught her.

"What the hell are you doing!" he demanded as he whipped her around with one arm. She had only an instant to collect herself, but it was enough.

"Leaving," she said calmly. "And what are you doing?"

"Don't play your games with me, damn it," he exploded, but behind his anger, the fear was starting to grow. He had seen the look that was in her eyes before, that first day when she'd walked into his office. Instinctively he knew that, somehow, she was gone from him. Somehow he had lost her to the shadows, and he didn't know how to get her back.

"Sabrina," he tried again. "Tell me what's going on. You owe me that much."

She tried to shrug it off lightly. "I just don't belong in this world, that's all," she said simply. "I don't belong wearing hundred-dollar dresses and going into thousand-dollar ladies' rooms. I tried this world," she told him, the coolness now fading from her eyes until he could see the pain. "It just isn't me."

"What about me?" he persisted, desperation edging his voice. Suddenly he felt as if it was all falling apart. This whole evening was supposed to be wonderful. It had been meant to convince her to stay. And yet, somehow, somewhere, he had failed miserably. Despite his best efforts, despite everything he'd hoped then, she simply didn't care for him after all. Feeling the fear reel up his spine, he tried one last time. "What about us?" he asked urgently. "What about the last three weeks? What about how well we seemed to work together?"

She dismissed it all with a wave of her hand. "This wasn't real life, Thomas. These have been three very odd weeks, that's all. In the end you're still a product of this world. And I'm still a product of mine. It just won't work. I'm sorry, Thomas, but I don't love you. And I'm sorry if you thought otherwise."

Perhaps, if he'd been calmer, he would have heard the false note of bravado in her words. Perhaps he would have been able to read between the lines, to pick out her own doubts from the words she so smoothly tossed in his face. But he wasn't. He was a man who was having his heart broken for the first time in his life. He was a man hearing the woman he had grown to care about, leave him. But beneath the dull roar of pain, he was still a man with pride. So she believed it wouldn't work. So she'd rather be without him. So she didn't care. It might hurt him, but he would rather die than show her how much. If she could be cool about it, then so could he.

"Then I guess it's just my mistake," he bit out slowly. "You'll have to forgive me."

She almost relented then, seeing the dull pain in his eyes before he covered it with icy civility. But she had come too far to back down now. "Fine," she managed to say levelly. "I think it would be best if I got back to my world and my life now. And you can get on with yours."

"No," he said slowly, catching her completely off guard. "You're still a witness to a murder, and the murderer still knows where you live. You can reject the man, Sabrina, but you have no control over the cop. I *will* return home with you, and I *will* remain at your house until this matter is resolved. Don't worry, though, I'll keep to the floor. I'd hate to impose upon you."

The sarcasm in his voice cut through her, crashing harshly into the steel ribbon of her resolve. She almost doubled over in physical pain, but managed to keep her spine straight.

Three years, she told herself fiercely. Three years of harsh and brutal education. She would not forget it now.

"That's fine," she told him, keeping her face and eyes completely expressionless. "Just fine."

"Good," he said curtly, and he whirled around, striding fiercely away. He didn't look back once to see if she followed, nor did he slow his strides to make it easier for her to catch up.

She half jogged to follow him, feeling the twinge in her feet as tender skin rubbed against the straps of her heels. She concentrated on the pain there, accepting it as her just punishment for the way she'd hurt him.

Three years. And still she bore the pain.

What was done, was done.

Chapter 11

The tension in the car on the way back was stifling, leaving them both rigid. Gone was the magic of the evening and the freedom of gliding along in a beautiful car. The Mustang had become a trap, closing Sabrina in with a huge, glowering man.

She couldn't meet his eyes, couldn't stand to see his rage and pain. Nor could she bear to think of her own. Someday, she told herself, they would both look back on this and know that she'd been right. As all things in life, it could only hurt for so long. And then the healing would begin, and she would learn how to make it through the day without seeing emerald eyes, and he would slowly forget his stay at a worn house with a worn woman.

Someday he would meet another woman, one who could make him smile and ease the lines of tension around his eyes. That woman would be able to give him everything he needed, everything he dreamed of. And maybe, on some dark and shadowy night, he would hold her close and tell her of the woman he thought he'd loved once, but who'd left him. The door of the past would close for him then, her ghost exorcised in the arms of another woman. He would leave her behind, completely and totally, as he should.

She could bear that, as well, Sabrina told herself. Because she was the one who had made the decision. She had looked at love, felt its magic, and let it go. She would get on with her life, too, losing herself in the children who needed her so. They had saved her once, they would save her again.

What was done, was done.

True to his word, Thomas spent the night on the floor of her room. The bed seemed much larger than she remembered and much colder. She tossed and turned endlessly, trying to get comfortable until finally Thomas's terse voice penetrated the darkness.

"Do you mind?" he bit out. "I'm trying to sleep."

After that, she lay perfectly still in the middle of the bed, afraid to move, afraid to breathe. Finally, at some odd hour of the morning, she crept downstairs, found Ricko's cigarettes and padded silently into the kitchen.

She smoked most of the pack, one right after another, until she felt so dizzy she thought she would be sick. And then, just for good measure, she smoked one more. She could barely hold the last one, her hands trembled so badly. But at least this time, she could blame it on the nicotine.

She spent the rest of the evening there, just sitting, staring out of frosty windowpanes. When dawn finally came, her violet eyes were weighed down by huge black smudges. Her face was much too pale, and her hands were still shaking violently.

Ricko summed it up nicely as he strolled into the kitchen with rumpled jeans and T-shirt.

"You look like hell."

She gave him a wan smile. "Isn't this a little early for you?"

"Yeah, but I figured if I wanted a cigarette I'd better come in now and rescue it."

"Sorry," she said. "But it was one of those nights."

He nodded, rummaging through the refrigerator until he found the orange juice. He poured himself a large glass, then after contemplating her ashen features, poured her one, too. He handed it to her without a word, then boosted himself up to his usual seat on the edge of the counter.

"So what happened?" he said at last. "The clock strike midnight?"

"Close enough."

"So are you guys like, broken up?"

"I guess you could say that."

"You break up with him?"

She nodded.

"Big mistake," he informed her with a shake of his head. "Very big mistake."

"No," she told him. "It just looks like it."

"So how long will he stick around?"

Sabrina paused, not knowing what to say without revealing that Thomas was a cop.

"I still work here," Thomas said from the doorway. He looked almost as bad as Sabrina, except that his eyes were still hard with anger and his jaw was clenched tightly.

"Bull," Ricko told him, looking almost cheerful. "Honest, folks, none of us buy that routine. If we were really that stupid, we wouldn't be alive by now."

Sabrina could see the truth in his words. She only wished she had bothered to figure that out earlier.

"We know he's a cop," Ricko continued. "But since he hasn't arrested Suzie and leaves the rest of us alone, we figured he was cool. So what's the deal, anyway? Do you call him a volunteer to keep yourself out of trouble?"

Sabrina almost had to laugh. If only life were that simple. She didn't say anything, just glanced over at Thomas. He was giving Ricko an assessing gaze, then he finally spoke.

"Have you ever felt like you were being watched while you've been here?" he asked intensely.

"Yeah. Once. But it went away, so I forgot about it."

"Have you seen anyone lingering about? Say, a tall, thin man?"

"And if I have?" Ricko quizzed.

"I'm sort of a witness to a murder," Sabrina spoke up. "Well, we might as well tell him everything," she told Thomas, seeing his dark look. "As long as you're going to give him the third degree, he deserves to know."

"A murder?" Ricko said, looking impressed. "That's cool."

"Did you see a man?" Thomas prodded.

"Nah, but I wish I had."

Thomas's shoulders drooped slightly, and Sabrina realized just how tired he must be. They certainly made a fine pair, she thought to herself. Together they were a walking advertisement for the *Night of the Living Dead*.

"Well now you know what's going on," said Thomas wearily. "I'm not going anywhere until this man is caught and that's that."

Ricko just nodded, looking from one to the other. Then he sighed, and shook his head instead.

"Man, oh, man," he said to himself as he jumped down from the counter and walked back into the living room. "Man, oh, man."

The kitchen seemed much smaller with Ricko gone. Sabrina found herself staring at the walls, the window, the floor, anything but Thomas. For his part he seemed intent on avoiding her, too, as he yanked open the refrigerator door and peered inside. The silence seemed to stretch on endlessly, tightening Sabrina's nerves beyond all hopes of sanity.

She could still remember all those mornings they'd sat here together, quietly talking and sharing before Thomas had to go to work. Obviously those times were long gone. Get used to it, she told herself firmly.

But neither could quite manage that. The sound of cereal being poured cut through the silence, making them both jump. At any other time she would have laughed over it, but now she simply sat quietly. She just didn't know the words that could soothe the pain she'd inflicted.

She was almost at the point of fleeing from the kitchen when the phone rang. While the first ring frayed her nerves, she picked it up gratefully.

The phone call was short, draining the color from her face. She hung up the phone to find Thomas staring at her.

"A kid I know—Mike—is in the hospital," she said. "He asked for me. They said he overdosed on acid. An entire sheet's worth."

Even Thomas blanched at that. One sheet of acid contained one hundred squares, each square equivalent to one hit. Essentially Mike had consumed one hundred hits of acid. There wasn't a need to say anything more. Thomas grabbed their coats and led her to the car.

The journey to the hospital did little to ease Sabrina's nerves. It went like the rest of the morning, with each of them remaining silent and tense. There was a yawning chasm between them now. The simple intimacies and smiles of before were gone, and in their place was an emptiness that could never be filled.

She wondered what he would do if she reached out to brush a fallen lock of hair out of his eyes. Most likely, he would snap off her hand at the wrist. The anger within him was as powerful as his passion had once been. It consumed him, turning him into a mountain of rage, just waiting to explode. Except every now and then, she would catch him staring off, looking lost and tired. Those moments were even harder to take than his silence.

She could handle his anger, could even handle violence, but not his confusion, not his pain. She wanted to reach out and smooth his brow, to hold him close until all his pain disappeared. But that wasn't her place anymore. Would never be her place again.

What was done, was done, she reminded herself. But the words seemed hollow now, an unfit epitaph for the most magical days of her life.

When they finally pulled up to the hospital, she was grateful.

They found his room easily enough, it was the only room with a police officer outside the door. Thomas drew the man aside, and talked with him briefly. He came back looking very grave.

"That was Detective Garrison. He said that Mike was discovered in a raid on a suspected crack house two days ago. The house was empty except for him, and they couldn't find any traces of drugs, but they're keeping him for questioning anyway."

Sabrina sighed deeply. So she had been right and Mike was in over his head. She wondered what he planned on doing now. Taking another deep breath, she walked in, Thomas right behind her.

Lying helplessly on the white hospital bed with an IV needle in one wrist and a respirator in his nose, Mike didn't look too good. The police had found him unconscious on the floor of a suspected crack house during a raid, but so far Mike hadn't talked much, and his attitude didn't improve any even after Sabrina and Thomas's entrance.

"I just wanted you to know that Shadow was okay," he muttered sullenly to Sabrina while giving Thomas suspicious glances.

"Shadow?" she asked, cocking one eyebrow. "I saw him just the other night. He was fine then."

"Well, that was before things went down. But don't worry, Shadow's a smart guy. He got out okay."

"Got out of what okay?"

Mike gave her an exasperated look. "The bust, what else?"

She gave him a sharp look. "So he's into drugs, too?"

Mike simply shrugged. "He doesn't do them, if that's what you think. But every now and then, he'll run an errand or two. Nothing major."

"How deep is he in?"

"I don't know. Nobody knows a damned thing about Shadow. He just shows up. And when he does, they give him something to do. He doesn't ask questions or make any demands. He just does the errand, and then he disappears. Just like that."

"And they still trust him?" Thomas spoke up.

Mike gave him another mistrustful gaze. "Not at first, but they do now. He's never given them a reason not to. Hey, man, in the drug business the silent types are the best types."

"So Shadow's okay," Sabrina repeated. "What about you, Mike? What are you going to do now?"

"I can take care of myself," he informed her with bravado worn a little thin by the pain.

"How deep are you into the drug business?" asked Thomas.

"Deep enough," the kid replied.

"What are you going to do about it?"

Mike just shrugged, refusing to comment. And as much as both Sabrina and Thomas tried to prod him, neither could change that. It was clear that he knew people in the business, but wouldn't consider turning state's witness. Nor would he commit to counseling or rehabilitation. In the end he was just as sullen and uncooperative when they left as when they had arrived.

Sabrina could only sigh in frustration, wanting so desperately to help him but realizing it just wasn't possible until he was ready to help himself.

"Do you think he'll be okay?" she asked Thomas as they made their way through the hospital lobby to the parking lot. But he only shook his head, his face equally grim.

They each remained silent for the drive home, the day's events resting heavily on their minds. Tired, Sabrina barely said a word to the group upon arrival. She just headed for the stairs.

And since she was the first to enter the room, she was the one who found it. If she hadn't glanced over, she probably would have missed it herself. After all, there'd been no warning, not even a small premonition. She had simply walked into her room the way she must walk into her room a dozen times a day.

Somehow that made it all the more nerve-racking. Because she did walk into her room a dozen times a day. And because her room was supposed to be safe.

But there it was, lying perfectly in the center of her bed, tied with a crimson ribbon. A single black rose.

Thomas raced up the stairs at her call, hearing the shakiness in her voice. Lunging into the room, he was ready for violence or mayhem. He wasn't ready for the rose.

It brought him up short briefly, then he exploded in a burst of colorful phrases. But they didn't do any good. The rose, and all it implied, remained.

Going back down the stairs, Thomas questioned everyone thoroughly. No one had seen anything. Woof had never barked, and Gord, even with his experience in the marines, had never heard a thing.

Striding outside, Thomas glared at the grass beneath the window. There were no imprints, no footsteps. But then he turned to stare at the huge oak tree to the side of the house. It would be nothing to climb it, he realized. It could easily take someone to the roof and from there they would just have to force the bedroom window open and slide into the room. And in a house this old, opening the window would be easy.

For good measure he tested his theory, heaving himself up onto the lower branches, then climbing nimbly. The roof felt solid under his feet, though he had to tread carefully to keep from slipping. Lying on his stomach at the edge, he reached down and touched the window. Applying pressure with his hands, he lifted it slightly and then slid it smoothly open.

Cursing royally, he closed the window and climbed back down. Without a glance at anyone, he marched back into the house and worked on jamming all the windows from the inside.

But it didn't matter to Sabrina. The killer's point had already been made. He had gone from flowers on her doorstep, to corpses down the street, to haunting her yard, and now this. Breaking into her house. His point was clear. He was homing in on her now, showing her just how fragile the illusion of safety could be. That way she would sweat more before he made his ultimate move. Before he killed her.

But she was about to force his hand, she thought grimly. Three years on the streets had taught her more than he would ever realize. It was time for the games to end.

Tonight, she told herself firmly, and for the first time in the long week, she felt the tension within her ease. There was no more debating, no more wondering, no more worrying. The decision had been made. Once and for all, it would finally end.

By the time Thomas returned downstairs, she was almost smiling.

The night crept stealthily up on Sabrina, even as she tried to avoid it. The shadows lengthened and the hour grew later and later. She could no longer meet Thomas's eye, no longer bear to be near him.

But she could feel him watching her, feel his hunger and longing as his gaze blazed into her back. It would be over soon, she tried to tell herself. But that made it even worse. In many ways the murderer had been her salvation. Once he was caught, Thomas would leave, and this one chapter of her life would truly be over.

Night fell. Soon she would be able to delay it no longer. Careful not to touch, to look, she made her way, followed by Thomas, to the bedroom.

By unspoken agreement, she used the bathroom first, coming out in her nightclothes to crawl beneath the protective covers. Thomas disappeared next, coming out wearing only a pair of shorts and sliding into the covers set up on the floor.

And then the waiting began. Sabrina lay there, waiting for him to fall asleep, waiting for the moment to come. Closing her eyes briefly, she was certain the last thing she would do was fall asleep, but she did. Sleep claimed her, carrying her away into a velvet dream.

The dream turned into silk and satin that tantalized her bare skin, whispering against her ear of things long forgotten. It brushed her lips and hair with a shivering caress that heightened her senses. Then it slowed to a languorous tenderness that pulled at her heart. She moaned softly, rolling over to reach for what she needed.

And found emptiness.

It woke her up with a cold start, stifling her passion and filling her eyes with tears. Looking over the edge of the bed, she found who she had been seeking. She got up quietly and padded over to the windowsill to see him better.

In the dim ribbons of moonlight, his chest lay bare and silver. His face was tight even in sleep, lines of pain and worry creasing his brow.

Her heart pulled at her again, bringing pain to her own eyes. And she knew why. Under cover of the night, she could admit to it.

Love.

In the dark of the night, looking over at the sleeping man, she could feel it creeping up on her, let loose from some deep, hidden part of her.

From her perch on the windowsill, she watched Thomas's vulnerable form with her heart in her eyes. She wanted to stroke his forehead in soothing comfort. Only it wasn't her place anymore.

Her thoughts took flight, entwining themselves around her, whispering in her ear with painfully sweet promises. Holding, comforting, soothing. Tenderness, caring, healing. Love. After all these years, finally love.

She had searched for it for so long. They all did, all the shadows in the streets below. Perhaps that was what the streets were all about. Searching, but never finding. Destroying themselves in the desperate hunt.

So many things she'd done, endured, and all in the hopes of finding love. But here, in the darkness, love had found her.

With his huge frame deep in slumber, Thomas looked innocent, harmless. But she knew better. Somewhere along the line, he had stolen her heart. Or maybe she had given it to him, she didn't really know. Either way, she wouldn't be getting it back.

After tonight the case would be closed. She knew, because she was going to end it. End the waiting, and the wondering. She had run once when she was sixteen years old. She wasn't going to run anymore. Somewhere, in the dark of the night, a man was threatening the life she had so carefully built.

But it would be over soon. She would see to that.

The shadows grew longer, and she turned to look at the street below. It was too cold. The last week in February had begun and with it had come a bone-chilling frost that had cleared what action the street by her house saw.

The frost glittered, the dim streetlight reflecting colorful prisms of light across a sparkling street.

Beautiful. But oh, so dangerous. Too many things were like that. The kind of things that tugged at her heart, making her vulnerable with longing.

Love.

How had it ever happened? After all those years of drifting from foster home to foster home—dreaming that this would be the family that would keep her, that this would be the family that would love her—only to be evicted time and again. Not enough food, not enough money, not enough love for one lost little girl.

Then there'd been the years on her own, but she'd still been searching. Daring to dream that two girls at a bus station would care enough to help her. Then, still alone and frightened and desperate, forgetting her own self worth, forgetting her own dignity.

She would be dead now, she knew that with certainty, if not for that one transient. His single act of compassion had given her the strength to get out of the gutter. She had cheated the drugs, the streets, and perhaps even destiny, out of her death.

And in the process, she'd remembered, remembered the dream of both the little girl and of the woman. To find love.

In the rehab center, there had been a class for ex-prostitutes on making love. It had been the biggest joke there. After all, with years of meeting every kind of man, what did they need to learn about sex? But they'd found out that was exactly the point. They knew everything about sex, and nothing about making love.

The right to demand tenderness, the right to demand satisfaction. The intimacy of sharing, the togetherness of the act had all been denied them. Sabrina would never forget the mind-numbing shock of hearing a young teacher explain that making love was exactly that. *Making love.*

But she understood it all now. Understood it all too well, because that was what she'd been doing all along with Thomas. Making love.

She hadn't consciously thought about it, but it rang true in her heart. The tenderness, the awe, the intimacy had all been there. The pure wonder of exploring his body, and the possessive thrill of his huge frame laboring over hers, couldn't be denied. The closeness afterward, being snuggled up against the hard length of his body, those warm feelings clinched it.

Love.

But why now? Why with this man, a man she could never have?

Because he's what you've always wanted, her heart whispered. Because he's the dream you searched your whole life for. Because he's the hope that beckoned you out of the gutter. Because he is everything.

She couldn't help herself. "I love you," she whispered into the shadows. "God, do I love you."

Maybe she'd said the words too loud, for Thomas stirred in his sleep. One arm came out, blindly searching next to him. But then awareness came to him, and he sat up, groggily blinking his eyes.

"Sabrina?" he questioned, seeing her dim shadow halfway across the room.

At that moment she wanted him more than she had ever wanted anything in her life. She wanted one last memory to savor, one last memory to carry with her later on when she would need its strength. One last time to let her body tell him everything she could not.

Thomas was really starting to come awake now, his senses picking up the dark undercurrents in the room. Suddenly his anger didn't seem so important. He could feel Sabrina's pain, feel her longing, and he could not deny it.

He lifted his body from the cold harshness of the floor and moved to join her across the room.

Watching his approach, seeing the soft light reflect off the smooth lines of his muscular frame, she felt the love swell in her throat, filling her eyes with tears.

She found she couldn't swallow, couldn't breathe. She could only watch the most beautiful man she had ever met come straight to her.

"Are you okay?" he questioned softly.

She heard the concern, the tenderness, and incredibly, felt the love within her grow.

And because she knew her heart must surely be in her eyes, she buried her head against the comfort of his warm chest and wrapped her arms securely around his lean waist.

But it wasn't enough. She could never get close enough.

"Make love to me," she whispered, hearing the tremor in her own voice, the desperate edge of longing.

But she was beyond caring, beyond anything but the fierce need to have him. To truly, truly, have him.

She arched her head back and reached up, bringing his head down to hers and kissing him savagely, aware of the almost bruising pressure of her mouth, tasting the salt of her unshed tears.

Her lips were demanding, consuming him with a rage of passion he could only respond to with raw, hot emotion.

As her hands flew across his body in desperate need, he fiercely grabbed her worn T-shirt between two massive fists and ripped it from her shaking body.

She moaned under the onslaught, pressing her now naked body even closer to his. She needed him, needed him with fury, with gentleness, with savagery, with anything she could get. So she took. With her hands, with her mouth, she claimed him over and over again.

And as he swung her over to the bed, then plunged desperately into her fevered body, she clawed at his back.

Closer, her mind cried out as she arched her hips upward to meet his burning thrusts. And with her desperate aching, she took him even as he took her, until both swirled into a realm of madness where there existed only the taste and touch of the other. Closer. Closer. Until they exploded into oblivion.

Thomas didn't question her mood afterward, when both had returned to the reality of the aftermath. He didn't question the desperation, the fierce longing, the need.

And even when he felt the burning saltiness against his chest, he didn't question her tears.

He just held her.

And when he awoke, just a little later, she was gone.

Chapter 12

She shivered slightly as she slipped out the door onto the unsteady porch. She shut the door silently behind her, hearing the last click as the latch caught and held. There was no going back now. But then, there never was.

She restrained herself from a last lingering glance at the upstairs window. She didn't want to see what she was leaving behind, didn't want to remember the huge man slumbering peacefully in her bed.

Sleeping, at least for now. She wasn't a fool. Thomas had the sixth sense of a seasoned cop. Sooner or later he would awaken, already knowing that something was wrong. Hopefully, by then, it would be all over. All said and done.

Whatever that would be.

With one last deep breath of resolution, she stepped into the night. She walked steadily out into the street, taking slow steps, allowing the night to seep into her blood. The darkness was heavy, the black clouds of a coming storm raging above her, giving the night a thick, almost tangible feel.

She accepted it, letting it swirl around her. God, it had been a long time. Eight years to be exact. And how far she had come. She had even found love.

At the end of the street she had to turn, had to take that last look at the house now so far away. The window was black in the night, an empty eye without even a light to see her off. She felt the tears sting, felt the heaviness in her throat thicken until she wanted to fall down and cry out in pain.

He was love, he was everything. How could she let him go? But then, how could she ask him to stay?

Abruptly she turned away. That, after all, was the crux of the matter. How could she ask him to stay? She couldn't, she wouldn't. Resolutely she repeated to herself that this was her world now, and began to walk, feeling the slight pitter-patter of the rain as it started to fall.

The rain soon became a downpour, flattening her hair, pummeling her cheeks, soaking her clothes. But still she walked, straight and firm. Her head was up, her chin squared in determination. And at her side, she clutched her handbag securely with black gloved hands, feeling the alien outline of the chrome pistol even through the fabric.

She had never used the gun before. She had bought and registered it merely as a precaution. And so far, it had remained so. Until now. Until this night. She didn't want to kill the man, it wasn't her way. But she wasn't a fool. She knew that the man meant to kill her, sooner or later. So she'd just as soon it be on her terms, on her territory.

This night, with all its wet wonder, was her world. Here she was invulnerable, a veteran of a three-year war. Here she was taking action to stop the waiting. She refused to spend weeks peering into the shadows and over her shoulder, wondering when and where he would pounce.

Instinctively, she knew he would come, if only to taunt her. She knew she didn't even have to find him. Sooner or later, he would find her.

So she moved quickly now, smoothly gliding along dark and stormy streets. Her tennis shoes squished with every step, slowing her down slightly. Her clothes were damp against her, sticking like cement to the delicate outline of her body. But the briskness of her walking and her own thoughts kept the chill at bay.

The first order of business was to lose whatever escort Thomas might have seen fit to arrange for her. Patrol cars still alternated passes by her house and the surrounding neighborhood, so she had to be careful of them. She didn't think Thomas was still having her followed by anyone on foot, at least not at night. He expected her to be safely tucked away under his supervision during those hours. But just to be sure, she whipped her way in and out of the old parking lots, deserted buildings and side streets that riddled the area by the shelter.

She had the advantage. She knew the area well, and she was even familiar with it by nightfall.

She did have an eventual goal in mind—a deserted warehouse not far from where the first girl had died. Once, a lifetime ago, she had slept there occasionally. These days, it had become so treacherous even the vagrants stayed away. But she knew it well, knew which floors were safe to walk upon and which ones were likely to crumble. And she was small, light, giving her more of an advantage against her tormentor.

She could lead the killer places where the boards would give under his weight, even as she walked on them. And there was enough action not far from there that she could be certain assistance would be relatively accessible. She didn't want to kill the man, she just wanted to trap him, to render him immobile until help could arrive.

And then she would return to an empty house and an empty bed. Then she could start trying to pick up the pieces and get on with her life, even though things would never be the same.

The rain had slowed to a thick mist that collected on her eyelashes. The streets glowed wetly under the light of the streetlamps, beckoning her on. Every now and then a car would roar by, splashing her with mud and water until her pantlegs were thick and heavy.

But still she kept walking, eyes penetrating the dark, nerves adjusting to the rhythm of the night. Then, to her right, a shadow moved a bit too quickly and she knew she was being followed. Cop? She paused the slightest bit, and the shadow failed to advance. Someone was waiting for her.

She waited to feel the fear, waited to feel it shaking up her spine in never-ending chills.

But it didn't quite materialize, only hovering on the edges of her mind like a thought she couldn't quite grasp. And then it hit her in the gut, hard and heavy, bringing her up short and gasping.

Her blood raced with a surge of adrenaline and she darted desperately forward, with only one more block to go. She could hear the pounding behind her, wet and clear in the darkness. Puddles whizzed by, scattering crazily as she dashed through them.

The shadows were moving now, thick and fast, keeping up with her even as the pounding of her heart rang in her ears. The building loomed ahead, a dark gray tombstone in the night. The last sentinel for a last stand. She was almost to the doorway when he caught her.

His arm was long and thin, bringing her up short in a snapping halt as he caught her arm. There was an audible pop in the darkness and for a minute, Sabrina was afraid that she had dislocated her shoulder. But then his grip relented a fraction, allowing her to roll her shoulder, feeling everything grind into place.

He stepped forward, out of the shadows, and for the first time, she saw his face.

Something wasn't right, she thought instantly. True, his features were thin and long, with an angular, hawkish nose. And he had a high forehead, topped with short brown hair. He even looked like a tall, thin man, but he wasn't the right tall, thin man.

She studied him carefully. His angular frame was encased in torn jeans that were loose, as if he had recently lost weight. The simple cotton shirt he wore was stained in the front, with the sleeves rolled up, revealing thin blue-veined arms.

"Who are you?" she whispered. He didn't answer, he just pushed her into the warehouse.

Maybe it was the way he walked, she thought as he shoved her along. She could feel his hands shaking upon her shoulders, and his blue eyes dashed to and fro, afraid to rest. He didn't stand straight, or walk smoothly. Instead his shoulders hunched protectively forward, and he moved with slow, shuffling steps.

The floor trembled underneath them and she slowed, beginning to pick her steps carefully. Around them stood the eroding remains of the support beams. Rats and termites had worked hard over the years, turning the solid trunks into spongy lengths riddled with holes. Here and there, Sabrina could see the broken floorboards where the last wanderers had fallen through.

Then she felt her captor stumble behind her and instinctively turned to help. He recoiled at her touch, blue eyes growing wide in horror. She backed away, sensing finally the wildness lurking under the surface. He was scared, his eyes once again dashing around the empty warehouse. Hysteria rimmed them in a bright sheen that sent beads of sweat to her own brow.

"Please," she tried again. "Tell me who you are?"

"I know who you are," he told her accusingly as his eyes raced over and around her. "I know what you do, I know how you do it. You must want my name so you can use it against me. Jack warned me about you. Don't think I don't know. He told me."

"Who is Jack? Told you what? What did Jack tell you about me?"

But he only shook his head furiously, pushing her forward once more. This time, they moved slower, testing the floorboards gradually before resting their weight on them.

Carefully, they made their way to the far side of the warehouse. Coming into the east side of the building, the holes became fewer and farther between, and the boards stopped groaning under their feet. The building was in much better shape here, and the moon poured through broken windows to settle like a spotlight upon the open room. When they reached the middle, the man abruptly shoved her forward so hard that she stumbled, handbag flying from her grasp as she used her hands to break her fall.

Out of the corner of her eye she watched the bag tumble in the air and then land, the latch jarred open with the impact, letting eyeliner and lipstick spill forth. Slowly she got up, panic dark within her. She could barely make out the silver handle of the gun, but it was there, resting at the mouth of the bag.

Quickly she turned and looked at her assailant sharply, but he hadn't noticed anything.

She took a deep breath, feeling confused and out of her element. She hadn't found the killer, but another madman. How the hell was she going to get herself out of this mess?

"Obviously you know who I am," she said slowly, keeping her tone carefully even. "But honestly, I don't know who you or Jack are. Could you at least give me a hint?"

"I saw what you did to the girl," he said abruptly. "I talked to her. I tried to tell her about you. But you'd already brainwashed her."

"What girl?" Sabrina said softly, willing him to answer.

"The pretty girl," he said, and then sighed almost wistfully. "She had golden hair like an angel. She was nice to me," he said, his voice full of wonder. "She was actually nice to me."

"Suzie is a very special girl," Sabrina agreed, understanding now who he was talking about. She racked her brains for a common link with which to establish some conversation. If she could only keep him talking— He must have met Suzie before she'd returned to the shelter. Or perhaps... Then she had it. The night that Suzie disappeared. That night, she'd talked to a man. Sabrina couldn't be sure, they were one and the same, but it was a start. "What did you try to tell her about me?" she asked gently.

"The white slavery ring, of course," he said. "I know you sell the kids into slavery. Jack told me," he repeated emphatically. But suddenly he frowned and his hand went up to clutch at one temple. He pressed it against his forehead briefly. Then, when that wasn't enough, he pounded his fist against the temple.

He was becoming more agitated, and Sabrina began to get seriously worried. He was thin and shaking, and obviously deeply disturbed. Slowly, she took a step forward.

"I didn't sell Suzie into slavery," she said, edging forward to where he'd sat down. "In fact, she's at my house right now. Would you like to come see her?"

He eyed her suspiciously. "It's a trap. Do you think I don't know about the trap? Do you think I'm stupid? Everyone thinks I'm stupid. 'John's stupid.' Well, I'm not stupid. I'm just forgetful, that's all. Just forgetful."

"I know, John," she said soothingly, testing out his name. When he didn't protest, but remained seated, looking nervous and angry and hurt, she reached out her hand to touch his arm. Then, out of the corner of her eye, she saw a shadow stir on her right. For a moment she almost could see a face and then it was gone. The hairs on the back of her neck began to ripple and the chills snaked up her spine in full force.

I've got to get out of here, she realized suddenly. Somewhere she'd made a big mistake. And now, she had a feeling she was about to pay.

Without thinking, she surged forward.

"No," boomed a loud voice, and an arm reached out, grasping her tightly, stopping her flight. The arm was thin and surprising in its strength. Bewildered, she looked up to meet John's gaze.

Except, she realized, it wasn't John's gaze. Anymore. The eyes were now a hard, brilliant blue. His shoulders were back and his jaw rigid with burning anger and steely strength.

And suddenly she understood. John was Jack. And Jack was the killer.

Then she saw the knife. He held it high, the serrated edge gleaming in the moonlight. Except that the edge wasn't a clear, shiny silver. Darkness rimmed the cracks with a deep sheen. Dried blood, she thought faintly, and could no longer swallow.

"John," she tried, licking her lips. "John, please. Talk to me."

But the man before her now just smiled coldly and brought the knife closer.

Swallowing tightly, Sabrina watched the serrated edge approach.

"Do you think I don't know all about you?" he hissed out, taking a step forward. "Do you know how long I've watched you, waiting for my chance? You thought you could outsmart me, but you can't." He took another step, the knife now skimming across her throat. Her eyes closed convulsively. "People underestimate me all the time—doctors, the police, even my mother. But in the end, I'm smarter than all of you."

"John—" she began cautiously, but he cut her off with a quick thrust of the knife, piercing the top layer of her pale skin until a small trail of blood trickled down.

"Don't try it," he snarled at her. "Do you have any idea how many women I've killed?"

He paused, waiting for her answer, and finally she managed a small shake of her head. *Think,* Sabrina, *think,* her mind shouted. *You have to find a way out of here.* Suddenly, from far off, she thought she heard a small noise, but then there was only silence. She bit back a cry of fevered desperation. *She was alone with a killer.*

"I've killed twenty-two women," he informed her. "Here, California, Washington. Always using different methods, different styles, so no one would ever put them together. That's because I'm smart, very smart. And I've never had to worry about a witness, until you." He moved the knife again, drawing a stinging red line across her throat, watching almost curiously, as she flinched. "You do know what this means, don't you?"

Unfortunately she knew too well, and the fear was paralyzing her. This wasn't how it was supposed to go, she raged inwardly, tears welling in her eyes. She was supposed to lead the murderer in here, trap him in the collapsing structure, get the cops, and then be free to get on with her life. It wasn't supposed to end like this. She wasn't supposed to die. Her mind raced, sweat dripping down her brow and neck, mingling with the blood, stinging. She licked her lips, but no matter how hard she tried, she was unable to come up with a way to get out of the madman's clutches.

"Why did you kill them?" she asked weakly, valiantly stalling for time. *That's right. Keep him distracted. Now think, Sabrina think!*

Jack's face darkened, turning into a scowl. "Women are evil," he spat out. "No-good tramps. Bringing life and pain into the world and then just abandoning it, leaving it alone against the world. Because you don't care.'' His voice raised, becoming harsher, angrier. ''None of you care.''

''No,'' she said desperately, trying to reach him. ''We—*I* do care, and right now you need help, John. I can help you. Remember Suzie, John? Remember the girl with the golden hair, the sweet girl you met the other night? She told me about you John. She said you were a good man. Together we can help you. I can take you to her.'' She held her breath; for an instant she thought she saw something flicker in his eyes, but then the coldness came down again like a hard wall, shutting him off from her.

With a sinister smile, he drew the knife back, his eyes turning black with anticipation. ''You're evil. You need to pay.'' And then the knife came down.

Sabrina watched it slash toward her, dimly registering with odd detachment the moment of pure terror, of watching the knife fall, of witnessing her own destruction. Then all of a sudden the shadows around them heaved and moved, materializing into the unmistakable form of a wiry boy.

''No,'' she screamed, even as she saw Shadow dart forward. Jack turned suddenly, caught off guard. Not waiting another instant, her only thought to protect Shadow, Sabrina gave John a furious push. Halfway to Shadow already, John teetered slightly, but regained his balance quickly.

A scream of pure rage, emerged from his throat and he whirled around, lunging for her, knife outstretched with deadly intent.

''Sabrina, look out!'' cried out a deeper voice. Then there was the blast of a gun, a flash of gunfire and down Jack went with wide, disbelieving eyes.

Shadow stood behind him, chrome gun gleaming hotly in his hands. On his left Thomas materialized slowly, stepping cautiously forward, gun still held in front, a tendril of smoke coming from the barrel. But Shadow didn't notice. He watched the crimson stain spread across the top left of the thin man's shirt, watched the body fall. His eyes never changed, his face never moved. Then slowly, he walked forward to peer into bright blue eyes.

John looked at him in confusion, feeling the pain that ripped through him like a giant claw. He saw smoky gray eyes, but they were the eyes of a child. Then it came to him, one last feeble grip on the reality that had eluded him so often.

"It's okay," he murmured to the boy. He tried to reach out a hand to pat the boy, but couldn't manage. The pain gripped him, widening his eyes in a sudden spasm. "Really," he gasped out at last. "It's better this way. Better." And then he heaved a long gasp, blood rushing forth from his wound. His face fell forward onto the dust-thickened floor.

"He's dead," said Thomas flatly, and the words rang hollow in the emptiness of the warehouse. "I'm sorry, Shadow," he said softly. "I'm sorry you had to see this." The echo of his own voice made his stomach tighten with the awful thought floating on the edge of his mind. If he had been but one minute later...

Shadow stared at Thomas a long time, then looked back at the man fallen on the floor, emotions flickering dimly behind his eyes. Sabrina watched him, feeling the pain in her own throat. Fourteen years old and already a witness to violent death. Then he looked up, and she felt his fear.

"No, Shadow," she said, even as he walked forward and placed the gun quietly at her feet. "Don't run from this, please. I know it's hard, but Thomas and I will help you. We will. Tell him how we will, Thomas. Tell him." She could hear the desperation in her voice, hear the tears that collected there.

Shadow looked at her long and hard, his eyes deeply gray. Then they flashed with the first emotion she had ever seen on his face. Regret.

Thomas stepped forward, hand raised to gently lay it on Shadow's shoulder as he opened his mouth to speak, but Shadow had already turned away, fading into the night. Thomas tried to call out after him, tried to explain that it was his own gun that had fired the mortal shot. But the boy was already gone, and if he heard the echo of Thomas's words, he still did not turn back.

Then Thomas turned and looked at Sabrina, looking pale and shaky in the empty night, a thin trail of blood trickling down her throat. He felt as if he'd aged a million years since he'd woken up and found her gone. He'd known instantly in that split second of awareness, where she'd gone. And it had only increased his fear.

Now, somehow, looking at her standing just ten feet away, he wished he could explain exactly what he felt, but words failed him. So he waited in silence, half hoping that now that it was indeed over, the danger past, that she would want him back.

"How did you find me?" she asked softly.

"Your hair," he said simply. "It's so light. Like gold."

"Next time I'll wear a hat," she whispered. Another pause. "Is he really dead?" *Is it really over?*

"Yes."

"What do we do now?"

Come back to me. Stay with me. Don't ever leave. "There will be a lot of questions," he said softly. "Questions about him, questions about your gun, and since I killed him, there will be a routine investigation of the circumstances surrounding it. You will probably have to testify."

"The gun is registered."

"Good."

Another pause. A growing sense of the uncertainty, of the wanting, of the waiting. And yet still she didn't move, made no approach toward him.

And suddenly, looking at her in the shadows, he felt the realization hit him like a low blow to his stomach. She wasn't coming back. It wasn't about the murderer, it was about him. She didn't want *him.* He hadn't lost her, he'd never had her.

Suddenly he felt old, looking at the woman he loved, trying to let her go graciously, without a fight. But he couldn't do it. She'd come to mean too much to him. She was the woman who had taught him of hope, the woman who had taught him of courage. Since meeting her he had regained his enthusiasm for his job, he had regained his faith. He needed her. With her by his side, he could do anything. Take on all the bad guys, even learn how to lose the battles, without losing the war.

Please, God, let her come to me.

But she didn't move. She stayed rooted to the spot, looking lost and alone. Finally he couldn't take it anymore.

"I have to call it in," he said softly, and then he was gone.

Sabrina felt the loss, felt it tear at her heart. It was really over now. All over. A man lay dead at her feet, and she had lost both Thomas and Shadow.

She sat alone in a ray of moonlight on the warehouse floor, watching the blood pooling around the dead man, and felt the tears run down her face.

It had been two weeks.

She hadn't seen him since the night of the shooting. All the questions had been handled by Seth, endless questions about things she didn't want to remember. And the more they found out, the harder it became.

John had been in the state mental ward once. He had been diagnosed as having a tendency toward multiple personalities, given medication, and eventually released. But they had found no medication in his rundown apartment. Nor any prescriptions. They could only assume that he had never followed up on his drugs, that his illness had progressed, drowning him in darkness.

His mother, a prostitute, had abandoned him when he was seven. According to county officials, she'd simply left him on a street corner and never come back. John had gotten lost in the bureaucratic system after that. He had drifted in and out of foster homes and different schools, despite an extremely high IQ, never quite bringing his world into focus.

And that was the life of John, who had turned into the alter ego Jack. Sabrina still couldn't reconcile the two in her mind. Still couldn't match the nervous man she had met with the man who had brutally killed three women—more, if his ramblings held any truth to them.

Eventually all the lose ends had been sewn up and the case was considered closed.

Except for one thing. Shadow was nowhere to be found. None of her contacts were able to produce a bit of information on his whereabouts. For all intents and purposes, the fourteen-year-old boy had simply disappeared.

The other kids were doing great. Ricko still promised to leave every morning, and was still there every night. Just this morning, he'd casually announced that he and his group would be working for Mrs. Jacquobi starting Monday.

She hadn't cried. Not once since the warehouse. She felt too empty inside, as if she was filled with a huge vacuum that tears could never possibly fill. She kept waiting for the emptiness to go away, kept waiting for the longing to ease, but it never did.

She kept looking up, expecting to see Thomas in the doorway, a smile on his lips, eyes bright with welcome. In the mornings, she would go downstairs, half expecting to see him at the table, steaming coffee in one hand, newspaper in the other. And often she woke up in the middle of the night, reaching for him, needing him and finding only emptiness.

There were times that she thought the longing, the need would never cease. She wanted to see him so badly it hurt beyond her comprehension, immobilizing her with pain. She wanted to touch his cheek, stroke his hair, hold him close. She wanted to wake up in the dawn with his arms warm around her, his breath in her hair.

She'd wanted too much.

Two weeks, too many packs of cigarettes, and she was back where she'd started. It was 2:00 a.m. and she couldn't sleep. Actually she had fallen asleep, but she'd dreamed. It had been a curious dream, floating around her in a languid caress. It had stroked her gently, held her tenderly, coaxing her into a writhing mass of need and desire. But then she'd awakened to emptiness. Small wonder she no longer wanted to dream, or sleep.

She had done this to herself. She should never have become involved with a man like Thomas. But how could she have known that it would go this far? That he would be this addictive? She had thought that letting him go would be like saying goodbye to a favorite pet. What she hadn't realized was that it was more like turning her back on a part of herself, turning away from her dreams and desires.

And she wondered, for the millionth time, if she had done the right thing. Perhaps she should tell him. Perhaps she should just tell him everything, the entire truth. Chances were, he would still let her go. But at least then he would know. Know why she'd had to turn her back on him. Maybe by easing his pain, she could ease her own.

Over the past few weeks she'd learned a thing or two about love. She'd always known that everyone had their own horror stories. Everyone had their feelings of neglect, vulnerability and rejection. While her past might be worst than most, it was also better than others. So perhaps the secret was in being able to let the anger and pain of the past go, and let the love in.

In the end, she had. That last precious night, in this very room, she'd felt the love, let it touch her, let herself return it in kind.

If only her past was completely the past. If only it didn't affect the present . . . and the future. For everything, there is a price to be paid. . . .

The rap on the window startled her out of her reverie, jangling her tightly strung nerves. She looked up to see a face peering in the window and almost screamed.

But slowly, she began to make out the features in the dark. It was Shadow.

She opened the window quickly, helping him ease in, not bothering to ask why he hadn't knocked on the front door. The past two weeks had apparently not been good ones for him. There was a dark bruise on one cheek and a ragged scratch that started by one ear and disappeared under his collar. He looked scraggly and tired and infinitely dear.

His face was as composed as ever, but there was a hardness to it now, a look of fierce determination that took her by surprise.

In one short motion he reached into his back pocket and took out his knife. He laid it firmly in the palm of her hand. Then he leaned over and rolled up his pantleg, carefully easing the lead pipe from his calf. Giving her a square look, he deposited that in her hand, as well.

Then he took a deep breath and nodded. It was all she needed to see. She threw her arms around his small frame.

For a moment he was rigid in her arms, folding up into himself. But then, after a long minute, one hand moved hesitantly up. And in a rare gesture of comfort, one she instinctively knew he hadn't offered for perhaps years, he awkwardly patted her on the back.

"It's going to be okay, now," she told him. "Honestly, Shadow. I promise you things will be better."

The boy's eyes weren't completely convinced, but he nodded nonetheless.

"Shadow," she began slowly. "You do understand you didn't kill that man, don't you?"

He froze before her, shooting her a penetrating look.

"I want you to understand that it wasn't your fault," Sabrina continued carefully. "The final reports and analyses show that it was Lieutenant Lain's gun that fired the fatal shot."

Shadow didn't look completely convinced at that, either, but he considered it for a solemn moment and then nodded again.

"Do you still want to stay?" she asked softly. "You know I would love it if you would."

There was a longer pause, a pause of deep thinking. This time, the nod came slowly, but inwardly Sabrina rejoiced. It was a start, and so often that was the hardest part.

Looking down, Sabrina was overwhelmed at the courage of the boy before her. Just fourteen years old, he had spent God knows how long on the streets, and yet he'd already found enough courage deep inside himself to change, to pull himself up, to give himself a shot at a better life.

And in that instant, she suddenly wondered if she wasn't robbing herself of that same chance.

"I blew it," she told Shadow softly. "I pushed him away without giving him a fair chance. I think I was afraid. It's hard, isn't it?" she asked, half to herself and half to Shadow. "Hard to change, and even harder to hope."

Shadow didn't answer her, she had a feeling that maybe he never would. And yet the silence was probably the best answer anyway. It played the words back to her, forcing her to think.

She missed Thomas more than she'd ever thought it possible to. She really didn't want to let him go. And perhaps he *did* have doubts about her, perhaps he wanted more than she could ever give him. But she didn't know that for sure, did she? And instead of trying to find out, she had simply given up. She, of all people, knew just how important it was to fight. But she hadn't.

"You're right," she said abruptly, and Shadow simply nodded. "I did cop out. I expect so much from you guys, so much courage, the least I can do is show a little myself. Well, it may be a little late, but I can still try. That's the beauty of it, Shadow. It may be late, but it's rarely too late. At least I hope not."

The decision finally made, she found that she couldn't wait. Leaving Shadow in charge of the fort, she briefly ran a brush though her tousled curls, then grabbed a raincoat and headed out the door. There were no buses this time of night. She splurged and flagged down a beat-up taxi.

By the time she arrived in front of Thomas's building she was incredibly nervous. She only knew his address because Seth had written it down for her several times. Just in case, he had said.

Well, here she was, with rain-flushed cheeks and damp hair and sweaty palms. It was four in the morning, and the solid oak door loomed imposingly in front of her. She raised her hand three times before she finally managed to knock.

At first all she heard was the familiar bark of Woof. It brought a sweet smile to her face, easing the tension in her muscles. But there was no further noise, so she knocked again.

Finally she heard the beginnings of life.

"All right you damned dog," a voice was mumbling. "Who the hell made you my mother?"

The door swung abruptly open. "Now what the hell do you—" Thomas stopped, speechless, his jaw hanging down.

If Sabrina had thought that he'd looked bad the first time she'd met him, then he looked infinitely worse now. His hair was a tousled mess, and three days' worth of beard littered his face. His eyes were almost completely bloodshot and he was wearing nothing but a pair of rumpled shorts that had wrinkled almost to the point of nonexistence.

But he looked like heaven to her.

"Can I come in?" she asked softly. He nodded dumbly, absorbing the sight of her shiny blond hair and violet eyes. Under the open black raincoat, she was wearing a thick plum sweater that darkened her eyes and brought a pink flush to her cheeks. She looked like a slice of perfection.

He wanted to touch her, to see if she was truly here after all these weeks of waiting. Instead he closed his eyes and clenched his fists at his sides, controlling himself with an effort. He followed her to the living room.

Looking at the jade elegance around her, Sabrina once again felt intimidated. Living in this modern luxury, she wondered how he had stood the bareness of her own house. Money. Wealth. It was his world, and it scared her.

But then she saw the bottle of Scotch, almost finished and lying on its side on one of the tables. She saw the collection of shot glasses scattered about and noticed for the first time, that the tangy scent of whiskey permeated the large room.

So it hadn't been easy for him, either.

He motioned for her to sit down. She eyed the black leather sofa suspiciously, then stiffly obeyed.

"I wanted to talk to you," she began.

He closed his eyes, running his hand through the mop of his hair. The last two weeks had been a hell beyond hell. How many nights had he come awake, reaching for her? How many times had he reached for the phone to call, only to remember she wanted nothing to do with him? And now she was here, yet the distance between them was still as great, and he found he didn't know where to begin.

"Are you here to explain it all, Sabrina?" he asked finally. "The *whole* truth? Because I know that what went down at the warehouse couldn't have been the real reason behind your walking out on me. Are you ready to trust me now?"

She smiled wanly at him. "I always trusted you, Thomas. But I want the best for you, and I'm not so sure that's what I am."

"Oh, hell, don't start that—" he began.

"Just listen to me. Please."

He couldn't refuse her. Not even now, after two weeks of trying to drink himself into oblivion.

He had tried to forget her. A million times he'd reached over to call Raquel. A billion times he'd told himself that it didn't matter. But damn it, it did. He had gone through two weeks of sheer agony, missing her, wishing that by some small miracle she'd come back to him. *Please, God, let this be it.* He nodded slowly, letting her know he was willing to listen.

"Remember that first night we went out, when you took me to the Rose Gardens?" she began hesitantly. "The night you talked about your dad and all the wonderful things he'd done, and how someday you wanted to have a son so you could teach him all those things as well?"

"Sure," he said with a shrug, trying his best to be casual. "I remember."

"Well," she replied, taking a deep breath. "That can never happen if you stay with me. Thomas, I can never have children."

His head came up, the truth washing over him all at once. He looked at her sharply, his attention now fully focused as he absorbed her words.

"Can't, or won't?" he asked finally.

"Can't. Oh, God, Thomas, I would sell my soul to have children. I would give anything. It was my dream, too, you know. I wanted to start a family, to have the family I'd never had before. But I can't."

She finished quickly, slightly breathless, her hands curling up at her sides, her eyes large and sad.

She'd never felt so vulnerable in her entire life. *Reach for me,* she thought somewhat desperately. *Tell me it's okay.*

But he didn't move. He just sat there, absorbing the words, trying to sort through them. It was something he had never considered. Somehow in all the pictures he'd ever had of the future, they had included finding the woman of his dreams and building a family with her. Somehow, he had managed the first part, at the expense of the second. It was a lot to consider.

"How?" he asked her quietly.

"When I was seventeen," Sabrina whispered, feeling miserable. You have to fight, she reminded herself and took another deep breath. You have to be strong. "I miscarried," she managed to say. "Very badly. I hadn't even known that I was pregnant. I hadn't taken care of myself or tried to eat better or anything.

"I killed it," she told him and the pain and guilt broke through to echo in the room. "God, it was something I had always dreamed of, and I killed it. I was malnourished, stressed out, living such a desperate existence that I destroyed a life form I didn't even know existed. One morning I woke up and felt this warmth on my legs. I was bleeding. And I just couldn't make it stop. I grabbed one of the girls and yelled for help. Then I passed out. When I came to, I was in the emergency room of a hospital. It turned out that Pretty Boy hadn't wanted to take me to a doctor so he'd taken me to a friend of his instead. She practically killed me. The doctor said too much damage had been done. I...I can't have kids. Not now, not ever."

Her voice faded with the last words, and he could hear the quiet despair that settled there. Looking at her now, sitting so close to her, so close he could smell the rain on her hair, he found himself once again wishing that he could protect her from the pain, but he was a decade too late.

"So you thought I should find someone else," he finished for her. "Someone who could have kids."

"You would make such a wonderful father," she said, and he could hear the wistfulness in her voice. "I can see you trying to teach your son how to play baseball. And I can see you bouncing a daughter on your knee. How can I ask you to give all that up?"

"You never asked me to," he said gently. "You never gave me that option. Look, Sabrina, I'm forty-two years old, I've earned the right to make my own decisions by now."

"I know," she said, tears in her voice. "I know. But I couldn't see how you would want me once you knew the truth, so I just never told you. I'm sorry I've been so inconsiderate. I just couldn't bear to lose you on those terms."

"I don't want to lose you, either," Thomas admitted. "God, Sabrina, do you know what hell these past two weeks without you have been for me? I mean, before I met you, I was just some burned-out cop. I felt about twice my age and half my ability. I was considering retirement, I was even considering marrying a woman just because everyone else thought it was such a good idea. And then I met you. In just a few weeks, you turned my life around. You taught me hope, Sabrina. You helped me rediscover my faith in this world and myself. When I'm with you, I feel like I can do anything. I feel like a whole person. No one has ever made me feel like that before."

"Then what do we do?" Sabrina asked. "Maybe if you still looked for someone else, they would make you feel the same. That way you could have kids, too."

"Sabrina," Thomas said softly, and even as he thought the words, he felt the conviction wash through him. "Sabrina, I don't want anyone else."

For a moment the words didn't quite sink in, and she simply looked at him blankly. Then slowly at first, then a little quicker, the meaning penetrated. "You mean—" she began.

"I don't want to lose you," Thomas repeated, the conviction becoming stronger and clearer, ringing in his voice. "It's like losing a part of myself, a part I've spent a lifetime looking for. I do want children, I have always wanted children. But—" And here another thought struck him. "Why, at the moment, you have a house full of them, and they need us as badly as any child ever will. And maybe someday we could adopt a child. There are other choices, Sabrina. Maybe not our first choice, but considering how lucky we've been just to find one another, good enough choices."

She looked at him, eyes growing wide as his words swirled around her. He wanted her. Wanted her enough to give up any hope of having his own children.

"Do you think you could be happy?" she prodded, still not quite able to believe his words.

"Sabrina, honey, the only way I can be happy is to stay with you. Sabrina, I love you."

She couldn't hold back any longer. She threw her arms around his neck, and hugged him fiercely.

"I love you, too," she cried into his neck, then drew back to look into the green depths of his eyes. "I love you. I love you."

There, at long last, the words she'd wanted so badly to say for so long. And saying them out loud seemed only to make them grow, taking on permanency. It had taken her eight years of waiting, eight years of loneliness, but here at last, was what she had spent a lifetime trying to find.

Here, with Thomas.

So those were the words, the only words she had ever really needed to find. Words of love. It surged through them both now, mingling with heady desire as he caught her lips in a burning kiss. It was deep and long, and only the tip of everything they needed.

With a groan, he scooped her up into his arms and strode toward the bedroom.

"Do you like diamonds?" he asked as he threw her onto the low futon. "Or how about amethysts, to match your eyes? Hell, how about both?"

She pulled him down, heavy and wonderful above her. "How about a warehouse instead," she whispered as her lips came up to claim his in another searing kiss.

"Hell, yes." He groaned and kissed her deeper, consuming them both in a sea of desire.

The kisses merely fanned the flames of their passion, sending them both into a world of love and desire, searing their souls, binding them one to the other with emotions that ran deeper than any words or vows. Now and forever.

* * * * *

Silhouette Intimate Moments
is proud to present
Mary Anne Wilson's
SISTER, SISTER duet—
Two halves of a whole,
two parts of a soul

In the mirror, Alicia and Alison Sullivan both had brilliant red hair and green eyes—but in personality and life-style, these identical twins were as different as night and day. Alison needed control, order and stability. Alicia, on the other hand, hated constraints, and the idea of settling down bored her.

Despite their differences, they had one thing in common—a need to be loved and cherished by a special man. And to fulfill their goals, these two sisters would do anything for each other—including switching places in a life-threatening situation.

Look for Alison and Jack's adventure in TWO FOR THE ROAD (IM #472, January 1993), and Alicia and Steven's story in TWO AGAINST THE WORLD (IM #489, April 1993)—and *enjoy!*

SISTERR